Vein
Fire

Lucia Adams

FreakShine Press

New York

For all of the Hannahs in the world.

ACKNOWLEDGEMENT

Special Thanks to Carolyn Violet for the use of her stunning photograph on the front cover.

SPECIAL NOTE FROM THE AUTHOR

Some of the scenes in *Vein Fire* depict drug abuse, sometimes in quantities or combinations that could possibly result in death. The author does not advocate that anyone should mix or consume the drugs as portrayed in this novel and by reading this novel, you are acknowledging that you are solely responsible for your own actions.

vein fire

lucia adams

CHAPTER 1
CINDER BLOCK
1988

New Florence, Pennsylvania

Hannah Simmons played the fainting game all summer. Bent in half, she inhaled thirty-five times until the air rasped and panged in her lungs. She exhaled hard and held her breath until she tipped backwards, and her thoughts were swallowed into the black belly of unconsciousness.

If she missed the bed, she'd have dusk-purple kisses from the floor or her nightstand. Her parents ignored the unexpected thumps until the repetition began blistering their time in front of the television. Regaining consciousness, she'd wake to their yells expanding up the staircase. Once, they sent her little sister, Lorri, to see what she was doing. Hannah woke up to several kicks in the ribs by her sister's small sandaled foot. The sudden flutter of her opening eyelids sent her sister pattering down the steps, tattling before Hannah could grab her and make her promise to keep it a secret. She could hear the murmur of Lorri's snitching as her lungs crackled like ice breaking while they became reacquainted with air.

"Knock it off," her father yelled. Neither parent left the television to educated Hannah in the dangers of self-asphyxiation. It was nothing they were concerned about—just a game played by a thirteen year old and an annoying disruption while they were watching the news. They believed her wholesomeness would keep her safe from what the seclusion of their rural house didn't.

Hannah wanted to feel like she did something well. Her best friend, Olivia, could hold her breath the longest before she passed out. Even at thirteen, their guy friends elbowed each other and whispered when Olivia collapsed. As she fell, her long, shimmering blonde hair would wave out behind her. When she landed, the dirty mattress puffed out a cloud of dust and leaf crumbs.

Five playmates practiced the game over the summer: Hannah, Olivia Parks, Joel Boland, Matt Hansen, and Brian Weiss. They hung out behind the auto salvage building at the end of the dead end street they all lived on. After a new highway was put in, the township closed the road. The pavement was cracked and thick brush staggered with teenage trees stamped the end of the road.

The sparse traffic rarely disturbed the children, allowing them to ride their bikes in-between their houses without much bother.

Across the street from the auto salvage was an old cemetery. The graves were all dated in the early 1900's, but once a month, a volunteer from some church in town mowed the grass in a neat plaid pattern. The deep-set engraved lettering on the white marble headstones melted into the rock over the years, puffing them out so they were barely legible. Most of the graves belonged to children with old-fashioned names. Matt scared the other kids with stories of a serial killer in the woods until Brian's mom explained they died from an outbreak of the Spanish Flu.

The three boys had always been friends, but Hannah was only included once Olivia moved into their neighborhood. The boys couldn't resist the lovely Olivia. Her legs were long and tan, with thighs so thin they didn't rub together at the top like Hannah's did. Olivia was not the kind of girl who typically lived on a dead-end, isolated road. She was smart and popular, and should have lived in one of the new housing developments like the other cheerleaders did.

The kids took turns passing out onto an old mattress they found behind the auto salvage. They kept it propped up against the building, under the deep roof eaves and would take it down to play the fainting game. Joel found an old wristwatch with a broken band in a junk drawer at his dad's house. He timed how long each of them could hold their breath, and he kept a record of it on the cardboard back of an old legal notepad.

An old biker guy owned the auto salvage. He'd come behind the building and ask the boys to help him carry parts occasionally, so they coexisted peacefully. They spied on him through the dirty windows—he was usually grinding metal or welding. Both jobs created an orange waterfall of sparks that extinguished themselves on his leather welding gauntlets and the smell of flux hung like smog. He wasn't any more interesting than other adults, but the things in his salvage yard were useful for making ramps they could jump their bikes off.

Since the age of eleven, the five friends raced bikes, invented ways to entertain themselves, and often swam in Olivia's pool. Olivia lived in a newer brick house with a paved driveway; everyone else lived in old farmhouses with peeling paint and dirt lanes.

It was 1988 and the summer before their ninth grade year. The boys joked and made innuendoes about expecting one of them to start dating one of the girls soon. Hannah knew they meant Olivia—she didn't think she'd be the first one asked out on a date, but she hoped it would come soon after Olivia took her pick.

Hannah started watching Matt before she developed a crush on him. His crystal blue eyes were accented by his summer-browned skin. Matt climbed with a slinky ease, conquering every tree with worthy sighing branches. He out-ran, out-threw, and out-biked the other boys, and Hannah noticed. Once in a while, the group would endure the long bike ride to Buttermilk Falls and swim in the cool, dark pool at the base of the waterfall. Matt was the only one brave enough to climb to the top of the rocks and jump off, so he teased the others, except for Olivia. One day, Hannah blurted, "I'll do it." The group was quiet as Matt shrugged and said, "Follow me."

Hannah decided to follow Matt. When she struggled climbing the mossy rocks, he took her hand and pulled her behind him. His hands were cold when she expected them to be warm and they were soft despite the calluses. At the top, he let go of her hand and pushed her near the ledge. "Don't get a running start or you chance falling the wrong way. Just stand on the edge and jump...unless you're too scared."

Hannah looked down at the tiny versions of Olivia, Joel, and Brian kicking ghost-like limbs under the water's green surface. "I'm not afraid." She narrowed her eyes at Matt. He smiled at her—the first real smile he'd ever given just for her, and she jumped. The rush of the wind blew her shirt up, and the water swallowed her feet first. She kicked for the surface and sucked the air in as soon as she reached the top. Seconds later, Matt's body plummeted into the water near her. When he emerged, he was laughing.

"Holy shit! Hannah really did it. She didn't even hesitate," Matt gasped and smiled.

Hannah smiled back at him, but Olivia swam between them, "Will you take me up, Matt? I want to try it, too."

The entire group made the climb up the mossy rocks,

but Matt only helped Olivia this time. Joel hesitated, and Olivia kept making people go ahead of her, but eventually they all jumped and Hannah's moment of being special lasted a whole seven minutes.

Living across the street from Matt, Hannah witnessed the horrors of his home life. There were beatings, but the things Matt and his brothers experienced at the hands of his stepfather were near killings. The kids skipped school sometimes when the bruises were too bad; they'd wait until their faces healed before returning.

At night, through the illuminated windows, Hannah saw Matt taking the majority of the abuse to prevent one of his younger brothers from getting it. The beatings came with a stick, a rock, a wrench, or anything the stepfather might have in his hand.

The worst came on the day Hannah heard Matt getting yelled at for not cleaning up after the dogs in the back yard. Hannah was jump roping on her front sidewalk and watched his stepfather exit the house with two slices of bread, shovel poop onto it, and reenter the house, screaming, "Eat it." Minutes later, Matt rushed out of the back door, gagging and vomiting.

The crush Hannah developed on Matt was inevitable. Many of her days were spent spying on him. The view she had from upstairs covered most of his yard and the surrounding woods, but was filtered by the sheer curtains in her bedroom. Matt spent a lot of time outside, playing baseball with his younger brothers. In the back of their house, there was a wire dog kennel pieced together with old, gray wood scraps. The small area housed nearly two dozen dogs, and at least double the number of ratty-furred cats lurked just beyond the kennel fencing, teasing the dogs into endless barking fits.

The previous year, Hannah had sat behind Matt in English class and one time, the tag on his sweatshirt stuck out. She took note of the size and wrote it down in her notes about O. Henry. An urge to take care of Matt lurked within Hannah. Nearly every day, Matt wore the same dirty, holed sweatshirt. Hannah wanted to buy him a new one, but wondered if it would offend him. Most of her notebooks were decorated with his name and hearts. Once, a loose page fell out of her tablet onto the bus floor. One of the younger boys picked it up and gave it to Matt. Minutes later, Matt called Hannah's name. When she turned around in her vinyl bus seat, her eyes widened with horror as she saw him holding up a piece of paper with "Matt + Hannah" scrawled in her handwriting. With all of the kids on the bus watching, Matt tore the paper in half several times. Hannah slunk down into her seat, mortified by the rejection everyone witnessed. When the bus driver reached their stop and swung the doors open, she bound off of the bus and ran to her house. Accepting Matt didn't like her back was difficult, but experiencing his torment made it worse.

*

Olivia's parents were taking her to Italy for a two week vacation and she announced it the day Hannah's mom had a cookout for the kids. Everyone was surprised to hear about the trip, not because her parents didn't have the money, but because her father rarely took days off of work, much less two full weeks.

"Hey Livie, do you think your parents would mind if we still swam in your pool when you were away?" Matt asked as he rotated a golden weed between his fingers, rocking back and forth on his bike casually. The sun caught the red tones in his brown hair and made him squint his light blue eyes.

"I'm not sure. I can ask."

"No!" Brian exclaimed. "Don't ask. If you don't ask, they can't say no."

"True," Joel said. "We can just sneak in and pretend we didn't know it wasn't okay until someone catches us."

Everyone started nodding their heads.

"Okay, just remember—the pool guy comes on Tuesdays and don't leave any evidence behind," Olivia said.

"What's in Italy anyway?" Hannah asked. "Isn't the Pope in Italy?"

"Shut up. Olivia's not Catholic and her parents wouldn't make her do something so stupid," Matt said.

"Um, I don't know. My mom said we'll shop and sightsee, probably eat lots of interesting food. I guess I'll have to let you know."

"You'll come back all fat and stuff," Joel joked.

"Ha, ha, very funny," Olivia said. "I'll race you to the back of the cemetery."

Everyone took off on their bikes with Olivia in the lead, heading for the cemetery. The volunteer from the church had just cut the grass two weeks ago and it was still low enough to ride bikes through.

The group rode between the headstones, chasing and dodging one another. Matt watched Olivia's back tire because he rode so close behind her. Hannah swerved out of the riding loop and paused under the shade of the trees and watched. All of the boys were chasing Olivia, and she understood why; she looked like a doll, or an angel— maybe an angel doll.

"Did your fatty legs get too tired?" Matt shouted at Hannah. Her cheeks fired red and she kicked off after him.

"Hey! Don't say that," Olivia said, pulling out from the circle, with the other boys stopping behind her.

Matt raced faster than Hannah, pulling ahead of her, laughing. She knew she didn't have a chance to catch him, so she slowed to a stop.

"I gotta head home. It's almost dinner time," Joel said.

"Yeah, me too," Brian said, following Joel.

Hannah didn't say anything, but followed the boys out, cycling down the road. She paused and looked back. Matt got off of his bike and was standing, talking to Olivia. His head hung down and he kicked some rocks with his sneaker. His shoes had been duct taped together since springtime and his toes were beginning to stick out again. Hannah lagged behind, waiting for Olivia. She wondered if Matt was apologizing to Olivia for his behavior. All of the boys offered their apologies to Olivia when they made fun of Hannah—not because they were sorry, but because they wanted her approval.

Hannah was almost home when she heard someone peddling furiously behind her. Before she had a chance to turn around and look, Matt whizzed past her, kicking up dust and rocks behind him. Hannah stopped to avoid the large dust cloud and peered over her shoulder. Olivia steadily pedaled towards Hannah.

"What was that about?" Hannah asked.

"Nothing, he's just upset."

"Upset about what?"

"He asked me to go out with him and I turned him down."

"Oh," Hannah said, looking at the ground. It was another thing Olivia experienced first.

"Hannah, don't tell anyone. He's so embarrassed. Plus I think he's mad at you."

"Why me?"

"Because I told him I wouldn't go out with someone who calls my best friend names."

"You said that?"

"Yes."

"I guess I never realized you thought of me as your best friend."

"Well, you're my best friend over the summer. When school starts back, Sera will be my best friend at school and you'll be my best friend at home."

"Oh," Hannah sighed—this made more sense. "Well, how did he ask you?"

"He was nervous and just said he needed to ask me something. He kept stalling as he said, 'um' over and over again. He picked me a few daisies and said, 'I wondered if you'd want to go out with me.'"

"And that's when you turned him down?"

"Hmm…it took me a few moments."

"Why? Did you have to think about it?" Hannah sounded frustrated.

"Well, yes, I did."

Hannah rolled her eyes.

"I also told him my parents wouldn't allow me to date him because of the stuff you told me about how he lives and his family."

"Olivia! How could you say that to him? I only told

you to see if your parents could help. Now he'll hate me for it."

"Stop it, Hannah. He doesn't care what you say."

Hannah was furious. She kicked off and peddled away from Olivia. Olivia called after her, but did not follow.

*

Hannah knew there were four things going right for her that week: first, Olivia was in Italy; second, her braces had been removed after two long years; third, her brown hair had a new spiral perm; and lastly, she had bought the new Cinderella tape before anyone else on her street. Music was becoming more and more important to the boys and Hannah didn't want left behind.

She hadn't seen her friends all weekend. Olivia was too busy packing before she left, and the boys didn't want to be bothered with her. A new, white off-the-shoulder shirt waited patiently in her closet for her big reveal in the afternoon. She brushed and flossed twice, proud her teeth hadn't yellowed beneath her braces like she'd seen happen to other kids at school. Several times, she straightened her clothes in the mirror, checking herself, hoping the boys would see more than just the chubby neighbor.

It was hot, but the tree-lined road broke the sunlight into manageable fragments. She could smell the grass releasing the sunshine. Hannah heard the boys up ahead before she saw them. They were practicing the fainting game; no doubt to impress Olivia when she came back.

Brian had just collapsed onto the mattress; his hand still loosely pinched his nose shut.

Joel stood over him with his watch, carefully recording the time on the piece of cardboard. "Oh hey, Hannah," he said without giving her as much as a second glance.

Matt stood back and didn't acknowledge Hannah. She could see his jaw moving under his cheeks—he looked angry. Brian woke up almost immediately. He gazed up at Hannah and smiled wonkily, "Wow. You look different."

Hannah smiled and blushed. "Thank you."

"Your time's getting worse instead of better," Joel said.

"What are you doing here?" huffed Matt.

"I just came to hang out," Hannah said.

"Well, why don't you leave—we're busy and no one wants you around. We only put up with you so Olivia will hang out with us."

"Matt, c'mon man, relax. Hannah's cool," said Joel.

"No, it's okay. He's just pissed off because Olivia refused to go out with him," Hannah retorted.

Matt clenched his fists, rotating three different shades of red before settling on one moderately flushed color.

Joel tried to change the subject. "Brian got the sheet music to *Long Cold Winter*."

"That's cool. I just bought the tape yesterday," Hannah said happily.

"Aww, man! I wanted to buy the tape, but I only had enough money to get the sheet music. I started to learn 'Gypsy Road' last night on the guitar, but I didn't get too far before my dad yelled at me to stop playing."

"Yeah—well it's not 'cuz you're a budding Ace fuckin' Frehley," Matt said.

"Well what do you play besides your cock? 'Oh Olivia! Olivia!'" Brian imitated Matt masturbating.

"You'd better shut your mouth," snapped Matt.

"Why don't you, dog shit breath?" Brian laughed. Matt's veins surfaced his neck. He glared at Hannah.

Hannah panicked and held her breath. Olivia must have told Brian. She worried Matt would think she had told the others.

"Guys, let's settle down," Joel said.

"Yeah, let's settle down. If the cunt wants to play with us, let her play. You're up, Hannah," Matt said, nodding towards the mattress.

Everyone was silent because of the word Matt had used. It wasn't something any of them had ever said before. They watched as Hannah dismounted her bike and walked over to the mattress, readying her hand over her nose.

"Will you catch me?" she asked Brian.

He nodded and stood behind her, ready with both arms to ease her down.

"Okay…" Joel posed with his watch, "On the count of three…one….two…three!"

Hannah inhaled sharply, filling her lungs to capacity, over and over, determined she could hold her breath the longest this time. She exhaled and waited for the blackness.

"Thirty seconds," Joel yelled.

She looked around; Matt was pacing back and forth in front of her.

"Forty-five! You can do this Hannah, you're going to break your record!" Joel squealed.

"C'mon! Hang in there," Brian whispered into her hair.

"One minute! You broke a minute! Keep going Hannah! Keep going."

The sky faded to black static as she tipped back into Brian's arms. He was partially beneath her, and broke her fall, allowing his body to fold as her weight transferred on top of him. He was staring at her parted lips and didn't see Matt come around to the front of them with the cinder block in his hands. Hannah's entire body convulsed after the first swing splintered the tibia bone out of her right leg. Her scream shattered through the cemetery when Matt brought the cinder block down on her left leg. He held the bloody block hovering over his head for the third strike when Joel yelled and dropped the watch. After the fourth swing, Joel tackled him to the ground.

Joel was much smaller than Matt, and they quickly stood up, but Matt turned and ran when he saw Brian had jumped up from underneath Hannah and started chasing him.

"Joel, we have to help her. Knock on the auto salvage door and see if anyone's there."

Brian ran back to Hannah, knelt down, and cradled her head on his lap. Her screams were the worst. Tears surged down her face and the veins in her temples puffed under the skin in lightening strike patterns. She rocked back and forth because of the pain, but with each movement, she screamed even more. Hannah's arms flapped as she grabbed for Brian's hand and then squeezed. Her legs were a jumbled mess of pulp and bone. Bright red blood saturated the mattress and was splattered up the gray block which rested a few feet from them.

Joel raced around the corner and the man from the auto salvage followed a few seconds behind him.

"You God-damned kids! I knew I shouldn't let you play back here. Oh Jesus. Jesus," he said when he saw Hannah's legs. He began choking back vomit, but coughed up snot and spit it into the dirt.

They couldn't pry Hannah's hands from Brian's until the morphine settled into her veins. She quickly passed out as the paramedics put her onto the gurney. Joel and Brian stood in the cemetery as the ambulance pulled away.

CHAPTER 2
THE PUDDING OF A PLAN

Matt waited patiently on the picnic table in his front yard for the police to arrive. He didn't go inside to say goodbye to his family and he didn't try to hide. It was a small town with a minimal local police force, so he was taken quietly, and without handcuffs. The officer might have been bringing Matt home for staying out past curfew, as he had many times, but he held the back door of the cruiser open for him instead of the front one.

Matt slid onto the seat and examined the red stains on his sock. There were also specks of red up and down his legs that he counted before the police arrived. He could have counted as high as he wanted to—there seemed to be an infinite number of splats, but the police pulled up before he tallied further than four hundred and twenty-three.

The police station was one partitioned room inside of the municipal building. The walls were bare and the single holding area was a cinder block enclosure with a reinforced steel door. By the time his mother arrived, the waiting area was chaotic. Matt was sure he was locked in a holding cell to protect him as much as contain him. Hannah's uncle showed up with a baseball bat, shouting, trying to get past the deputy. The silence returned when he was removed, except for Matt's mother, whose drunken cursing blubbered from the back office.

The local district magistrate arraigned Matt later that same afternoon. It was, after all, the middle of the day, in the middle of the week, in the middle of an ordinary July.

The public defender was a nervous woman with slender legs. Matt leaned back in his chair so he could peek up her skirt when she tried to speak to him. The peculiar attention, and knowing what he had done, made the petite woman uncomfortably cross and uncross her legs. He didn't offer her much help: yes, he had done it, on purpose; yes, he intended to harm Hannah; no, he was not sorry for what he had done.

Matt's life became a series of chess moves which he didn't make himself. From the holding cell, to the magistrate's office, to solitary confinement of the juvenile detention center where he was evaluated by a psychiatrist and then shipped off to Oakmont State Hospital's violent juvenile criminals ward—they were just moves on a checkered board to progress Matt from where he was, to where he was going. His rights were neutered to a minimal amount of decisions which they spoon fed to him with a great deal of limitations.

The ward was locked down. Visitors were infrequent and the doctor's hand was heavy when it came to pushing the medications. They could only keep Matt until he was eighteen, and he had already begun planning his exit.

He didn't sleep at night. Often, he'd replay the cinder block coming down on Hannah's legs. Her thighs responded dumbly, with a rippling echo of fat. Her knees and calves were different. They popped bone and blood immediately. Bone shards frayed her skin and the blood melted down her legs and onto the mattress. If he remembered it in slow motion, it was quite beautiful.

Matt didn't see the situation as "right" or "wrong", he saw it as necessary. Hannah *needed* it done to her. He could have killed her by striking her face with the cinder block instead of her legs, or by luring her into the woods and strangling her. He didn't see the point in ending her—she didn't need to be killed; she only needed to be taught a lesson. Taking her life would have been an act of anger; he wanted to deal back the humiliation.

It took Matt one day to realize medication time should be followed by two things: cheek and spit. Anyone who wasn't doing this spent their time sleeping on the chairs in the common room or dozing off during group therapy sessions. These were the people Matt believed neither the doctors nor he could help; they were hopeless.

Everyone sectioned off into cliques, just like high school. The fire starters huddled in groups, whispering and giggling like little girls. The real lunatics walked around talking to themselves and were shunned by everyone. There were the budding pedophiles who sat in writhing groups, palming their clothes until they could sneak off in pairs for gratification. Lastly, the watchers were people like Matt who quietly observed others, lost in the pudding of their next plan, or savoring the joys of what they had already done. The watchers could pass as normal and possessed the most chance of slipping back into society.

After a month, Matt had made one friend, Jared. Jared watched the others, like Matt. His pale blond-hair and small build made him look like one of the elementary aged boys, but he was only a year younger than Matt. The way his face pinched inward reminded Matt of a rat, mostly because it accentuated his slightly bucked front teeth and his beady eyes.

Jared explained that he liked to see people fly, and that's why he was in Oakmont. He had a theory—if someone was special enough, they could fly. He said he thought it was some sort of unconscious power all humans had, and it only needed the right catalyst to emerge. Jared was the catalyst. At first, he dropped his younger brother over the banister of their porch. After numerous attempts, he decided his brother's palsied-like falls meant he wasn't special enough to fly, and he moved on to trying to pick out the extraordinary people.

Jared was sure a classmate named Clarissa was one of the special ones. He watched her for many months at school—she was beautiful. Patient, his chance arrived at a football game. Clarissa and her girlfriends crowed at the top of the bleachers. They had jumped over the railing and were talking to the boys down below them on the ground. She was wearing white jeans and a white windbreaker over a little pink top. Perfect. Jared made his way up to the top of the bleachers and positioned himself behind Clarissa. Quickly, he gave her one good push, and she fell. Her windbreaker caught the air, and for a second, she looked like a little white bird with a pink belly. She seemed to pause for a second before she hit the ground in a crunch of bone and failure. She died. Jared was certain she was almost able to fly—maybe she only needed a few more tries. He said he was glad she hadn't screamed…it would have ruined it.

Only one boy saw him push Clarissa. When the psychiatrist evaluated him and sensed something was "off" with Jared, he committed him to Oakmont for long-term placement. There was no court hearing and no jury, just an article in the daily newspaper and an agreement with his parents that he should stay until he was eighteen.

Jared explained it to Matt…it wasn't much of a choice really; getting pushed was something Clarissa needed. Matt understood him perfectly well. He shared his story about Hannah, the smug, chubby neighbor who was always talking down to him. The surplus of time they had in the institution allowed Matt to retell the story almost daily. After hearing it so often, Jared could have made it his own.

In Matt's first year at Oakmont, Jared became a

semblance of a best friend. Had it been a different time, and a different place, Matt would not have befriended Jared, nor would he have spoken to him. He didn't like him very much and he thought he was creepy. Among the few watchers living on the secure unit, it was slim pickings for a worthwhile conversation, so Matt remained Jared's friend.

Without anyone to push, Jared said he became restless. He devised a plan where he and Matt would save their pills for a few weeks, crush them up, and put them in juice to feed to one of the lunatics. Matt wasn't sure about it. He had never killed anyone, and wasn't certain he wanted to, but he played along, having an urge to make things 'right' or to get 'even' for the placement in Oakmont. He recognized that his thoughts were very different from Jared's, who seemed to not value human life.

For an entire day, the two sat and whispered about who they should choose.

"Why are we doing this again?" asked Matt.

"Because there are no ledges and there are no cinder blocks here, and this is what we do," answered Jared. After a long pause, he inhaled with excitement. "It has to be Danny."

"Danny? He never bothers anyone."

"I know, but I've watched him and I'm certain it wouldn't be a waste. Danny has no potential to ever learn to fly. Plus, we'd be setting him free in a sense. Because he's a ward of the state and no one visits him, he'll be stuck in here forever if we don't get him out. Think about it—he doesn't speak and he carries that pathetic rag of a stuffed bunny around with him."

Matt considered it, and nodded his head. "Danny it is then."

They picked Danny because they liked him, but also, he would be easy. He loved grape juice and would drink whatever they mixed in with it. Matt wasn't sure what pills he was prescribed, but after he swallowed them once, he slept for two days and felt like shit.

Matt figured they didn't need to use all of the pills they had stashed, but it was Jared's plan, so he went along with it. They crushed the pills between two shiny magazine pages until they were a fine powder. Jared saved his grape juice from breakfast, and they dissolved the pills in it.

Jared only had to leave it in Danny's room for him to find it and drink it. When he wondered out of his room again, Jared retrieved the cup, rinsed it out in the bathroom and tossed it in the trash where it landed among dozens of other similar cups. Within one hour, Danny returned to his room, sick. He lay on his bed, convulsing in violent seizures for several minutes.

"Do you think he'll swallow his tongue?" Jared asked as they watched Danny die.

"I'm not sure, but I don't think he has much time left."

Indeed, he did not. The death rattle they had never heard before became a symphony they'd never forget. Danny was dead. They snuck out of the sleeping area and went to the common room to play chess. The two boys were calmer than usual, almost satisfied.

Danny's body was discovered and the place was locked down. Everyone was questioned, but no one remembered seeing anything. Matt almost believed the administrator suspected him, but nothing came of it. He, after all, had just been playing chess in the middle of the day, in the middle of the week, of a typical month, in a place where one day could not be distinguished from the next.

It took one week before the autopsy results came back and showed a high level of medicine in Danny's system. Out of all the patients on the floor, Jared was the only person prescribed the pills.

Jared was removed unceremoniously. Two orderlies held him down while a nurse thrust a shot into his ass cheek. He was limp when they walked him out, his pants still slightly pulled down, exposing a red bead of blood where the needle had plucked into his buttock.

They only questioned Matt once before Jared confessed—stating Matt had no part in poisoning Danny. Matt was sure they were still suspicious of him, but the full confession by Jared made the investigation easy, so they gave up on outing Matt as an accomplice.

Because there was no other place for murderers who

were mentally ill children, Jared returned, but to the restricted ward—in solitary confinement, indefinitely.

Occasionally, the two would see one another and grant a respectful nod towards the other, but they were always kept separated. Matt didn't mind getting rid of the crazy fuck. Jared was an unnatural sort of wrong and if Matt ever wanted to get released, he knew he needed to stay clear of him.

After several months of 'successful' therapy, Matt was moved to the integrated floor. This only meant was he was a mouse in a larger cage, but with girl mice as well. Two way mirrors were the norm on this floor, but the same reinforced steel and glass doors only opened when someone in an office pushed a button. Electric clicks on doors became a familiar background noise.

Here, Matt was given a job—not a real job where he earned money, but more like a chore. Correctly completing the tasks earned him neat red checkmarks in pre-printed boxes. His initial assignment was to clean the bathrooms. At first he was pissed off about it, but after he figured out the perks to the job, he asked to keep the chore longer than the first month.

Marilyn Bennet was his unofficial welcoming host to the integration unit. Her huge double D breasts earned her the nickname 'Bubbles'. Even the nurses had taken to calling her Bubbles instead of Marilyn. She told him she couldn't make the bad stuff go away, but she could make him forget he was there for a little while. Matt wasn't sure how crazy she was, or why she was committed to

Oakmont, but he did know she promised to suck his cock. It would be his very first blow job and he wanted it more than he'd ever wanted anything in his life.

There wasn't much opportunity to be unsupervised, and with cameras mounted in the corners of each room, it took Matt three days to figure out a way he could get Bubbles alone. Every day at lunchtime, she worked in the cafeteria, assembling sandwiches. He told her to complain that she had to use the bathroom and he'd meet her in the girl's lavatory at 12:15. Most of the other people ate lunch at that time, and if he posted the 'cleaning in progress' sign outside of the bathroom, they could steal fifteen minutes alone—at least.

He asked her if it was enough time, and Bubbles giggled, "That depends on you, silly!"

Matt was sure it would be the best fifteen minutes of his life.

They arranged to meet the next day, and Matt mounted the sign on the door. His heart pounded and his chest flushed in anticipation as he waited for Bubbles. He kept picturing his hands on the back of her head, and her curly blonde hair sticking up between his fingers. He didn't know what else to expect, but he was ready to find out.

Bubbles showed up at exactly 12:15, still wearing plastic food service gloves. She suggested they go into a bathroom stall in case anyone snuck in. Locking the door behind them, she turned, popped her tits out of the top of her shirt, and waited for Matt. He did nothing, so she sighed, placed his hands on her tits, and unbuttoned his pants. If she hadn't already guessed he was a virgin, she knew for sure by then.

Matt got his first hand job from Bubbles while she was wearing food service gloves. She didn't seem too eager to actually suck his dick, but since it only took him a minute before he blew his load, he wasn't sure.

Bubbles met Matt nearly every day to give him a hand job. She kept insisting she really did want to give him a blow job, but confessed to having some sort of germ phobia, so he had to settle for hand jobs while she wore the food service gloves. He adjusted to the sound of the plastic and didn't mind the crinkle noise so much.

One day, while Matt sat in the commons room watching TV, one of the newer vegetables kept bothering him. He towered above Matt and emitted these low, gravely laughs. Eventually, Matt had enough, stood up, and punched him in the face. The vegetable hit the ground like a sack of shit, and within minutes, the door locks clicked, a needle poked him in the ass, and two orderlies escorted him off to the restricted unit where he was tossed into solitary confinement.

CHAPTER 3
FRANKENLEGS

Hannah was skilled at pretending she was a good girl. He parents didn't know about the criss-cross of scars on her arms, the drinking binges, or the careless way she passed out blow jobs. If only the perfect daughter act were true. Hannah was just like any other girl who had a playmate smash her legs with a cinder block. She was good at hiding everything, even from herself.

Inside, she blamed herself for the incident behind the salvage yard. If she had only kept her mouth shut. Hannah never started school that year. She spent months in the hospital, undergoing surgeries to put pins into her shattered legs, and to reconstruct her right knee cap. While she was still in traction, she was allowed to go home, and she completed the eighth grade with a homebound teacher.

Whatever popularity she could have gained through sympathy was forgotten by the time she entered high school. The gym class uniforms didn't hide her scars and her nickname quickly caught on—Frankenlegs. Anyone who wanted to befriend her was afraid of the fallout from being associated with the class freak. She did have a few people courageous enough to talk to her regularly, but when the boys would yell "Frankenlegs" down the hall, those friends scattered.

Hating herself was easy. She could even do it during Sunday mass where her mother insisted she wear dresses. The pantyhose made her scars look an odd shade—ridges and pocks where scalpels and pins had split her flesh to make her whole. Hannah was very aware of all of her shortcomings, as well as a few she made up in her head. With all of the trips to the orthopedic surgeon, no one bothered to get her psychiatric help to overcome the trauma she lived through. Hannah smiled often, and was a pleasant and cooperative child, so she didn't outwardly seem to need therapy.

She was relieved when her mother told her Matt would not be released from the psychiatric facility until he was eighteen. His family still lived across the street and she often felt awkward whenever she was in her yard if they were outside, so she stayed inside a lot. Brian and Joel still waved to her in the hallways and talked to her on the bus, but Olivia was on the varsity cheerleading squad and didn't bother with anyone who didn't wear the cheerleader's trademark black and red pleated skirt.

It wasn't until the end of her junior year of high school when she started doing her Spanish partner's homework that she finally broke into a group of friends. Her partner's name was Sam and he wore black motorcycle boots with a long knife tucked into them. Quickly, he became her best friend. Each day as his bus passed hers, he waved, and he ate lunch with her every day. Sam intimidated the other students, and those he didn't, he beat up when they muttered "Frankenlegs". Sam was two years younger than Hannah, but he was her protector.

At the end of the school year, she gathered the courage to ask him to a mutual friend's keg party. He hesitated, and she wasn't sure why, but he said yes and they agreed she'd pick him up Saturday night.

Sam took Hannah's virginity the night of the party, but on Monday morning, he asked another girl out. They never spoke again, but she remained in his circle of friends, and they quietly acted as though the other was invisible.

The experience cut Hannah—literally. She waned between blaming herself and thinking she was ugly—never settling on which feeling made her more miserable. These cuts would become the deepest ones on her arms. By this time, she had learned how to cut herself properly. She'd take a disposable razor, hold it in a towel and snap the plastic apart, and bend the razor blades until they were free of the plastic. Often she had done this without the towel, but it led to cuts on her fingertips. Although

31

she rather enjoyed the accidental cuts and she'd smile from the thought that she 'deserved' them, she knew purposeful cuts were better. She'd sit cross-legged on the bathroom floor—head down, with her hair falling like curtains on the sides of her face. Her tears buckled under their own viscosity, concaving the view of her task as they perched on her eyelashes. One blink and her vision cleared. It was a splitting of cells, out of necessity, really. She hated herself, and the guilt was overwhelming. This wasn't want. It was need.

If she could brand this sort of euphoria, she'd be wealthy. The necessity of it would fill voids like plaster in wall-holes. Bottles of it would hover in the corner of every medicine cabinet, next to the other band-aids and aspirins. The satisfaction of a job well-done meant blood, burning cuts, and itchy scabs. They were nice to look at later on, but for her pleasure and no one else's. The cuts on her arms meant long sleeves; the scars on her legs meant long pants—Hannah's body lived in an eternal winter.

Hannah begged her parents to allow her to transfer to another school, but they thought she was over-reacting. She, after all, had one friend who showed up to her birthday parties—Angela. Hannah made an attempt to get close to the odd girl with dirt under her fingernails. Angela's pale skin was dotted with black moles that matched her coal-colored hair. This distracted Hannah from maintaining eye contact with her, so Angela often snarked, "Are you listening to me?"

In an effort to bond with Angela, Hannah invited her

to hang out at the mall. After her mom dropped them off, Hannah drug Angela into a dressing room inside one of the anchor stores. She pulled out two plastic soda bottles, now filled with vodka and orange juice, and gave one to Angela as she chugged the other. Angela took one sip and handed the bottle back, so Hannah drank them both.

Hannah liked the mall. Kids from different schools hung out there and she felt like she had a chance to pretend she was normal. Angela whined she was hungry and wanted to go to Foxmoor to look at clothes, but Hannah took her to the arcade. That was where the *boys* were.

Angela refused to play anything besides Frogger and Pac Man. Hannah despised that it made them look like kids. They were, after all, nearly sixteen.

The employees walked around with clips of quarters on their belts and aprons stuffed with paper bills customers had exchanged for quarters. One Hannah had never seen before kept approaching the girls and commenting on their game.

"He's kinda cute," Hannah said.

"Eww…no way! He's old. He must be thirty or something," Angela squealed.

"I like older men." Hannah turned and smiled at the guy. Within a few minutes, he was behind her, looking over her shoulder at their game.

"You girls need some help?" he asked.

Hannah arched her ass back until it rubbed against his cock. "I always need help," she giggled. "Hey! Do you guys have a bathroom in here?"

"Nope, employees only."

"Aww…c'mon…I won't tell and I'll be *so* fast," she begged. Hannah didn't even try to hide that she was drunk. She swayed from side to side and her eyes kept going out of focus.

"Okay, I'll take you," the guy said.

Hannah smiled as he led her through the maze of machines towards the back. As they passed another employee, he motioned towards the rear door and yelled, "Hey, cover for me for a few." The other guy nodded in return.

First, Hannah went pee, and giggled so she could hear it echo off of the walls in the bathroom. When she emerged, the guy was leaning against the wall, waiting for her.

"See, I was fast."

He smiled, "Have you been drinking?"

Hannah laughed and held her finger to her lips, "Sshhh."

"C'mere." He pulled her close and kissed her. His tongue tasted like cigarettes as it explored her mouth until the vodka tang disappeared.

Hannah unbuttoned his pants and when he didn't resist, she dropped to her knees and passed the entire length of his cock between her lips. She sucked...she sucked for a long time and he still didn't cum. It was taking so long that she was getting bored and her mouth was going numb. Her mind wandered to Angela and if she'd still be waiting at the Pac Man machine, gobbling dots and running from ghosts, then her eyes focused on the guy's curly brown pubic hair, but the image disgusted her, so she closed her eyes.

Her pace slowed as her mouth tired and he told her to stand up. Hannah didn't want to fuck the guy, but she knew that if she kept sucking, she was going to vomit. He didn't tell her what to do; he simply turned her around, pushed her against the wall, and pulled her pants down to the middle of her thighs. Hannah was thankful he didn't yank them down completely, or else her scars would show.

In one smooth movement, he was inside of her. Sam was the only other person she'd slept with and this guy was much larger. Her body stiffened from the pain as he pushed further into her and she tried to move away, so he gathered both of her wrists into one hand and pinned them to the wall above her head. Each thrust hurt more than the last, and her body started to resist him, so he kicked her legs apart and pressed the full weight of his body against hers until the air was emptied from her lungs and he was fully inside of her.

The room was spinning and Hannah felt like she was going to pass out. The orange painted block wall felt cold against her cheek and the sensation kept her tethered to consciousness. Finally, the guy leaned back and Hannah inhaled. He reached his free arm around and started rubbing her clit as he sucked on her neck. Both acts aroused Hannah and she began to enjoy the stranger fucking her. When he started pounding her hard, the coins and paper bills rained at her feet. At the end, he took his finger off of her clit, gathered her long hair into his hand and twisted it until he had control of her head. He forced her head around so he was kissing her when he came inside of her. Hannah's eyes were open and she saw his hat had fallen off of his head. The light shined off of the bald spot on his crown. *Angela was right, he is old.*

*

It took Hannah nearly twenty minutes to find Angela. She was standing at the fountain, throwing her left over quarters into the water. The silver glistened as they floated to rest among the other coins on the bottom.

"Sorry I took so long."

Angela looked up and down the length of Hannah's body. "You fucked that guy, didn't you?"

"No," Hannah laughed, "I didn't."

"You don't have to lie. And besides, I can smell him on you."

"Listen, I'm sorry—I"

Angela cut her off, "Can we just walk to where your

mom is meeting us? Maybe she'll show up early."

"Okay."

The walk to the bench outside of the food court was the grueling sort of silence that filtered out the background chatter in the mall. When they exited the building, Hannah's mother hadn't arrived yet. The girls sat on the bench for ten minutes before Angela started to cry.

"I'm sorry, Ang. I'm not very good at being a friend."

"Why do you do that fucked up stuff?"

"I don't know." Hannah felt horrible...sober and horrible. She wanted to explain it all to Angela to make her understand it wasn't her that she dumped. "I hate myself so much. It's worse than anyone knows."

Angela sniffled and wiped away her tears, "Really?"

"Yeah, really. I hurt myself all of the time. It's not just drinking and what I do with guys."

"What do you mean?" Angela looked at Hannah.

Some things translate better with an image. Hannah couldn't say it anyway, so she pulled the sleeve up on her shirt and showed Angela the rows of fresh cuts she'd made that week.

Angela's eyes widened. "You do that...to yourself?"

"Yes." Hannah pulled her sleeve back down as her

mother's car parked alongside the curb. Both girls jumped into the car. Angela politely replied to the motherly inquiry about what the girls did, and the clothes they looked at, but was quiet otherwise. When they pulled into her driveway, Angela bolted from the car yelling, "Thank you!"

Over the weekend, Angela didn't answer Hannah's phone calls, and that Monday at school, she realized why. Exactly twelve minutes into first period, Hannah was called down to the principal's office. Angela and her mother sat to the left of the principal's desk and Hannah's parents sat to the right. The only remaining empty chair was in the middle. Hannah sat in it and let her eyes sway towards the left, then the right. *This is a kerfuckle sandwich.*

Lie. Deny. Run. None of the alternatives to telling the truth seemed like viable options. *Too many adults in the room.*

The principal spoke first, "Hannah, Angela and her mother are worried about you. Angela told us some disturbing stories about the trip to the mall you two had over the weekend. Would you like to tell us about it?"

"No." *That was easy.*

He continued, "Angela, why don't you tell Hannah's parents what you told me."

Hannah narrowed her eyes and looked at Angela. *She wouldn't. She'd not tell them. It would be too embarrassing.*

Angela cleared her throat, looked at her mom, and then focused her eyes on Hannah. "Mrs. Simmons dropped us off at the mall and the first thing Hannah did was take me into a dressing room to drink bottles of vodka and orange juice. I didn't drink any, so Hannah drank both bottles."

Liar! She did drink some. Well, just a sip.

"Then we went to Time-Out and Hannah went into the back with one of the workers and had sex with him." *Bitch! She doesn't even know that for sure.* "When she came out of the back with him, I overheard him telling another worker that he had sex with her and she…she…put her mouth on his penis."

Fuck. I thought she'd left. My dad is squirming. Fuck. Why did I have to be sitting next to him?

"When we went outside to wait for Mrs. Simmons to pick us up, Hannah told me she does that sort of thing all of the time AND she showed me these cuts all over her arms. She said she did it to herself with a knife."

That bitch! I never told her that. Besides, I use a razor.

The silence was a peculiar soundtrack for a nightmare, and that's how Hannah knew she wasn't dreaming. She kept her eyes focused on the white paper dots on the floor—refugees from the three-hole punch sitting on the desk.

The principal sighed. "Hannah, will you please pull your shirt sleeves up?"

Hannah doubled over. He might as well have punched cramps into her stomach. She inhaled deeply and straightened herself in the seat, but winced because her cunt still hurt. *I should tell them THAT.* Instead, Hannah slid her sleeves up to her elbows, stretched her arms out, and turned them palm up.

Hannah's mother gasped and Angela nodded at the principal.

Cry. That was the fourth option Hannah hadn't thought of. It was as good as confirming that everything Angela said was true, but slightly less humiliating. Tears and snot gurgled out of her as Angela and her mother were ushered out of the room. Hannah's mother pushed tissues into Hannah's hands and alternated between telling her daughter not to cry and answering the principal's questions.

Hannah was taken home and met the first of many psychiatrists that week. He was a friendly man with straight gray beard hair that he kept neatly trimmed. Hannah called him The Wizard because he wore green suits and on his wall hung a large painting of hot air balloons. Most importantly, he introduced her to a new friend—Xanax. Sometimes he wrote her excuses so she'd not have to participate in gym class and this pleased her.

The Xanax did make school easier. Hannah would just put her head down on her desk and sleep through class. She knew they weren't going to fail her; allowing her to graduate only assured they'd be rid of her brand of crazy sooner rather than later.

At home, Hannah's parents took great care to hide all of the sharp objects in the house and to never again mention what was said in the principal's office. For the first month, they wouldn't even allow her to be alone with Lorri, but that ended as soon as they needed a babysitter so they could go to their bowling banquet.

Hairy legs and not having a knife to cut a bagel open was equally annoying. Hannah's father complained about it almost every morning. Finally, Hannah took her mother into her bedroom and showed her all of the things she could cut herself with...a broken light bulb in the trash, the hinge on her jewelry box, the screws in her walls, and the hooked end on her wire hangers.

"There's a lot I can do with a wire hanger," Hannah remarked.

Her mother's jaw snapped shut and she gave Hannah her razors back. The kitchen once again became a dangerous place for bagels, and not a single person spoke about any of it.

Angela never gossiped about what had occurred, but her snitching landed her a choice volunteer job in the office and this catapulted her popularity to new heights. Suddenly the male students were interested in the girl who could sneak them excuses and there was nothing the female students loved more than a girl who was popular with the guys.

Hannah encountered Angela in the office a few times, but only spoke to her when she had to. Part of Hannah was thankful that Angela taught her two very important lessons: Trust no one, and life is easier when you don't let anyone in. She smiled when she noticed...*She still has dirt under her fingernails.*

CHAPTER 4
MONSTERS

Matt didn't look forward to being reunited with Jared. In their time apart, he contemplated the Danny incident. He was angry at himself for agreeing to follow Jared's idea. Part of him wanted to exercise the guilt by riveting punches into Jared, but he knew that would only raise suspicion. Since they were both in solitary confinement, he didn't have to deal with him. He was only on the restricted floor for a week before they allowed him to return to the integrated floor, and even reinstated his job.

Mopping piss splatters off of the urinals was worth his fifteen minutes with Bubbles every day. She promoted him from hand jobs to full-on sex. They never made the pit-stop for blow jobs, but he figured with her germ phobia, it was a dream that had to die.

Losing his virginity was epic. He had Bubbles

practically folded in half, pinned against the wall in the bathroom stall, her toes kicking up over the top of the metal barrier, as he slammed angry thrusts into her. She looked terrified. He didn't care. Since she came back the next day, he knew he must have done something right. From then on, he only called her Marilyn. His fifteen minutes with her was the best part of his day, and if you pushed the moments together like slices of bread, it still didn't amount to a loaf of time.

Nothing filled the days. The patients attended a school of sorts—one room with one teacher who struggled to teach several different grades at the same time. Homework was nonexistent and no one could be trusted with a pencil. Marilyn would take the markers and color her fingernails during class. Matt watched her out of boredom as she avoided the cuticles and would color the little white half-moons with a different marker.

Almost as bad as school, group therapy was the second biggest waste of their time. Junior therapists who didn't know how to handle the diversity of the group directed the sessions. One day, when the people gathered in their seats, he was surprised to see Marilyn among them. She usually had group therapy in the mornings, but they must have switched her to the afternoons.

She twitched. Two more people and it would be her turn. Matt didn't take his eyes off of her. In the bathroom, standing so close, she looked much taller. She was small, and from the other side of the therapy circle, she looked like a fairy, despite her oversized tits.

"Marilyn?"

"Huh?"

"It's your turn."

"Oh, yeah, right," she paused.

"The beginning? We're talking about your first action in the series of things that necessitated your hospitalization." The therapist rolled her eyes. She was a cunt.

Marilyn looked off into nothing as she tried to recall what it was.

"Marilyn?"

"Um, Squiggles, our guinea pig."

"Your guinea pig?"

"Yeah, she caught ringworm and her fur fell out. We weren't allowed to touch her."

"And did you—touch her?"

"She squealed a lot at night. I guess they don't sleep much then...nocturnal or whatever they're called. She kept me awake and she was squealing like she was in pain."

"So what did you do?"

"I put my mother's rubber gloves on—the yellow ones she used to wash dishes with—and I took Squiggles out

45

of her cage."

Marilyn stopped and swallowed, clearly uncomfortable with sharing her story. Matt wondered if it was because he was in the group.

"Continue, please—what did you do with Squiggles?"

"I—I was going to set her loose in the woods, but it was so cold; I thought I was doing her a favor. I—I just took her outside to our goldfish pond. I had to break the ice to make a big enough hole to fit Squiggles. My fingers nearly froze and the goldfish swam around her like green ghosts. I held her under the water until she stopped moving."

"So, what do you feel was your pivotal decision point?"

"I don't know."

"Well, when did you decide to kill Squiggles?"

"When I was laying in bed, listening to her squeal."

"Would you identify this as your pivotal decision point?"

"Yes, I guess so."

"What do you think some alternative actions would have been?"

"I dunno. Maybe wearing leather gloves instead of rubber gloves so she couldn't bite me."

"Do you feel that being bitten was the worst consequence of your actions?"

"I guess not."

"What was, then?"

"Winding up here?"

"If you back up, at what point did someone else in your family do something different than what you did that night?"

"They stayed in bed?"

"Correct. Having the thoughts of killing the guinea pig—Squiggles—wasn't the critical point until you acted upon those urges."

"But if I hadn't worn the rubber gloves, I wouldn't have tried to set them on fire. The fire was the consequence."

"No, Marilyn, the fire came after you killed Squiggles. Killing Squiggles was your first consequence."

"Well then, I'm glad she's dead."

Everyone in the group laughed quietly. Marilyn looked up at them and then quickly lowered her eyes.

"Okay, Paul—you're next."

Paul droned on about his pivotal point—something about being caught masturbating in his sister's room.

Matt ignored him. He stared at Marilyn, who looked too embarrassed to meet his gaze as he contemplated what she had heard. Matt thought, *Humph. Who knew? I lost my virginity to a guinea pig killer. And those fucking rubber gloves…I'm not surprised she wore them long before she came here. And what's with the fire? I wonder if she'll tell me if I ask. Freaky. Oh well.*

"Matt?" the therapist said.

"What? Oh, yeah, my turn."

The bitch rolled her eyes again.

"My pivotal point was when I picked up the cinder block and smashed it on Hannah's legs."

"Okay, very good. But, did you think about it, or plan it?"

"Nope, she was passed out; I saw the cinder block, and it came to me."

"So your arc of action was short and without a period of planning, correct?"

"Yeah, I just thought about it and did it."

"Okay, now what were your other options?"

"I could have killed her."

"Yes, you could have, but that's a *negative* option. Can you give me a positive alternative?"

48

"Um, I could have just gone home."

"Very good. Identifying these critical points will help you recognize them in the future. Okay, Chad, you're next."

Marilyn's eyes darted to meet Matt's and then back again. Matt wasn't able to guess what she was thinking, but he was also sure he didn't care.

The next day, in the bathroom with Marilyn, he found out.

"So who's this Hannah girl you were talking about in therapy circle? Was she your girlfriend?"

"Are you kidding me? No, she wasn't my girlfriend."

"Well, who was she?"

"Just some girl from the neighborhood."

"Did you like her?"

"She was okay for a while, but no, I didn't like her."

"Then why did you do that to her legs—with the cinder block?"

"She pissed me off. Listen, can we drop it? It's bad enough I gotta go over this shit in therapy, can we just spend time together?"

Marilyn wasn't satisfied. She refused to fuck Matt and gave him a half-assed hand job while she wore those fucking food service gloves. He had already made a mental note to not eat any of the sandwiches after their first encounter.

Marilyn would bring Hannah up occasionally. Matt realized she was jealous of Hannah, but it was another thing he didn't care about. He liked Marilyn, but was more interested in her willingness to get him off than her jealousy trips.

He was right—Marilyn's hesitation in group therapy was because she was uncomfortable speaking in front of him. After several weeks, the real reason she was in the facility erupted from her—literally. Marilyn had the stomach flu. She was a mess of snot and tears, with both fluids glistening in stray hair strands. As she sat in the recreation room with a bucket between her legs, she contracted the sharing disease. Matt sat across the room from her as she explained how she set the yellow rubber gloves on fire in her basement the night she drowned Squiggles. She drew designs with the lighter fluid, and didn't bother to tell anyone when the house was on fire. Her little sister died, and Marilyn seemed detached from the incident. Matt knew he had issues, but he was not a monster like Marilyn.

*

Two and a half years after Matt was admitted to the state hospital, Marilyn told him she was pregnant. They stood crammed into the last stall in the bathroom; the smell of disinfectant stained his tongue. Marilyn was a slobbering mess of blubbery and drool. Matt didn't

50

experience the elated anticipation of becoming a father. He didn't feel anything.

The next blow Marilyn dealt was confessing Matt might not be the father of the baby. She fucked one of the orderlies—Ronald. Matt would have taken this harder if she wasn't pregnant. Not knowing if he was the father or not was a relief.

"What do you want to do about it?"

"Ronald says…"

Ronald says? echoed in Matt's head.

"…he says I should tell them I'm pregnant, but say I don't know who the father is. I'm—I'm going to get an abortion."

Matt didn't hesitate, "I think that's a great idea."

"You do?"

"Absolutely."

Marilyn was a trouper. She aborted the baby and only missed three days of hand jobs. After two weeks, she was freshly medicated with birth control and back to fucking Matt in the bathroom.

"So what's with this Ronald? He's an orderly on the female ward?"

"Yeah."

"And how often do you sleep with him?"

"Just once or twice."

"Once or twice a week, a month, or what?"

"Just once or twice a month. He caught me sneaking off to meet you and that's how I keep him quiet. Why, are you jealous?"

"No, should I be?"

Marilyn had a disappointed pout on her face. "You still love that Hannah girl, don't you?"

Matt sighed. "Why would you think that?"

"You crushed her legs. You must feel something for her."

"Well, it wasn't love."

"She has your scars though. I've been fucking you for a year and I don't have that."

"Hey—didn't you have my baby cut out of you?"

"Yeah." Marilyn looked down.

"Look at me." Matt lifted her chin with his fingertips. "Those scars are more beautiful than anything I could have done with a cinder block."

Marilyn smiled at Matt and kissed him.

CHAPTER 5
PALMS
1994

All of Hannah's pills were yellow. She was sure it meant something significant, perhaps a secret message of sorts. Yellow Xanax was prescribed for her panic attacks, yellow Zoloft so she wouldn't off herself, and yellow Percocet for her leg pain. She didn't know how she lucked out getting the Percocet, but it wasn't something she was going to start complaining about. Hannah was nineteen and worked as a filing clerk at City Hall—not exactly a job she couldn't do high.

Donna was the only other person who worked in the basement filing area with her. Hannah liked Donna—she had trained her and they always took their lunch breaks together. After a year of lunches, Donna told Hannah about her splitting migraines. Hannah was happy to offer her a handful of Percocets. Donna learned quickly. She had other pains from all of the bending she did over the filing cabinets, and her husband's back aches would frequently reach emergency status. Donna could have just asked for the pills, but Hannah figured it made her feel better to mention a story before an outstretched palm.

The friendship didn't go one way; Donna often invited Hannah over for dinner, or they'd meet Donna's husband, Bob, for beers after work. A few times a month, Donna and Bob took Hannah to drink with them at the bar near their house. The plan was always that Hannah would sleep on their couch instead of driving to her apartment, but willing lips and the inability to say no always led to Hannah going home with some guy she'd not remember when she was sober. Bob always had a use for anything yellow Hannah had in her purse. He was friendly and always made her laugh. During the week, he was a construction worker with a voracious appetite for neatly rolled joints. He could out-smoke Hannah and Donna and still drive home.

Bob met them for lunch every Friday. Afterwards, he always convinced them to smoke. The three of them crammed into the cab of his pick-up truck and passed the joint back and forth as they sat parked behind the post office's dumpster. Hannah wondered how Donna didn't notice Bob staring at her. His fingers lingered on the joint as he handed it to her, and he'd rub his leg against hers. She cursed herself for not being more assertive about wanting to sit on the end. She tried to figure out if Donna and Bob had an open relationship. Donna had slept with one of their co-workers for a few months over the winter, but still carried on with Bob like she was happily married.

The attention from Bob made Hannah feel insecure. Donna was far more desirable than she was, with her tiny, petite, doll-like figure, and her curly blonde hair. Her suntan never faded in the winter and her smile lit up her entire face. Hannah's body was round in some places, scarred in most areas, eternally pale, and she hardly ever smiled. Even though she wondered what it would be like to sleep with Bob, she quickly shook the thought out of her head—Donna was her closest friend.

"Bob! We're gonna smell like pot," Donna giggled.

"Tell those City Hall crooks to go fuck themselves."

Donna and Hannah laughed. It was Bob's answer to most problems. He didn't hesitate to tell people to fuck off at the slightest indication they were going to bother him.

"Did Donna invite you to our barbeque this weekend?" he asked in-between puffs.

"Yeah, I mentioned it to her."

"Well, are you coming?"

"I don't know," Hannah hesitated.

"What do you mean you don't know? Of course you're coming."

There was no arguing with Bob—Hannah would go.

*

Donna didn't know about Hannah's scars, so she dragged her around the barbeque, trying to introduce her to different men. A lot of Bob's c-workers came, and his son's friends were there as well. Bob was in his forties, so his son was slightly older than Hannah. When Hannah's conversations with Bob's friends didn't last long, Bob crooked his arm around her shoulder and walked her over to his son's friends.

"We'll find someone you like," Bob said before he pushed her towards the crowd of guys and gave her a smack on her ass. "Listen up, everyone; this is Hannah. She's lonely. Someone talk to her—she's a good girl." Bob tousled Hannah's hair and walked away.

Self-consciously, Hannah smoothed her hair down and smiled.

"C'mon, Hannah—we don't bite. Let's get you a beer," some guy in a baseball cap said as he reached into the cooler and popped the top off of a Rolling Rock.

"Thanks." She took the bottle and drank from it.

"We're about to play beer pong—you can be on my team," the same guy said.

Even though it was her first time, Hannah had fun playing beer pong. She lost with the lowest score. The wooden picnic table was on a slant and no matter how exact she thought her aim was, she always missed. By the time she had six beers in her, she was no longer walking to the house when she had to pee, but squatting in the dry leaves in the woods. She'd already taken a break to give the guy in the baseball cap a blow job behind Donna and Bob's camper. Soon after they resumed their pong game, an obnoxious guy in cowboy boots rubbed up against her.

"Hey!" she said, "You're making me mess up my pong shot."

"It's okay, darlin', your pong shots were off before I came. I've been watching."

"You have?" Hannah gave him a drunken smile.

"Yes, I have. You wanna go for a walk?"

"Maybe in a little bit. I need another beer."

"In a little bit? Can't we go now?"

"No! I need a beer."

Someone stuck a beer in her hand and she chugged it.

A group of guys who had been playing horseshoes all night joined the pong crowd. Hannah froze. She wasn't sure—her facial recognition skills were terrible—but the one guy looked like Matt—cinder block Matt. His eyes met her stare and the surprised look that seeped across his face confirmed who he was.

Hannah turned and spoke to the guy in the cowboy

boots, "How about that walk now?"

He grinned and pulled her towards the woods with him. She wanted to walk deep into the trees to avoid any spot where someone had already pissed, but the cowboy stopped when the light ended and laid on the grass, not bothering with going so far as the woods.

Hannah was sobering up—too afraid of Matt to leave the safety of the man she was with, but not drunk enough to fuck. The man tasted like cigarettes and calluses ridged his fingertips. He started to annoy her when his slobbering kisses wet most of face. He stopped, leaned back, pulled a flask from his back pocket, opened it, and took a swig. He handed it to Hannah. "Drink this."

She took a sip and tried to hand it back to him, but he pushed the flask towards her and said, "No, drink all of it."

Hannah hesitated, but opened her throat and poured the whiskey down, allowing it to burn in a flood as it emptied into her stomach.

"Now, what's your name, little girl?

"Hannah."

"Hannah…nice. Well, com'ere Hannah." The man pulled her close, kissed her again, and his spit soaked her face. She could feel his hard-on grinding into her leg. He pushed her shirt up and pulled her pants down. His jeans were around his ankles when he mounted her. She could feel him struggling to get his cock into her, so she stretched her legs back as far as she could. He rocked onto his knees and started rubbing himself.

"Come suck this a little bit. I've had too much to drink."

Hannah leaned forward to rest on her palms and stuck the limp dick in her mouth. She sucked and ran her tongue over the man's shaft, but it was useless. He was flaccid.

"Fuck! Not again! Listen, I drank too much. I got something in my truck that'll help. You stay right here and I'll be back."

Hannah wasn't sure if she should get dressed or not. The whiskey kicked in so she stretched back onto the grass, and looked at the stars. After a few minutes, she started to feel scared and cold. She was in the dark, away from the rest of the party—and Matt...he was somewhere out there. Months had passed since Hannah last thought about Matt being released, but they were over eighteen now, so it made sense.

The cracking sound of a twig made Hannah look to her left. A man's black silhouette stood between her and the rest of the party. She couldn't see his face, but the lights blared around his shape.

"Hannah Simmons?"

Hannah could smell her own fear and her piss released in a warm stream into the patch of grass beneath her. It wasn't the man in the cowboy boots. This guy was much shorter.

"Don't be afraid, Hannah. That's all I wanted to tell you—don't be afraid."

Hannah did not move, and she did not breathe. The man, who appeared to be Matt, turned and walked back to the party. After his figure was swallowed by the crowd, Hannah stood up, put her pants back on, and ran. She sprinted to the opposite side from which he came—back to the beer pong crowd, leaving her panties on the grass. She stopped and went back for them, undressed, put them on, and redressed. If she had forgotten them there, she knew Bob would have hit them with his lawnmower, shredding pink onto his green yard.

"Whatssa mattta?" Bob greeted Hannah when she snuck herself back into the crowd. Her head spun from the liquor and her stomach lurched. She swallowed back the vomit and closed her eyes, but the darkness cycloned, too. She opened them and Bob was smiling as he handed her a beer. She drank it, fast, and her empty hand was filled with another bottle.

"Shit, Hannah, you can really drink." Bob lit a joint. He passed it to her and she inhaled deeply before passing it back to him. "Nah, pass it that way; I got more."

Hannah felt safe standing next to Bob. He fed her beers and joints over the next hour until she was lost in the ever-changing flicker of the campfire.

"Hannah, have you met Matt yet? He works with me."

Hannah turned her stare from the fire and looked at Bob. Matt was standing next to him.

"I know Hannah. We went to school together."

"Damn, I didn't know you graduated from Laurel High, Matt."

"Yeah." Matt didn't say anymore. Hannah knew he wouldn't want to explain to Bob why he hadn't graduated from there, but from the program at Oakmont.

"Well, if you know where she lives, she might need a ride home," Bob laughed and lit another joint. He handed it to Matt first who took a hit and passed it to Hannah.

Hannah took the joint and placed her lips where Matt's had been. The paper was slightly wet. She took a small hit and held it in front of her for someone to take. Bob took it, puffed on it twice, and handed it to Matt.

"Here, you guys finish this, I gotta go find Donna."

Matt stared at Hannah. She hoped he couldn't tell she was breathing like a rabbit—fast and full of panic.

"Calm down, you're going to give yourself a heart attack."

Hannah didn't speak.

"It was years ago. It was a mistake. Look, can we just finish this joint and talk?"

Hannah nodded her head and took the outstretched

joint.

"So, have you seen any of the old gang? Joel or Brian?"

"Joel moved to Philadelphia to play in some band. I haven't seen him since high school. Brian is at Penn State studying accounting."

"Ack, Brian and his fucking numbers."

"Yeah."

"How 'bout Olivia?"

"Pregnant."

"Pregnant?" Matt laughed, "Would I know who the daddy is?"

"Nah, some hippy artist guy from Pittsburgh."

"Oh, I bet her father's pissed as hell."

"Of course, why do you think she did it?"

They laughed and Hannah was calm. Once in awhile, the yard would spin."

"What about you? You work with Bob now?"

"Yeah, I've been doing that for a few months. How about you?"

"I work with Bob's wife, Donna, down at City Hall."

"Oh, that's cool."

"Yeah, it's a pretty decent job…boring. The hours are good, so I'm not complaining."

There were a few minutes when they didn't speak, but nervously drank their beers.

Hannah staggered a little bit and almost fell. Matt grabbed her arm, "Whoa! Be careful."

"Thanks. I'm drunk as hell."

"You'd better not drive home."

"Yeah, I'd better not."

"Where do you live now?"

"Downtown." She nodded her head, trying to move the awkward conversation along.

"Yeah, me too."

"Oh, that's cool." She kept nodding, but it didn't speed things up.

"Yeah."

"Listen, if you want, I can drive you home. I know you probably are still scared of me, but I swear, I'm a different person now, and if you'd ask Bob, he'd vouch for me. He's known me for months. He even helped get me my job."

"Wow, that's impressive, he wouldn't even do that for

his son."

"Yeah, we've been cool for a long time. So, can I drive you home?"

"I—I don't know."

"Aw, c'mon. My ride left without me. I could really use a lift downtown."

"Your ride left you?"

"Yeah, he was drunk though, so I think he forgot about me. I've been looking for someone to take me home for the past hour. I promise—you have nothing to be afraid of."

Hannah hesitated, "Okay."

"Cool. Really?" Matt smiled and looked happy.

"Yeah. As soon as you're ready, I'm about to pass out."

"Okay, my jacket's over on that chair, I'll be right back." Matt trotted off, and Hannah dug deep into her little red purse for a bottle of pills. She opened them, dumped six into her palm, and swallowed them with her beer. Xanax and alcohol shouldn't be mixed—and Hannah knew this, but it stopped her from having a panic attack.

Matt came back and smiled at her. After they said goodbye to Donna and Bob, they walked to Hannah's car. Hannah was still sipping from her bottle of beer when the car turned onto the highway. She finished it and tossed it out the car window, briefly sticking her head out so she could feel the wind on her face. As soon as she plopped back into her seat, she passed out.

Matt couldn't wake her as he entered the city. He knew he could check her purse for her driver's license to find her address, but then he'd have to find a ride home from her house or walk. He pulled behind his house and parked the car. He got out, unlocked his back door, and returned for Hannah. For a minute, he considered leaving her in the car to sleep, but sighed as he slung her over his shoulder and carried her inside.

CHAPTER 6
EMULSION

"Will you show me your scars?" Matt asked as he tugged her pants off.

Hannah didn't answer him. He ran a greedy finger along the splintered paths of her healed wounds. His crooked finger tugged the crotch of her underwear to the side.

"Did you shave for me?"

Hannah didn't hear him. He knew she hadn't shaved for him— *the slut kept herself bare for a devil called opportunity. My, how she'd grown.* Matt rubbed the outside of his jeans. This was easy for him.

He leaned into her until his face was inches from hers and blew on a chunk of hair caught in her eyelashes. She didn't move. He took her panties off. This was Hannah, the girl who ruined his life. The doctors could reason how it was actually his fault, but in the end, they ran on a circular track in his head, and all roads led back to Hannah.

In the room only lit by a television, her skin was a creamy blue color. The lines of scars on the inside of her arm were a lighter color, and they looked like army soldiers lined up, locked and loaded. It was time.

Matt pushed Hannah's legs up until they framed the sides of her face. He spit on her cunt, twice, and watched as she inhaled when he penetrated her. Still, she slept.

"You're going to let me do this to you every day, aren't you?"

Hannah didn't answer; she was hidden away behind closed eyelids, lost in a dream that smelled like candles burning in a cathedral at Easter.

"Sshh, now," he said, even though she was quiet. His hands slid down from her ankle as he lowered her leg and kissed it. He sunk himself in deep, but she was bottomless, like him.

*

Hannah slept on the couch that smelled like dog, only half aware of shapes in red light that moved and whispered.

When she woke up, she didn't know what happened,

only that something *had* happened. The sun illuminated the silence in the room and she immediately sat upright on the couch and realized it was morning. She was dressed, but wondered if she had been naked at some point because her shirt was on backwards, and her pants were crooked. Matt was asleep at the other end of the couch and his head rested on his folded arms. Hannah realized she pissed her pants, but it must have been hours earlier because the piss was nearly dried. As she carefully rose from the couch, she touched where she had been sitting. It was damp, but just barely. Her hear raced and she hoped it would dry before Matt noticed. Hannah took broad, soft steps as she tip-toed around the house until she found the kitchen and saw her shoes next to the door. Easing her feet into them slowly, she slipped out of the house without waking Matt. After she took two steps off of the porch, she bolted across the yard, only to fall forward into the grass. Standing up in a panic, she ran the rest of the way to her car. She was cold and she felt sick—like she could vomit. Whatever happened, she knew it was her fault.

When she got home, she shed her clothes and showered. Each bead of water pounded their tiny fists into her skin, screaming at her to remember. She didn't hear them. Hot soap and water steamed away any doubt she had, and erased the prior night's smells: cock, smoke, and beer. There was nothing to think about; it was all gone after the shower. When she stepped out of the shower and wiped the fog from the mirror, the questions came back. She had a purplish hickey on the side of her neck. Her muscles were sore. She thought she knew, but wasn't sure. She fought through her memory of blurry red images, but they quickly dissolved and then there was nothing. In her head, it was settled—she would ask Matt.

Hannah was happy to stretch out on her own bed. She wondered if her muscles were sore from sleeping on the couch. Her bed felt good, and she fell asleep trying to piece the events of the previous night into a firm memory, but it was like flan.

*

Matt and Hannah were an emulsion; they'd never combine together in their fluid existence, yet they surrounded each other. Even when they occupied one another in the same moment in time, they remained two distinct immiscible entities—not able to be fully blended. Their overlapping could be volatile or it could be verdant, however, they rarely had the same take on the flickering procession of film clips which had become their lives. The mixture was remarkable as Matt and Hannah never held the same perspective on their encounters.

*

Hannah woke up and looked at the clock—she had slept for hours. She began searching for her purse, but couldn't find it. Hannah went out to her car, but didn't find it there either. After hesitating, she called Donna, who said Bob had already picked up the garbage and didn't find a purse. The only thing left to do was to call Matt. Bob gave her Matt's phone number and she wrote it on a corner of an old newspaper.

She nervously held the scrap of paper in her palm, but was angry as she dialed. When he answered, her mood smoothed.

"Hey, it's me—Hannah."

"Hi, Hannah, what's up?" His voice was scratchy, as if he just woke up.

"I was wondering if I left my purse there last night?"

"Um, red thing, small, long strap?"

"Yeah, that's it." *Great, Hannah—of all fucking places to leave your purse.*

"Would it be alright if I came over to pick it up? I really need it."

"Yeah. Remember where I live?"

"Yeah."

"Cool. How about in an hour or so?"

"Okay. Um, maybe we could talk about last night as well?"

Matt paused, "Sure. Sure, whatever. I'll see you in an hour. I gotta go jump in the shower now."

"Okay, bye."

"Later."

Hannah was frantic to get ready. She didn't know what

to wear, and she still had to fix her hair. Matt only lived a few blocks from her, so she had almost the full hour to get ready. Before she left, she wrote a note saying she was going to his house and stuck it in her freezer. If something did happen to her while she was there, at least they'd find the note after she turned up missing. The freezer was the perfect place—if Matt *did* do something and came back to her apartment, he'd never look there, but eventually someone else would.

CHAPTER 7
A SOUVENIR

Jared stood on Matt's porch, a backpack slung around his shoulder, and a chocolate bar in the opposite hand.

"What up?" Jared said, but Matt stared back at him dumbly. "Aren't you glad to see me?"

"Err…how did you know where I lived?"

"Doug Dubaey—from transitional living—the group home…remember him? I'm out now man, they stuck me in there and when I said I was from Oakmont, Doug asked me if I had known you. What? Are you that surprised to see me?"

"No, no…listen, come on in. Sorry about that. I was,

um, expecting someone to come over and I thought you were them."

Jared didn't sit; he took himself on a tour of Matt's downstairs, peeking into rooms and picking up random things, examining them.

"So, how long have you lived here?"

"About four months or so. They put me into the group home when I first came out too. It sucked, so I got out as fast as I could."

"Yeah, bunch of fat bitches telling me what to do isn't my idea of fun either. I'll be looking to get out ASAP as well."

"I didn't expect they'd let you out of Oakmont so soon."

"Huh?" he said, scanning the titles of Matt's VCR tapes. "Yeah, my mom got her lawyer on it. Plus, being a juvey helped. They can't hold shit against you for too long. But then again, you know that." He smiled sadistically at Matt.

A knocking sound caused them both to look at the door. Matt exhaled and hung his head. *Perfect fucking timing.* He opened the door and Hanna stood there, cautiously peeking around him at Jared.

"Is this a bad time? Do you want me to come back?"

"Uhhh..." Matt stalled to answer her while Jared stepped forward.

"You aren't interrupting anything, please...don't go away on my behalf."

Matt opened the door and Hannah walked in. "Jared, this is Hannah. Hannah—Jared."

"Nice to meet you," she said with a shy smile and a slight wave.

They all walked into the living room.

"So, Hannah, how do you know Matt?"

"We grew up by each other—you know, a long time ago."

"Oh, neighbors. How nice. Do you live around here now?"

"Yeah—just over on Linton Street, in the condo apartments. Do you know where that's at?"

Stupid girl. Matt couldn't believe she told Jared where she lived. *Doesn't she have any fucking idea that she shouldn't tell people where she lives?*

"I think I do. I might have passed them on the way over here. Are they the ones in a group of four?"

"No, they're in a group of six, but I live in the first one, so the noise isn't so bad."

Stupid! Stupid! Stupid!

"Do you live by yourself?"

"Yeah, I do. How about you? Do you live around here?"

More fucking stupidity. Does she really think everyone is safe?

"Yeah, in the neighborhood," he said, smiled, and locked on her eyes until she gave a nervous laugh. He mirrored her laugh.

"You've got pretty eyes."

Oh God.

"What? Um…thanks." Hannah looked down; her cheeks flared.

"Yes, you're a very pretty girl." Jared spoke as though he could devour her. "Are you two…?" he said, waving his finger between Matt and Hannah.

"No, not at all," Hannah and Matt said in an awkward unison.

"Really? Just friends then?"

"Yeah, just friends. But, listen, Jared, I have the number of the group home, so I can give you a call sometime, but right now I promised I'd talk to Hannah about something important, so we, um...we gotta talk alone."

"Oh! No! Please, don't make him leave on my account. I can talk to you some other time. I'd feel terrible if he left because of me." Hannah's words came out so quickly that Matt could tell she was nervous and wondered if she was glad Jared was there so she wasn't alone with him.

"That's so sweet of you, Hannah." Jared said as he looked at her and smiled, his head tilted to the side. She smiled back and lowered her eyes again.

JesusFuckingChrist. Does this girl HAVE to be so fucking nice to everyone? Can't she smell the steaming fucking predator in the room?

"I came over to see if Matt wanted to watch a movie. How about we all watch one together?" Jared directed his question at Hannah.

"Sure, I'd watch a movie with you guys."

Jared seemed to be imitating the faces Hannah was making without noticing it himself. He smiled and nodded her head, just as she did.

Really? These two are gonna be stuck together in the same

fucking room together for two hours? Stupid. Fucking. Hannah.

Jared dropped onto Matt's couch, directly in the middle. "Let's all get cozy. You pick something, Matt. I'm not up on what's good." Jared winked at Matt.

Hannah took her jacket off and draped it over the radiator. Jared patted the cushion next to him and she sat down.

"Hey," he said, smiling with a half-crazed look on his face, leaning into her.

"Hey." She laughed nervously, as she sensed something was off about him, and she positioned herself as far away from him as she could.

That's right, Hannah. Listen to that little voice in the back of your head.

Matt's phone rang and he took the call in the other room where they couldn't hear him. Jared picked up a section of Hannah's hair and rubbed it between his fingers. He pulled the hair up to his face and smelled it. Hannah squirmed and tried to move away from him even more without making it seem obvious. Jared wasn't smiling anymore. Matt reentered the room and witnessed the silent exchange. Panic A-bombed through his skull.

"Hannah, that was my mom. Her car broke down at the Dairy-Dale. Can you give me a ride to go and get her? She's with my little brothers, so I'd like to leave now."

77

"Can I come with?" Jared asked.

"Sorry, man, her car's small and we wouldn't all fit. But, hey, it's good you're in town, so I'll give you a call this week and maybe we can hang out."

Hannah jumped up from the couch without even answering Matt. *Of course she'd do it, she never said no to anything. Good girl.*

Jared looked angry. He froze, looked at Matt, and stared him down like he was trying to figure out if he was lying or not.

"Sure, Matt, I'll give you a call. Maybe I'll drop by sometime when I'm not too busy. How does that sound?"

"Cool. Just, um, give me a call or something when you're free; we can watch that movie."

"Yeah," he paused, "Hey, Hannah, you wanna watch a movie sometime?"

"Um, sure." Hannah looked anxious to leave the house, trying to occupy herself with re-buttoning her already buttoned jacket.

"Why don't I stop by your place sometime? Is that cool with you?"

Hannah froze. She couldn't look more like a helpless

prey about to be pounced upon. "Yes?" she answered with an upturn, so it sounded like a question.

"Great. Apartment one, right?"

Matt could see that Hannah finally realized she had made a mistake in telling Jared where she lived. "Yes, apartment one," she said in a small voice.

"Okay, well, we gotta go. My mom is waiting."

The three of them left together and Matt made sure he locked his door.

"It was nice meeting you, Hannah," Jared said as he paused to take her hand and raise it to his mouth, kissing it."

Hannah giggled. The situation was uncomfortable and she wasn't handling it very well. She hurried to her car and unlocked the doors. Matt didn't say goodbye to Jared, he just jumped into the car and said, "Drive."

Matt was furious. The tendons in his neck twitched. Hannah didn't make a sound. Matt, after all, suspected that he still scared her.

"My mom's not at the Dairy Dale. It was a lie to get us out of there."

Hannah swallowed, "Jared—there's something wrong with him, isn't there?"

"BINGO! DING DONG! Now you get it. Not everyone is fucking nice, Hannah. There are people out there that are fucking crazy and you DON'T want them to know where you live—and Jared? Jared's one of them."

"I'm sorry."

"Why do you always apologize? Just get smart—and quick. If you're on Jared's radar, you should be shitting yourself."

"How do I know if I'm on his radar?"

"Are you fucking kidding me? Didn't you see the way he was looking at you? Wasn't him smelling your hair enough of a clue? Jesus. You're fucking ridiculous. Pull over, I need to think."

By this time, Hannah was at the Dairy Dale, so she pulled into its parking lot.

"Do you have anyone that could stay with you for a week or so?"

"I—I don't know. Maybe. I'd have to call a few people."

"Okay, let's go back to your apartment and figure this out."

Hannah started the car and crossed town, back to her

apartment. "Is he really that evil? I mean, he's back in society, so he can't be that bad."

"Hannah, for God's sake. Some of the craziest fucks aren't locked up; they're out shopping at the fucking Dairy Dale, or walking their dogs down your fucking street. You don't know for sure. You just have to trust me. Jared's one crazy motherfucker."

"But people change. Maybe he changed."

"No, Hannah. He was born wrong. Stop trying to make this shit okay in your head. It's not okay."

Hannah was quiet. When they got to her apartment, Matt jumped out of the car and looked up and down the streets. Satisfied, he followed Hannah to her front door. Once inside, he didn't notice the mess, but Hannah scurried about, first picking up the laundry off of the couch, which he didn't complain about because they *did* need somewhere to sit, but after she kept cleaning, he yelled at her.

"Fuck that shit, Hannah. We need to figure stuff out. Don't worry about cleaning now."

Hannah sat on the couch. Matt held his head in his hands. He knew he'd have to play this one carefully. He didn't want to piss Jared off because he'd not snitched on him regarding Danny, but he certainly didn't want to be his fucking friend, or see Hannah take a sky dive off of some balcony.

"Do you got any of those zani's left?"

"Um, yeah, they're in my purse." Hannah stood up and grabbed her purse, dug the bottle out, and handed it to Matt. "Wait...how did you know I had zani's?"

"I was looking for your address on your driver's license in your purse when I went to take you home last night. I wasn't trying to snoop...just relax. I only looked for a second before I decided to take you to my house instead."

"It's okay. I understand. I don't mind that you looked in my purse and saw my Xanax."

"Cool. Care if I?"

"No, help yourself. I have plenty."

Matt pulled the cellophane wrapper off of his cigarette pack and set it on the coffee table. He dumped a few of the tablets out of the bottle, onto the table, placed the cellophane over them, and crushed them up with the butt end of his cigarette lighter.

"Can I see your driver's license?"

"Um, sure." Hannah's head lowered as she searched in her purse again until she pulled her wallet out and handed her license to Matt. He used it to separate the crushed pills into neat lines.

"Dollar bill?"

"Oh." Hannah hesitated for a second and went back into her purse, searching for the money. "Will a twenty do?"

Matt made a face and cocked his head to the side. He raised his one eyebrow and put his hand out. Hannah handed him the twenty and he began rolling it up tightly.

"What are you doing? Are you going to snort that?"

"No, *we're* going to."

"We are? But I've never snorted anything before."

"It's cool. I'll show you how." Matt lowered his head onto the table, inserted the twenty up his nose, and snorted the line. When he was done, he tossed his head back and coughed. "Your turn. C'mere. Use whatever nostril is clearer, and hold the other one closed. Put the bill up your nose, exhale everything out of your lungs, and then snort it up steadily."

Hannah was nervous. She was clumsy with following his instructions, but she started snorting.

"That's it. Keep it going. Snort the whole line."

Hannah finished the entire line, and then tossed her head back slightly, like Matt had done. "That feels good. I'm all tingly."

"Yeah, it's better than swallowing them."

Hannah giggled. "I like it."

"Yeah, wanna do another bump in a little bit?"

"Sure."

"What do you have to drink?"

"Um…iced tea, milk, grape juice…"

"Any liquor? Beer?"

"Yeah, I have some Jäger."

Hannah went into the kitchen and got the green bottle out of the cupboard and started looking for a shot glass.

"Two."

"Two?" Hannah asked.

"Two glasses."

Hannah's living room opened into her kitchen, so it was one big room. The back wall of her kitchen was mostly taken up by a double-wide sliding glass door. It opened into a back yard she shared with her neighbors. She only had a thin curtain pulled across the door, and Matt made a mental note—she'd need lined curtains with

Jared loose in the neighborhood.

Hannah carried everything into the living room and paused, "Wait. Should we be mixing Xanax and alcohol? I've only ever done it once before and not while I was snorting the pills."

"You worry too much." Matt took the Jäger from her and poured some into each glass. "Cheers," he said, taking his glass and throwing the liquid down his throat.

Hannah hesitated, but swallowed hers as well. She squinted up her face and shook her head. "Wow." She sat next to Matt on the couch as he poured them two more drinks.

"How do you feel?"

"Like a Lucy in the sky."

"Okay, Lucy, let's do another bump."

Matt started crushing more Xanax as he lit a cigarette and offered the pack to Hannah.

"No thanks, I don't smoke."

"You didn't snort until five minutes ago, either."

Hannah laughed, "Trying to corrupt me, then, are you?"

"Nah, I think I've done enough to you—time to move on to someone else."

"What? I'm not complaining. I like hanging out with you. Corrupt away!"

"You," he said as he playfully poked her in the nose, "I didn't mean I was done hanging out with you, I meant, you know, when we were kids—what I did. It was stupid and I can't tell you I'm sorry enough."

"It's cool. It's in the past. Forgive and forget—or whatever people say."

"It's just, as fucked up as I am, there's a lot worse out there. Normal people like you don't usually get one crazy motherfucker in their life, much less two, so we gotta keep Jared away from you."

"Hey, I don't mind crazy. It's not like I'm the picture of sanity."

"Yeah—I noticed the scars," he exhaled smoke from his cigarette. "Maybe one day you'll tell me about them."

"Yeah, sometime," Hannah paused, "but I don't want you to worry about me, I can take care of myself." Matt didn't respond. Of course he knew she *couldn't* take care of herself.

"Okay, it's zani time." Matt lowered his head and snorted the bigger of the two lines. "Next," he laughed with a big guffaw as he raised his head from the coffee table. He handed the rolled up twenty to Hannah. She moved around to the end of the table and knelt down. She was slow to inhale the powdery line, but smiled when she raised her head. *That's a beautiful sight*, Matt thought.

"Nice," she said, but then she lost her balance and slid off of her feet, onto the floor. "Whoa!"

"Shit goes right to your brain, huh?"

"Yeah, maybe I should slow down."

"Yeah, maybe. Let's do shots."

Hannah crawled to the couch and drank the shot Matt poured for her. She slouched back into the couch. "Damn, I feel nice. How about you?"

"I'm all right. I'm a fucking beast. I can do this shit all night and still walk straight."

"I can't. I can barely keep my eyes open."

"You can barely keep your eyes open?" Matt leaned into Hannah and they both laughed as she lightly pushed him away. He leaned back in, ignoring her as she tried to push him away again, and he kissed her.

"Matt, stop. We didn't even talk about this."

"What's there to talk about?"

"I don't know. It's just that I—I can't remember if we did anything last night."

"What does last night got to do with tonight?"

Hannah stopped in the middle of her next word and giggled, "You're right. Nothing." She continued to giggle as Matt leaned in for another kiss. She let him kiss her, but then she pulled away, "DRINK! Time for another drink."

"Okay,   okay.   I   see   how   you   are."
"What does that mean?"

"Nothing, you got me all worked up and then you leave me hard with nothing but my hand."

"I'm sorry. It's just that this whole situation is kinda fucked up."

Kinda fucked up? You don't know the half of it.

Matt didn't talk; he made two lines on the coffee table while Hannah poured them two more drinks. He hurried up and snorted the smaller of the two lines.

"That whole thing?" Hannah pointed to the long, thick powdery line. "How much is that? An entire pill?"

"It's cool—you can handle it."

Hannah didn't argue anymore, she snorted the line,

but this time like a pro.

"Oh-my-fucking-God, YES! That feels good."

"Yeah, it's sweet. How about we watch some television?"

"Okay." Hannah staggered back to the couch and fell onto it. "I'm soooo fucked up."

"Nothing wrong with that." Matt intently watched the television while he flipped through channels. After a while, Hannah's heavy eyes remained partially open, even though she was softly snoring. Matt knew she was asleep by the way her head bent at the neck at such an uncomfortable angle. *Lightweight*. He watched some rerun for half an hour before he picked her arm up and let it drop down onto her body. *Yep, sleeping-fucking-beauty*.

He wasn't slow or even careful this time. He didn't bother to redress her, or even cover her up. He returned the Jäger to the cabinet and washed both of their glasses. He dumped a few of the Xanax into his hand and pocketed them before he tossed the bottle back into her purse. He unrolled the twenty and placed it in her wallet, in between the other bills. There was a Polaroid camera on top of Hannah's fridge which he retrieved. He stood back and took a picture of Hannah, naked and sprawled on her couch. *A souvenir*. He was a little disappointed how the picture didn't show her scars, or the wet glistening between her legs, but it would do.

He was about to leave when through the sliding glass doors, he saw something move outside. He crept along the wall and flicked the outside light on. He scanned the back yard. *Nothing.* He flicked the light off. He looked at Hannah and considered trying to wake her up. *Nah, bad idea. Who wants to deal with that?* Matt checked the time. *Ten at night, one more hour until Jared would have to make curfew at the group home.* He sat on the floor by the couch and flicked the TV on. He'd wait.

At eleven o'clock, the news came on and Matt turned the TV off. He looked at sleeping Hannah. *So sweet. So dumb.* He lifted her arm and let it drop again. Still, no movement.

Why not. It wasn't a question, it was an option. Matt was an opportunist and didn't pass up chances like this. He moved her so her ass was on the edge of the couch, and he let her legs fall to the sides. He knelt before her and eased inside, not sure how much longer she'd be passed out. She didn't move at all. When he got a good rhythm going, she still didn't wake up, although her tits jumped with each thrust. Matt spit on her clit and rubbed it a little bit. She smiled in her sleep. *Slut.* Each time he'd rub, she smiled, but she never woke up. Although it was an interesting experiment for him, he wasn't rubbing her when he came. He took no joy in seeing her smile.

He twirled her legs back onto the couch and dressed. The puddle of cum pooled on the upholstery under her ass cheeks pleased Matt. He locked the door behind him and walked home. It was four blocks away and the air chilled the skin left exposed from him only wearing a t-shirt. He slept better that night than he had in years.

CHAPTER 8
SKYE

There were things Hannah liked to remember, and things that liked to remember Hannah. Her couch had a frowning sag from the weight of her torso after a night of sleeping on it and not moving. Her limbs ached, but didn't whisper any secrets. Waking up naked smacked her recollection of the previous night's events.

As she made her way up the steps, what remained of Matt which hadn't soaked into her couch, ran down her thighs. Her skin wasn't able to record where his hands had explored, so she imagined touches in the steam of the shower. Her palms were against the tiles as the water sprayed on the back of her head. She could hear the phone ringing, but she kept her eyes shut and her mouth open as she breathed between the streams finding paths down her face.

The water began to run cold and she exited, wrapping a towel around her body, not bothering to dry her soaking hair. She slid her feet into shaggy pink slippers and shuffled to the mirror. One hand swiped the condensation from the glass and she could see one section of her body. She undid the towel and bent over so she could see the purple sucker bites on her neck. There were three more than she had the previous night. She held her breasts in both hands and lifted them up, turning to the side. In the fog of her reflection, she was almost pretty.

She refastened the towel and went downstairs to find her phone. It was still in its cradle, but she grabbed her purse and looked inside—she checked quickly and nothing was gone. The missed call was from a number she didn't recognize. She dialed it back as she walked upstairs.

A female voice answered, "Maple House, this is Rhonda."

"Um, hello. Someone just called me from this number."

"Well, I don't know who called you."

"Uh, is this a business?"

"Yes. Wait—hold on."

"Hello?" a man's voice answered.

"Hi, I was returning a call I received from this

number."

"Hannah?"

"Err...yes," she hesitated.

"Hannah! Hey! This is Jared—remember? We met yesterday at Matt's house."

"Oh, hey." The enthusiasm was completely absent from her voice. "How did you get my number?"

"I stopped by Matt's this morning and he said I should give you a call."

"He did?"

"Yeah. I wanted to see if maybe I could come over and watch a movie like you suggested."

"Um..."

"I mean, it's Sunday and Matt said he'd be busy so maybe I should drop by and keep you occupied until he's done with whatever he's doing."

"He said that?"

"Yeah, so, what do you think?"

"I—I guess. I just got out of the shower, so I need some time."

"Cool. How about in an hour? I'll walk over."

"You know where I live?"

"Yeah—remember? You told me yesterday."

"I guess I forgot."

"Sure—well, I'll be over in an hour."

"Okay."

"Later."

"Bye." Hannah hung up after he did.

She thought about calling Matt, but stopped herself. Maybe he realized he was wrong about Jared and would be coming over after awhile. She rushed to dry her hair and to get dressed.

The knots in her hair wouldn't rip out, so she cut them out. Her hair stopped at the middle of her back and losing a few strands wouldn't make much of a difference. She wondered how her hair had knotted so badly. She felt well-rested and didn't think she had tossed and turned much on the couch.

Hannah needed to process the distance Matt kept from her as his way to give her time to get used to him. She couldn't see him as the Matt from before, or before that. She wasn't afraid of him anymore—well, at least no more than she was afraid of everyone else. She was sore and she knew he had fucked her two nights in a row. She hesitated to call it rape because she knew she wanted it— to be wanted, to be fucked. She pulled her calendar off of the wall and took out a red pen. She put a red x on the day before, and the day before that. Each x stood for each time Matt had fucked her. She only knew of twice, but put a small x on the line that separated the two days because she imagined he had fucked her more than once on at least one of the nights. She could give herself that— one extra x because it was more of a likely x than a hopeful x.

A knock at the door startled her, and she dropped the calendar. She quickly hung it back up and ran down her steps. She opened her door and Jared stood holding a buff-colored puppy.

"Oh! Look how cute! Come in. Is that your dog?"

"No, silly rabbit, she's your dog."

"What?"

"Yeah, I hope you can keep her. My sister's friend was giving them away and they couldn't find a home for the runt, so they were going to kill her. I thought you might be able to take her."

"What? They were going to kill her?"

"Yeah, just put her in a bag and toss her into the river."

Hannah stood, horrified, and took the dog from Jared. She held the dog to her face, inhaled its fur, pet it, and kissed it. "I'd love to keep her. You said it's a girl?" She held the dog up and tried to look to see what sex it was.

"Yeah, I'm sure it's a girl. I was thinking of you and hoping you'd like her and be willing to save her."

"I love her! Thank you, that was so kind of you."

"You're welcome. My sister was calling her Skye, but you can rename her."

"Skye? Aww, that's so cute. It's perfect. I adore her."

"So you can keep her?"

"Yes! And I love her little pink collar. I'll have to get a leash and some dog food today." Hannah carried Skye into the kitchen, chose a bowl, and filled it with water. She set the bowl on the floor and placed Skye in front of it. "Oh, she's thirsty. And look at her cute little tongue."

"So I did good?"

"Yes! She'll keep me company *and* you saved her."

"Can I get a hug then?"

Hannah hesitated. "Sure!" She moved forward and hugged him, trying to pull back quickly, but he held her there and nuzzled his face into the swan of her neck. Skye barked and Hannah pulled out of the hug. She felt creeped out.

Jared was smiling, "How about that movie?"

"Yeah." She didn't sound nearly as enthusiastic as he did. She started going through a pile of movies. "What do you want to watch? Action? Funny? I'll guess you're like most guys and hate romance."

"You got anything scary? I haven't watched a scary

movie in a long time."

"Umm...*Pet Sematary* might be cool since you brought me Skye. Have you seen it?"

"No, is it any good?"

"Yeah, it's a Stephen King story. I read the book and it scared the shit out of me."

"Sounds good, put it in."

"Can I get you something to drink or some popcorn?"

"I'll take something to drink."

"Okay. I have Pepsi, Mountain Dew, grape juice, and I think I have some liquor left."

"Mountain Dew, please."

Hannah went into the kitchen to grab the drinks. Skye was following her around. She brought them back, set them on the coffee table, and picked Skye up. She kissed the dog's head and looked at him. "Oh, she has some tartar on her teeth. How old is she?"

"I dunno. I'll ask my sister. She's an older puppy probably because all the others have been gone from the litter for a while now."

"Oh. Okay."

The movie started and Skye slept patiently on Hannah's lap. Her small furry chest rose with each breath.

Occasionally, Hannah would notice Jared starring at her. At first she ignored him, but then she started sensing something was off. She kept her eyes on the movie, trying not to flinch.

When the movie was done, Hannah jumped up and put Skye on the floor. "I have to go to the bathroom—I'll be back."

She saw the phone sitting on the vanity in the bathroom, so she shut the door and locked it. She dialed Matt's number, but no one answered. She sighed, and sat on the toilet.

After a few minutes, she flushed and went downstairs. Skye was perky and smiling; her little toenails danced on the linoleum. Hannah smiled at her. Jared stood in the doorway between the kitchen and the living room. She tried to walk past him and he moved in front of her. She took a step to the left, and he mirrored her movement. She moved to the other side and he did the same.

"What? You wanna dance or something?" Hannah joked.

"Maybe." There was no humor in Jared's voice.

"I—I need to go to my parents' house and I can't wait to show my sister Skye."

"No you don't."

"What?"

"You weren't going to your parents' house. You just

99

want to get rid of me."

"Jared—no, I have dinner with them every Sunday, they're expecting me."

Jared's eyes flickered. "I was just messin' with you, Hannah."

Hannah forced a laugh, "Yeah, I figured as much. I hate to kick you out, but maybe I'll catch you over at Matt's this week."

"I doubt that."

"Why?" Hannah smiled.

"Oh, Matt's girlfriend is in town; we probably won't see him again until she comes up for air. You know what I mean," Jared made a blow job motion with his hand and his face.

"Girlfriend?"

"Yeah, didn't he tell you about Marilyn?"

"Marilyn? No—no, he didn't."

"They go way back. You probably shouldn't bother them."

"No, of course not."

"Is it all right if I stop by again? You know, to check on Skye."

"Yeah," Hannah smiled through the pain. "Yes, sure."

"Cool. I'll go since you need to leave and all."

"Yeah, I'm going now."

Hannah gathered Skye up in her arms, grabbed her purse, and left. Twice, she made sure the door was locked, and walked to her car. Jared waited on the sidewalk. The thought of Matt with his girlfriend drained the blood from her body. She knew she was stupid to assume he felt anything for her, and she cursed herself for feeling so needy.

"Hey, Jared, can I give you a ride on my way out of town?"

Jared smiled, "That would be great," climbed into Hannah's car, and cheerfully gave her directions. When she stopped at the intersection he wanted dropped off at, he leaned over and gave her a quick kiss on the lips before jumping out. "See you later, Hannah."

And he was gone. Hannah touched her lips. Maybe she was wrong about Jared. Maybe.

CHAPTER 9
FACE DOWN IN A HAMSTER CAGE

Hannah hadn't seen Matt or Jared in four days, but she came home late—on purpose, trying to avoid Jared and she didn't bother calling Matt. She felt fucked and dumped, and it hurt. Her week at work was slow. Donna was on vacation, visiting her mother in Philadelphia, but Bob offered to take her to lunch on Friday like they usually did. Afterwards, they sat in his truck behind the dumpsters, passing the fat rolled joint between them.

"C'mere," Bob said as he pulled Hannah's head towards his. "It's shotgun time." The joint was backwards and in between his lips as he blew out. A string of smoke quivered before Hannah sucked it in and sharply inhaled.

Hannah pulled her head out of his grasp and coughed.

"Fuck me, that's hard on the lungs."

"Okay."

"What?"

"Okay, I'll fuck you."

"Ha-ha, Bob."

"How 'bout you give me a little head?"

"Are you kidding me?"

"No. C'mon. I'm fucking hard."

"What about Donna?"

"We won't tell Donna."

Hannah placed her hand on the door handle. Bob unbuttoned his jeans and slid them down a few inches. His erect cock popped out of his underwear and pointed up.

"C'mon, Hannah. I waited a long fucking time to get you alone."

Hannah knew she should leave—she should bitch him out for even imagining cheating on Donna. Instead, she slid across the seat of the truck and put her mouth on his cock. It tasted bitter and sweaty and his hand engulfed the back of her head until it forced her deep into his curly hair.

This is like being face down in a hamster cage, Hannah

thought. She squeezed tears through her tightly closed eyes and concentrated on getting him to finish. Bob dug his hand into her shirt until he freed one of her tits, pinching the nipple with the same intensity in which he thrust her head on his cock until he blew his load into her mouth.

When he was done, he let her up and she gasped for air. Her face was red and there was cum smeared around her lips. She wiped it off with the back of her hand and smoothed her hair down.

Bob buttoned his pants, "I'll drive you back. I gotta get to work—we've been short a guy all week. Hey, you know—your friend Matt. Did you know he got arrested?"

"What? Matt got arrested?"

"Yeah, on Sunday. He got picked up in Pittsburgh buying H."

"H?"

"Yeah, you know, heroin."

"Well, when's he getting out?"

"He was supposed to get out today, I'm not sure."

Hannah felt dumbstruck. She wondered if Jared had known, and she also wondered if he invented Marilyn. Bob dropped her off at City Hall and she stood on the sidewalk, looking up at it. The old, massive stone building had gargoyles perched on the roof's four corners. They were watching her, watching them.

Hannah went to the bathroom and washed Bob's scent off of her face with medicinal smelling hand soap. She gargled with orange juice—the only thing she had—and let it penetrate the film of his semen on her teeth before she spit the juice into the sink. She turned and looked at the toilet and considered sticking her finger down her throat to vomit what remained of Bob into the toilet, but the thought of tasting him again sickened her. She looked at herself in the mirror; she felt only disgust with herself. The sleeves of her shirt were pulled up and she saw all of the red cuts she had made that week, stupidly over what she felt was Matt's rejection. *More scars that can't be hidden. Dumb fucking bitch. How the fuck will anyone think you're pretty with all of those scars? But Bob said he had been waiting. Did he find her attractive? A week without Donna riding his cock...she often spoke of their active sex life—maybe he just wanted to be satisfied.*

She seemed in a daze the entire day. She felt guilty for sucking Bob's dick, but also for not knowing Matt was in jail. *Stupid! You should have gone to his fucking house. You could have helped him. And Jared—did he know about Matt's arrest?*

Hannah left work at the end of the day and drove to Matt's house. After two knocks, he answered the door, wearing only a tight fitting t-shirt and boxers. The fabric took notice of each move his lithe body made, and so did Hannah.

"Hey."

"Hey. Can I come in?"

"Yeah," he said, stepping aside and letting her in.

"Bob told me you got arrested. Are you okay?"

Matt laughed, "Yeah, I'm fine."

"What happened?"

"I was in Pittsburgh buying shit and I got pulled over after my first stop."

"Bob said it was heroin."

"Yeah, well Bob has a big fucking mouth."

"Is it true?"

"Yes, Hannah, it's true."

"How did you get out?"

"My mom posted bail."

"Oh, fuck." Hannah knew Matt's mother didn't have the money to make any amount of bail.

"Yeah, it cost a fuckload to get her car out of impound. She convinced my grandma to drain her savings and get one of those payday loans so she could come up with the money."

"Shit, Matt, I'm sorry. What's going to happen now?"

Matt laughed, "I wait for my hearing notice to come in the mail."

"What about a lawyer?"

"Public Defender, baby." Matt flopped onto the couch, picked up the remote, and shut the TV off. Luckily, the first guy didn't have much shit to sell me so I got busted with very little H."

"That's good, at least—and your mom?"

"She's pissed as hell, but I'm gonna pay her back."

Hannah took her coat off and sat on one of the chairs. "I have some money in savings if you need help."

"Yeah? How much?"

"About five thousand dollars."

"Shit, Hannah. You're like an old fucking lady stuffing money into an account, huh?"

Hannah looked down. The comment upset her and reminded her of the things Matt used to say to her when they were kids.

"Hannah, don't take that the wrong way, c'mon. It's a good fucking thing."

"It is?"

"Yeah, rainy day and all that shit."

Hannah smiled.

"When could you get that money out?" Mat slid to the edge of the couch and faced Hannah.

"Um, the bank closes in an hour, so before then, or tomorrow for sure."

"Could you lend me that money and give me a ride? If I borrow some of it, I could make it back over the weekend and repay you by Monday or Tuesday at the latest."

"You could? How?"

"Same way I was gonna make it before I got arrested."

"You're gonna buy drugs?" Hannah exclaimed. "But you just got arrested."

"Yeah, well I guess I didn't learn my lesson." Matt sat back on the couch. "I know it sounds risky, but it really isn't. I could double the money in a few days. That way I could pay you and my mom back. C'mon, Hannah. My little brothers are gonna starve this fucking month."

Hannah sighed and thought while Matt eagerly looked at her. "Okay."

"Yes!" Matt jumped up and clapped his hands once. He grabbed Hannah and kissed her on the cheek. She smiled, and they immediately left the house.

There was a brief discussion over who should drive, but Hannah argued they'd be less likely to get questioned if they were pulled over and she was the driver. Matt agreed, and they headed for the city.

Hannah didn't bring up the subject of Marilyn or Jared. She swore silently to herself over forgetting to stop at home and let Skye outside. She shrugged off the thought and with each passing mile, forgot about Bob.

They made three separate stops for the drugs—the first was for weed and coke, the second for bricks of heroin, and the third was for Percocets. On the way down, Matt had removed the panel behind the glove compartment and stuffed everything inside except the Percocet—they wouldn't fit. He removed his sock, dumped the pills into them, gently lifted Hannah's breasts up, and tucked the sock under them so her bra held them up.

"Don't worry, they'll be safe there."

Hannah smiled. He had touched her and she trusted him.

They were nearly home when Hannah asked Matt if he wanted dropped off at his house. The conversation had been light and fun, but Matt seemed puzzled.

"Aren't you coming in?"

"I'm sorry, I didn't know if you wanted me to."

"Hannah! God, you're so—well you're always apologizing and shit. Of course I want you to come in. What's wrong? Don't you want to?"

"Yeah, I do, it's just that I'm worried about my puppy."

"I didn't know you had a puppy."

"Yeah, I just got her. She's been alone all day."

"Fuck, yeah, stop and we'll grab her and take her to my house."

"Really? You wouldn't mind?"

"Fuck, even I like puppies."

CHAPTER 10
CARPET ANGELS
& CHASING DRAGONS

Skye had to pee so bad, she was shivering. Hannah let her outside and checked for accidents on the carpeting, but there were none. She ran upstairs and brushed the final traces of Bob off of her teeth. After she let Skye inside, she grabbed two clean bowls from her cupboard and some packets of dog food. With Skye in her arms, she returned to the car and handed the dog to Matt.

"Hey, she is cute. What's her name?"

"Skye."

"Skye? That's a cool name. Did she piss all over your house?"

"No. I even looked but couldn't find anything."

"Fuck, she must be one smart dog to get housetrained so fast."

They drove the few blocks to Matt's house and he instructed Hannah to park in the back. After he unlocked his door for her, he returned to the car, and removed the drugs. Skye happily ran around the house, smelling things before settling on Hannah's lap.

Matt came back in with his purchases, dumped them onto the coffee table, and motioned with his fingers for Hannah to give him the Percocets. She pulled them from her bra and handed them to Matt. He emptied them out of his sock, onto the table, and put his sock back onto his bare foot.

"Can you count these for me?" he pointed to the pile of yellow pills. Hannah knew them well; she had bottles of them in her bathroom. She picked her prescription up every month, but rarely took them. In fact, Bob and Donna took them more often than she did. She knelt on the floor and began counting them into piles of ten.

"These are worth money?"

"Yeah—I'll sell them for about five bucks a pill. Why?"

"Just wondering." Hannah decided not to tell Matt about her stash.

When she finished, Hannah took the bricks of heroin

apart and Matt weighed marijuana into sandwich baggies. The bricks were wrapped in pages ripped from porno magazines. Cocks rammed holes and ridiculous expressions decorated painted faces. Inside were tiny wax paper stamps filled with a small amount of brownish powder. Hannah counted them into buns—groups of ten, and placed a rubber band around them.

"Be careful with them—they're small and easy to lose."

"I will."

"I should make you strip down to your underwear like they do with the putas in trailers where they bag this shit up."

"Why do they do that?"

"To make sure they don't steal anything."

"Why would I steal something I bought?"

Matt smiled, "I was trying to get you down to your panties."

Hannah laughed and kept counting. Skye trotted over to Matt and he picked the dog up. "Hannah, you know this isn't a puppy, don't you?"

"No, it's a puppy."

"No, it's a fucking Pomeranian. They don't get any bigger than this."

"Oh," Hannah said quietly.

"So where'd you get the mutt?"

"Jared got her for me."

"Jared?" Matt put Skye down and cocked his head sideways at Hannah. "*Jared* gave you a dog?"

"Yeah, he said his sister's friend had puppies and they were going to kill the runt if they didn't find it a home. He brought it to me."

Matt's head cocked even further. "His *sister?*"

Hannah continued to count stamps and didn't look at Matt. "It was his sister's friend's dog who had puppies."

"Hannah, Jared doesn't have a sister."

"Oh," she whispered.

Matt stood up and grabbd a piece of paper off of the top of his television. He read it for a second, picked Skye up, and examined her. "Did she come with this collar?"

Hannah briefly raised her eyes and looked at Skye. "Yes."

Matt handed the paper to Hannah, but she hesitated to take it. "Some old lady came around today passing those flyers out. It seems as though she's missing her Pomeranian named Bebe."

Skye barked. Hannah read the paper and set it down.

"I don't care where she came from; I'm not giving her back."

"When did he bring the dog to you?"

"Sunday afternoon." Hannah was reluctant to give any of the details out. She kept counting the stamps and didn't look up.

"Hannah, for fuck's sake. Don't tell me you let him in."

"Yeah, I let him in. So what? Big fucking evil that he is just brought me a puppy, watched a movie, and left."

"You watched a movie with him?"

"Yeah, *Pet Semetary.*"

"*Pet Semetary*? Nice choice for a first date." Matt spit the words out.

"It wasn't a date. He's *your* friend, remember?"

"Hannah, stop your fucking counting." Hannah looked up at him. "Jared's fucking nuts. He'll hurt you, if not kill you, so you need to stay away from him."

"You keep saying that, but he seems pretty fucking harmless to me."

"He's already killed two people. Do you want to be number three?"

Hannah looked at the drugs on the table and then met

Matt's eyes, "No."

"Then you have to listen to me. Jared stole some old lady's dog and brought it to you because he figured I'd tell you to stay away from him."

"Well I'm not giving the fucking dog back." Hannah picked Skye up and put her on her lap, petting her.

"No, you don't have to give the dog back, but let's buy her a new collar…maybe get her fur shaved so she looks different, okay?"

"Like a lion."

"What?"

"I want to get her shaved like a lion."

"Yeah, like a lion." Matt placed a hand on Hannah's face and smoothed her hair back.

"She'll look cute as a lion," Hannah said.

"I'm just trying to look out for you, okay?"

Hannah nodded and stopped petting Skye. Matt moved closer to her, and she thought he might kiss her, but he didn't. He leaned back and Hannah resumed counting.

"I'm gonna roll us a joint, then we can stop counting until tomorrow."

"Sounds good."

Matt broke the buds of the weed up, and removed the stems and seeds. The rolling paper was thin, and creased easily between Matt's fingers. He sprinkled the marijuana on the paper, carefully rolled it, and licked it to seal it.

"Fuck, this shit is sticky with keef. Here, suck it off of my fingers."

"Really?"

"Yeah, no sense in wasting it."

Hannah moved closer to Matt until her mouth met his outstretched fingers. She sucked the sticky keef from them with her eyes closed.

"Now that's a beautiful sight."

Hannah opened her eyes and moved back to where she was sitting. She smiled at Matt, but looked down quickly.

"Maybe later, eh?" he chuckled and resumed rolling the joint.

They smoked the joint as they cleaned the drugs off of the table, and then Matt took them upstairs to his safe. He came back down and Hannah could see his gun shoved into the back of his pants.

"You have a gun?"

"Yeah, I had it with me when we went to Pittsburgh. Listen, don't be pissed. I didn't want to risk losing your money."

The gun frightened Hannah, but Matt had been so nice to her all night. She just smiled. He threw a small tied up balloon on the coffee table.

"We gotta try this."

"Try it? What is it?"

"It's tar heroin. I bought us a little bit for tonight."

"You mean we're going to shoot it up?"

"Nah, that's for junkies. We're gonna smoke it."

"You can smoke it?"

"You can smoke anything, but we're going to chase a dragon."

Matt went into the kitchen and came back carrying a few things. He took out his pocket knife, carefully slit the balloon open, and put some of the black tar onto a square of aluminum foil. He rolled a subscription card from inside of a magazine into a funnel and handed it to Hannah. "You first?"

Hannah smiled. "Wait. I don't know what I'm doing."

"I'll light this until it cooks and then you suck up all of the smoke that you can through that funnel. Okay? Ready?"

Hannah nodded her head, but wasn't sure if she was ready. She sat next to Matt and when he held his lighter under the foil, she tried sucking up as much of the smoke as her lungs could swallow. She didn't want to disappoint Matt.

*

The carpet felt like moss under her body. Hannah moved her arms and legs, "Look, I'm making snow angels."

"But there's no snow, Angel."

"Look, I'm making carpet angels."

"Yes, you are."

Hannah giggled and closed her eyes. The carpet was swallowing her into a sea of glowing jelly fish, and then spitting her back out to Matt. Spit and swallow, swallow and spit. She didn't know how, or when she had lost all of her clothes; she only knew she felt like heaven.

"You grew up pretty," Matt breathed into her ear. She smiled.

CHAPTER 11
PAISLEYS

In her life, she lived lucky days and good days, but Hannah never experienced ones like those that Matt gave her. The weekend rolled and she felt like clothes tossing in a dryer—round and round, in and out, like jelly beans and belly buttons.

Customers came and the paper stacked until Matt said they were even. Soon, the paper stacks were bundled and he said they were making profit. Hannah told him he was a prophet. He kissed her for it.

It was usually men who bought the drugs. Some would stay and indulge while others would take their stuff and leave. If they were smoking, sometimes they'd share with Hannah, but it made no difference because Matt always had plenty for her. Hannah passed out easily. Matt only let her have little rations of the stash because he said the drugs would eventually make her skin itch if she didn't have them.

After her first shower, she realized she hadn't brought clothes with her, so she wore one of Matt's long t-shirts and a pair of his sweat pants. He said she looked cute in them and liked how they were easy to take off. They hadn't had sex yet while she was awake, but she was almost sure all of the days on her calendar would need red x's.

Hannah called in sick on Monday, and Tuesday, and then she dared to call off on Wednesday. She wasn't eager to see Donna, and staying with Matt was too much like a dream she once had of things she thought she'd never do.

Matt had the tolerance of a horse. He smoked, snorted, and popped pills, but he could always function. Unlike Hannah, he went to work every day. Hannah slept on the couch when he was at work and she never answered the door. Tweakers would knock for what seemed a mouthful of minutes, but she ignored them. Matt was right—she couldn't protect herself, and he didn't want robbed. The gun was kept on the coffee table while he was gone. Hannah never touched it, but it was there if she needed it. She thought she heard someone calling her name and Skye's name once, but she went back to sleep and ignored the knocking.

Marcus was a friend of Matt's who bought in bulk to

sell on his own. Because of this, Matt said he gave him a discount. Marcus didn't sell out of Matt's house—it was Matt's territory. Since he was a good customer, Matt didn't mind that he hung out a lot, shooting heroin up his veins, and then spending an hour afterwards with his head doing a drug nod as he stared at the television.

Hannah knew Marcus was waiting on Matt's porch, but she didn't bother to let him in. Matt got off of work early on Wednesday and when he arrived home, Hannah heard him unlock all three locks before they entered the house. She was lying on the couch, half-asleep, her arm dangling down and resting on top of Skye. Skye jumped up to greet them, but Hannah didn't move.

Matt took the gun, went upstairs, and brought down a few buns. Marcus took them and held up a needle, "Do you mind, man?"

"No, go right ahead. I'm all sweaty from work. I'm gonna go upstairs to shower and then I'll be down."

Matt bound up the steps, two at a time, with Skye running behind him. Hannah opened her eyes and saw Marcus cooking his heroin in a spoon. She longed to inhale the fumes.

He saw her watching and he nodded towards her, "You wanna hit?"

Hannah nodded her head, but didn't move. As he methodically prepared the heroin for injecting, Hannah watched Marcus; it was the closest he'd ever come to her. The scent of his deep cologne traveled up her nose and she smiled. His skin was a lovely cocoa color and she noticed his impressive arm muscles. After he pulled the plunger back to suck up the heroin, he plinked the side of the syringe so he could force the air out. She nearly said, "Please don't," but knew the tiny air bubble wouldn't have killed her anyway.

Marcus removed his belt and tightened it around Hannah's calf. He pulled her sweat pants up and smacked a blue vein on the side of her ankle. She held her breath, terrified he'd raise her pant leg higher and see her scars.

The beveled end slid into her skin; a lightning strike of red flashed into the barrel and with a flick of his thumb, he pushed the heroin into Hannah's vein.

She felt it—a sticky warmth massaged her cells. Marcus took the tourniquet off and it swam through her body in a flutter. Hannah was in a waterfall of orange welding sparks again.

Sitting on the floor, Marcus hit himself, but in a large bulging vein in the crook of his arm. His body fell back against the couch, his head rested on Hannah's abdomen, and he closed his eyes for a few minutes.

The shower started and the rhythm sounded like rain. Marcus peeled the blanket off of Hannah in slow motion and crept a hand between the waistband of her sweatpants and her skin. Hannah was still swimming. She didn't care who was touching her because everything felt like cotton candy.

Marcus explored her and pressed his lips to the small mound beneath her belly button. Hannah smiled. Somewhere, behind closed eyes, she was floating on a little raft on a stream, surrounded by veil-tail goldfish. The rain stopped, and so did the touches and kisses. She wouldn't tell Matt. She had come to expect this sort of thing when he left her alone with one of his customers. She wasn't sure if it was part of his plan, or if they were all just opportunists doing things opportunists did.

Hannah kept secrets from Matt—things she should have told him. Marcus left and she didn't mention the hit he'd injected into her. The prick was on her ankle and he'd never notice it. He brought out the last of the tar and smoked it with Hannah, who was still high from what Marcus had given her.

Hannah sucked the smoke up like a good girl. When Matt told her to take her shirt off, she did that too. When someone knocked at the door and he laid her down and covered her with the blanket, she was still. When he let Jared into the house and argued with him in the next room, Hannah pretended she was asleep.

Hannah was under a tree with paisleys for leaves. They were fall colors and spring colors. They were delicate, and they were elaborate. In her mind, it wasn't winter—she didn't have to wear long sleeves or tights under her clothes. She lay under the tree and it shed its paisleys on her like cupcake sprinkles. She rolled around in them, inhaled their scent, and moved her arms and legs back and forth.

Between the paisleys were words. The words fell from a cloud hanging over the tree and were either purple, or blue, depending on whether it was Jared or Matt who spoke them: Murder. Blame. Institution. Fuck. Need. Want. Secret. Refuse. Permit. Hannah. Fly.

In the scatter of paisleys, the words didn't make sense to her, but she knew they were important.

Sometime later, her eyes flickered open. Matt and Jared sat on a couch, watching her contemplatively. She closed her eyes and remained still until she opened them and it was just Matt sitting on the couch. Something had changed. She could feel it.

"Hannah, I need you to sober up."

"I'll try."

"Do you want something to drink?"

"Yes, please."

"Coffee or grape juice?"

"Grape juice."

"I think you need coffee."

"Okay, coffee."

Matt stood up and walked into the kitchen. Hannah swung her legs over the side of the couch and sat up. Her head was heavy. Matt returned with the coffee and handed it to her.

"What happened?" Hannah's voice cracked and she took a sip of the juice.

"You passed out, I guess."

She smiled, "Hmm…it was nice. Was Jared here?"

"No." Matt's lips tightened.

"Funny. I thought I heard and saw him."

"You were really fucked up." Matt turned the television on.

The alarm that never seemed to sound in her, chimed like church bells. "Yeah, I guess you're right."

"Listen, I have to cook some of that coke into crack and it's best if you aren't here."

"You're cooking it into crack?"

"What I don't step on, I'm cooking."

"What do you mean, step on?"

"That means dilute it with baby laxatives. I'll make more money off of it that way."

"Why do I have to leave?"

"Hannah…" Matt hung his head and shook it from side to side, laughing. "This house is going to smell *really* bad and everyone in it is going to be high as fuck; you can't stay while I cook the crack."

"Okay, when do you want me to leave?"

"I don't want you to leave, you just need to." Matt looked at Hannah. She shivered in his clothes and starting to tear up. "You aren't going to cry, are you?"

"No," she said as tears eased from the corners of her eyes.

"Don't cry. You can come back; you just shouldn't be here for a while. Listen, let me cook it up and I'll come stay at your house."

"You will?" She perked up.

"Yeah. Hannah, you need to go back to work anyway. I talked to Bob today; Donna's starting to get suspicious."

"Donna's suspicious? About what?" She perked up and could feel the obviously guilty look on her face.

"Yeah, you've missed a lot of work this week. She's

worried about you. Go back to work, and it'll be no big deal."

"Okay, when I think I can drive, I'll leave."

"If you want me to drive you home and then walk back here, I will."

"No, that's fine."

"Are you sure?"

"Yeah, no problem."

"Okay, just wait until after eleven."

"Why?"

"Don't ask."

Hannah didn't wait until she was sober. After a half of an hour of watching TV in silence, she picked her purse up, grabbed Skye, murmured a slight goodbye, and went home.

The apartment was still and smelled stale. It was as though it slept and died in her absence. She showered and made neat red x's on her calendar before she went to bed. Facing Donna wasn't something she looked forward to.

CHAPTER 12
DIVULGENCES

Jared could smell Hannah's stupidity. She believed the whole bit about the dog and didn't even question him. Girls and puppies, puppies and girls—they were interchangeable. Usually. Except for Hannah. She might be a bird—a little blackbird in her long shirts and pants, hiding something he was eager to see. But first—first, he wanted inside of her in every way possible. She had secrets and he wanted to make them his before he heard her chirp.

Matt was a prick. Jared didn't mind taking all of the responsibility for Danny, fuck, it was his idea, but Matt could show his gratitude. He could *share*. Living in a group home made getting laid almost as hard as it had been when he spent his entire teenage years in near solitary confinement. The doctors didn't trust him. His blood tests frequently showed he wasn't taking his anti-psychotics and mood stabilizers. They labeled him as uncooperative and either shot his medicine into his ass, or made him drink it. They thought they were smart, but Jared was the one living on the outside now.

The group home sucked. He shared a room with Ben, who he kept catching masturbating into a hole he had cut into his stuffed teddy bear. It was disgusting. He told him to blow his load into tissues like everyone else did, but he just kept fucking the bear. The bear's insides had to look like a Jackson Pollock painting with the varying shades of dried cum.

The worst part was the staff. They were such fucks; they made him forget about the rules. He only had an hour long window to take his medication three times a day. They still didn't trust him to medicate himself. He missed his afternoon dose on Sunday when he was with Hannah, so they restricted his privileges for ten days. Because of this, he couldn't visit Matt or Hannah. He had only missed his medication by fifteen minutes and the staff woman, Carla, refused to give it to him. She was a fat bitch with three chins. He called her 'jowls' and it made her hate him even more. She had toothpick legs with a beach ball belly and she smelled like a mixture of cheap perfume and shit. Her arms were kind of short and he figured she might not be able to reach her ass to wipe properly. She brought in video recordings of soap operas and sat on the couch watching them when she should have been working for her pay. She wasn't the laziest, there was a tall skinny woman named Susan. She kept her hair in cornrows and started and ended her shift on the couch. At least Carla passed meds to the residents.

The everyday routine consisted of chores and day treatment, which was a circle-jerk version of group therapy. The day therapy was six hours long, so it consumed most of his time. Attendance was mandatory, so he went. He followed the rules because he didn't want to return to Oakmont. He hoped he could get his own place in a few months like Matt had done. Matt had left the group home in record time, but he wasn't court-ordered there like Jared was. Jared would live there for at least a few more months, depending on how well he played the game.

His time in Oakmont taught him about people and games, secrets and need. Want was a forbidden candy which tempted people to make mistakes. He could read others well—it was one of his strengths. The remainder of his time at Oakmont was spent as a watcher; nurses, orderlies, patients and doctors all operated on the same habitual matrix. People didn't change. Everything was a game and the trick was to not get caught, but to play better than everyone else. Every person kept secrets, and these were to be used to be a game player. Jared knew he needed things. He needed to satisfy his wants. And what he wanted was Hannah.

When he met her, he knew she was special. He could almost see her heart fluttering under her blouse. She scared easily and couldn't hide that she hid things.

Matt resisted giving Hannah to him. He asked if he could have her there, on the couch, like Matt had done in Hannah's apartment. Yes, he admitted to having watched them that night. Matt turned him down, saying he didn't want anything to do with it—that he had done enough to Hannah. Jared knew what Matt had done to her. They'd whispered their stories to one another, and since they only gave one and shared one, it was the only thing Jared had, so he remembered it well: Matt had crushed Hannah's legs with a cinder block. It wasn't Jared's thing; he didn't like messy middles to sandwich between clean beginnings and final endings. Still, the story was a lollipop in his mind, and he sucked it for almost six years.

Jared needed time with Hannah. The truth was, he didn't plan on blowing his load in her after two minutes and then moving on. He wanted to savor her for hours, even if it meant tying her up. *The drugs were a great idea— Matt's idea, but smart nonetheless.* If she was unconscious, it would give him time to put the ropes on her...unless she cooperated. *Oh, but no! She wouldn't cooperate with all of it; no, no, no. The ropes would be an eventuality, a guarantee, insurance, a divulgence of her future.*

Matt's anger made Jared laugh. There was no statute of limitations on murder and Jared had Matt by the balls. Matt understood the difference between want and need. He wanted Hannah, but he didn't need her, so he gave her up. Matt would leave Hannah alone and Jared would have his chance, not only without interference, but with help from Matt.

Jared knew Matt would bend to his will. He spent the

previous ten days constructing a plan, and he'd spend the next ten days carrying it out.

The visit to Matt's house was more productive than he could have imagined. Hannah was asleep, so it was easy for Matt to steal her house key. Jared said he was just using it to go through her house while she slept, and he'd return the key. He said he would leave it on the back porch so Matt could sneak it into her purse before she left. He agreed to keep Hannah there with him until after curfew, so Jared wouldn't have to worry about her coming home and surprising him.

Jared didn't go to Hannah's house right away. At the bottom of Matt's street was a hardware store. It had already proven to be a great place to purchase other needed things. Jared went there and had a copy of the key made. The extra time allowed him to sneak into Hannah's house and look around. He stole three things: a picture of her, a pair of her underwear, and an old diary. He would *learn* her. The key would allow him to return to covet what was no longer Matt's.

A first skim of the diary revealed to him one of the things she'd been hiding—her scars. She churned about them in her diary a lot; how to hide them and how ashamed she was of them. And she was a cutter. He took delight in that. Knives sang to her, and he was glad something did. He had spent so many hours in group therapy with little girls worshiping the pain they did unto themselves. He experimented with them in the institution—they fell the quickest to pain that wasn't from their own hands. Hannah would be more than just an experiment in nature, she'd be *fun*.

CHAPTER 13
RABBIT HOLE

Hannah woke up with thistles under her skin. Her sleep was restless. She dreamt a green ribbon snake kept coiling around her body, making her writhe and sigh. Two hours before her alarm went off, she climbed out of bed and went to her bathroom medicine cabinet. She dumped two Percocets into her palm, swallowed them, turned the sink faucet on, stuck her mouth into the warm running water, and drank.

She expected this might happen. There was a summer when she had four surgeries on her legs. First the pills made her itch, and then they made her want, and finally, need.

Despite hiding under her blankets, she couldn't sleep.

Her eyes were squeezed into little slits like a house with its shutters closed in anticipation of a tornado. Hannah was her own storm. Matt's rejection made her want to cut herself, but she didn't have the energy.

It was a divulgence to allow her thoughts to linger on Matt, and what his fingers felt like on her skin, but it was like a distant memory, fogged by drugs, with snippets barely blowing in the winds of her mind.

Hannah thought she loved Matt once, before the cinder block. She always believed that if he would love her back, she'd be the wanted one, and the worthy one. Too much of her time was spent thinking about what had happened and there was only one logical explanation: she deserved it. She was ugly, fat, mouthy, and a nuisance. Like the rats in the neighbor's barn which swelled from the smorgasbord of the oat bin, she needed clubbed.

Because she was, by most standards, a tall girl, she had grown into her weight by her late teens. Her mother said she had lost her baby fat, but Hannah knew it had more to do with the meals she vomited into the toilet. She wasn't bulimic, but she didn't always think she deserved the food she had eaten. In fact, there wasn't anything Hannah thought she deserved—even life. She found herself to be completely and utterly disposable.

The stress of work loomed and wouldn't allow her to fall back to sleep. She worried if Donna knew. Maybe Bob had told her, or maybe she'd read the guilt on Hannah's face. Hannah wondered how she could keep her job if Donna found out. She'd be too embarrassed to work there, and they worked so closely together that it would be bad—very bad.

Hannah knew it was her fault. *HerFault, HerFault, HerFault.* She could have said 'no', but she didn't. Skye wiggled under the covers with Hannah. She sighed. No matter what, the sun would still rise and the sun would still set. Even though the idea appealed to her, she couldn't hide in her apartment forever.

Unexpectedly, it dawned—the familiar sparkle from the pain killers. Her cells relaxed and she felt relief. Only two pills had done it—not too bad and she knew she could wean herself off of it like she had done before. Since she was in control of her own stash, it would be easier this time. There was nothing worse than having a mother dole your pills out to you and chide you for the missing ones. Addiction was easier when you played alone. Besides, this wasn't a full blown addiction, just a little scratch.

Her thoughts were like mud on shoes, leaving clumps and tracks as they paced in her head. She recognized they were the sick thoughts—ones she had which weren't 'well' or 'normal'. In the sparkle, she played with them anyway:

What if she really did become an addict? Would Matt like her more? And Marcus, with his hand down her panties, plunging a long finger inside of her—would he want her as well? Maybe it would be fun—just for a little while—to see if it made her confident. She could be the girl at the party who danced on the coffee table while everyone watched—the girl everyone wanted. But the scars—remembering the scars furrowed her brow. Nothing hid them but long pants or leggings. And the ones on her arms—how her sleeves would inch up when she stretched her arm out to pass money at windows of drive-thru restaurants and the cashier would pause to look down at the slashes in her skin, and then take the money. It was almost a guarantee.

Hiding things was as much of a coping mechanism for Hannah as cutting was. Emotions were things which needed to be stuffed down until she choked on them. The only person she could relax and expose them to was herself. Being alone brought her comfort, just as cutting and abusing her medicine did. She didn't mind not having friends, she was used to it. Close relationships brought questions Hannah didn't want to answer. Part of her was like the person she had invented in high school—the better version of herself—the Hannah who lived to her potential. When she was alone, she could feel like the better Hannah was able to emerge. She would turn the music up and dance, make faces at herself in the mirror, and wear the short, sleeveless dresses she kept hidden in the back of her closet. As crazy as she was, even Hannah knew that underneath the dysfunction was someone so happy, they could fly.

*

It was easier for Hannah to go to work high than not. Donna was all smiles and squeals when she saw her. She hugged Hannah, but Hannah didn't hug back. She was frozen from the numbness of being high, somewhat lost

138

in the particles of the moment.

Donna pulled back. "What's the matter, hon?"

"Don't mind me, I'm still sick. And my knee is bothering me today, so I took a few Percs and I think I might have overdone it."

"Aww, it's a slow day—perfect for your first day back. You'll be fine."

Hannah was fine. A fucking crippled monkey could do her job. Hannah laughed at the thought, for she *was* a crippled monkey. She was so high that she had to go through the bother of reciting the alphabet in her head so she could find her place: abcdefG! G for Gariety, Robert and his unpaid water bill. Next was abcdefghiJ! For Jameson, Catherine and her application for a choice handicap parking spot right in front of her house.

Filing wasn't serious business—just a well-used system which the members of city council kept insisting would be transferred to computerized documents in the near future. Until then, Hannah weathered paper cuts and sore fingers.

At lunchtime, Donna said she wanted to walk across the street to a café for a sandwich. Hannah declined lunching with her. Instead, she had apple juice from the vending machine upstairs and two more Percocets. Before her lunch break was over, Hannah had the sudden desire to ride the elevator to the top floor and back. The elevator rocked and jolted as if it was as old as the building. Hannah liked the way her red shoes looked on the black and white checkered floor tile inside the elevator. She concentrated on them so much that she forgot to notice the particular ding which signified she had reached the top floor. Because of this, she rode the elevator three more times to the top before she got the ride just right: alone in the elevator, and feeling the burp the elevator made when it hit the top floor.

The ride made her happy. She bounced to a song in her head as she made her way back to her work space. Donna was already there waiting. She had a tuna sandwich for lunch and the smell had followed her back. It made Hannah nauseated, so Donna tried to rectify it by sucking on a breath mint. Nothing could have been worse than the smell of tuna, except for peppermint tuna. After twenty minutes, Hannah vomited her apple juice into the trash can.

"Gosh, you aren't pregnant, are you?" Donna asked.

Hannah froze—the expression—absent from her face as she calculated when and with who she last had sex. Luckily, it was easy to remember. She hadn't had sex in awhile, except for Matt; she had only been passing out blow jobs liberally, and it was too soon for her to be experiencing pregnancy symptoms from fucking Matt.

Hannah and Donna worked in silence for the rest of the afternoon. Hannah dealt with Donna's tuna smell, and Donna dealt with Hannah's regurgitated apple juice smell. They were twins of disgust which went un-discussed.

After work, Hannah went to Matt's house. She stood, pathetically, on his porch, knocking over and over again, but he didn't answer. She thought he'd be home because after work was a prime time to sell, but she stood there for twenty minutes before she felt ridiculous enough to leave.

She stopped by her house, let Skye out, and then took him with her to drive to her parents' home. Skye needed time in their yard, and she knew her sister would enjoy playing with him. She decided to pass by Matt's house, again, in case he came home from work.

She carried Skye to the porch, and only knocked once before Matt swung the door open.

"Hey, c'mon in."

Hannah stepped through the door and saw a girl sitting on Matt's floor, near the coffee table, tearing aluminum foil into pieces. She had long, straight, strawberry-blonde hair and a body as thin and flat as an ironing board. *She's cute.*

Hannah set Skye down and she ran over to the girl. The girl exclaimed and started petting Skye, who enjoyed the attention a little too much.

"Hi," the girls said simultaneously.

Hannah nodded in the girl's direction, "That's Skye and I'm Hannah."

"Ohmygod," the girl laughed. "My name is Hannah

too."

"It is?"

"Yeah, funny that."

It didn't look like a typical drug deal; the girl looked too comfortable and she was preparing to smoke up.

"We were going to blaze one, do you wanna join us?" Matt asked.

"Yeah, sure." Hannah walked to the couch and sat down. She immediately stood up and looked at her hand. "Shit, did you spill something? I sat in something wet."

Hannah number two bit her lip and smiled. She looked at Matt and they both started laughing. "Um...sorry, that was from us, earlier."

Us?

"You might want to go and wash your hands," Matt said.

Hannah looked at her palm. Her heart was racing and her cheeks were flushed. She hurried and walked into the kitchen to wash her hands before they could see her starting to cry.

She stood at the sink, panting and trying to calm down. A small scrub brush on the sink's ledge would serve—she squirted dish soap on it. Hanah tried to scour the thoughts away. She inhaled until her lungs were bursting as she scrubbed several layers of skin from the tops of her hands. It was her punishment—punishment for being stupid, and punishment for not being the one Matt chose.

He fucked her—while she was awake. Hannah blinked the tears back and focused on her hands.

It was a lengthy hand washing session, by anyone's measure, and by the time Hannah reentered the living room, they were already smoking the heroin. She didn't want to sit on the couch again, so she sat on the floor next to the other Hannah.

Matt passed her the straw and held the lighter's flame under the foil.

Four, three, two, one...it was almost all gone—the bad things—facing Donna, vomiting the apple juice, and Hannah number two; they all disappeared with each scant of smoke which she sucked up the straw. She didn't even pause when she realized Matt *had* been home earlier.

Everyone was laughing. Happiness seeped into the group until the tension was like a cherry pit spit into a napkin, folded and refolded until it was hidden.

"You know what?" Matt said. "You two side by side gives me an idea."

"What?" the girls asked in unison.

"How about it's my lucky day and I get a two-Hannah blow job?"

"What's that?" asked Hannah.

The other Hannah giggled, "He wants us to both suck his cock at the same time."

Hannah didn't know what to say. As willing as she was, she had never done anything like it before and was nervous.

"C'mon, it'll be fun." Hannah number two elbowed her gently. "Is this your first time?"

"Yes."

"If you girls don't want to…"

Hannah spoke up, "I'll do it."

The girls knelt side by side as Matt lowered his pants, hard with anticipation. He stuck it into Hannah's mouth first. This pleased her. She could taste the sex on his cock and she tried to ignore it, sucking harder until the taste disappeared. He pulled it away from her and offered it to Hannah number two, who eagerly took it, thrusting her head on it until it all disappeared, over and over again.

Matt pulled away, "Kiss each other," he said.

Hannah didn't have the option of hesitating; Hannah number two grabbed her and kissed her deeply. Her free hands explored Hannah's breasts. Hannah didn't know what to do. She kissed her back, but didn't return the touches.

"Okay, back to me," Matt said.

Hannah number two was greedy and didn't share

equally. When Matt distributed his cum all over their faces, Hannah number two swallowed hers and licked the remains off of Hannah's face, ending it with another deep kiss on Hannah's mouth. She leaned in to kiss Matt, but he pulled away.

"Not on the lips—not after what you just swallowed." He kissed her on the top of her head and she smiled.

Running the situation over again in her head made her heart race. The panic was starting to envelope her in until she felt like she couldn't breathe. The best way for her to get through it was to pretend she was someone else. Imagining she was the better version of herself—the girl who wouldn't have given a two-Hannah blow job; the girl who would have kicked the other Hannah's ass after her first cute laugh—this would allow her to smile through the pain. She had to convince herself it didn't hurt as badly as it did.

They hadn't smoked a lot, and after that, Hannah needed more. She went into the kitchen, poured herself some juice to drink, palmed a few Percocets from her purse, and swallowed them like she needed a rabbit hole to disappear down.

CHAPTER 14
SNARES & SUBJUGATION

There was only one Hannah in Matt's mind—the scarred Hannah. The other one was just his boss's niece. She had stopped at the worksite, to drop something off for her uncle, and Bob asked what her name was. When she replied, "Hannah," Matt's interest was piqued and he approached her. He started talking to her, and she flirted with him, so he asked her to stop by his place when he got off of work.

Of course she agreed. Matt was good looking. He regarded her as he did most women—annoying, but useful. After they smoked up, she mentioned how she liked to fuck when she was high. He obliged her. He was angry anyway—angry at Jared, so pounding it to her helped to relax him.

He knew the original Hannah would show up at some point and it worked out well when she picked that day. He guessed it was her knocking at the door when he was grinding Hannah number two into his couch. He also knew precisely what time Jared would arrive. The double blow job was a bonus. It wasn't part of the plan, but it seemed like a good idea. He really wanted to fuck both girls at the same time, but the future was a sea of opportunity and as soon as he sorted Jared out, he could move on to such pleasures.

Jared had a plan and Matt respected how well constructed it was. *Fuck, it was pure genius.* The weak spots were only Jared and Matt—Jared because he was insane, and Matt because he had his own ideas. Hannah was too predictable; she'd easily follow the plan without even realizing it.

Hannah number two unknowingly existed as part of the scheme. Jared had told Matt to start dating someone so Hannah would feel rejected.

"Who the fuck am I supposed to date? Girlfriends don't grow on fucking trees," Matt responded.

Jared suggested Bubbles, but she was living two towns away, and Matt was relieved to be rid of her. Hannah number two was a gift from the universe—she loved to smoke and party, and was pretty enough to not only make Hannah jealous, but a bliss to fuck.

Matt had seen Hannah's face twitch when she figured out he had fucked someone else. He felt guilty, but it wasn't like he could take any of it back. All of it—everything he had done to her was lunacy. When Jared first told him of his plan, he was angry, but would rather protect himself than Hannah, so he agreed. After a night of laying in bed, thinking about it, Matt wondered if what he was going to do was crueler than the cinder block incident.

Matt knew Jared's routine at the group home; he had lived it for months. Mandatory attendance at dinner was at five o'clock. Afterwards, chores, and then Jared would be free to come over.

The trio was about to smoke up when the knock came at exactly 6:30. Matt let Jared in, and directed him to sit next to Hannah on the floor since the couch was still wet. Hannah number two laughed and leaned in to kiss Matt. He looked over at Jared and Hannah to make sure they were watching—they both were.

Matt pulled back, "Smoking time. You in, Jared?"

"Nah, you guys go ahead."

Matt knew Jared couldn't smoke. He still had to submit to weekly drug tests, and even if he didn't, he probably wouldn't be interested anyway. Jared got high on crazy.

The two Hannah's were almost cheek to cheek, sucking in the smoke as Matt held the lighter under the foil. His cock moved in his pants as he couldn't ignore the memories of the two-Hannah blow job.

When they were done, Hannah number two chuckled and whispered into Matt's ear. She offered to fuck him again. He had gone soft because her laugh annoyed him already, but he knew it was a perfect chance to show Jared his commitment to the plan.

Matt turned the TV on and pulled Hannah number two up by her arm. "You two watch some TV and we'll be back in a second. Matt led her into the adjacent dining room. The lights were off, but he knew there was a straight view from the living room, so they would be seen.

His pants weren't even unbuttoned by the time she was completely naked and reaching for her ankles. He shoved it into her over-stretched hole and started with a good rhythm. Jared watched, but Hannah tried to focus on the television. She twitched and blinked back tears. Even a room away, Matt could tell it hurt.

The look on Jared's face reminded Matt of something—and then he realized it—Jared had the same expression as he watched Danny die all of those years ago. Matt shook his head to get rid of the images. Just then, Jared put his arm around Hannah and moved closer to her. She leaned her head onto his shoulder, and when he placed his hand on her thigh, she didn't move it.

Matt could feel himself going soft. He couldn't stop watching Jared, who was watching him. It occurred to Matt that this was all a game to Jared and he was playing with him as much as he was with Hannah. Matt slammed a few last thrusts into Hannah number two and then held her hips as he remained inside of her for a few seconds. He pretended he had ejaculated; he quickly pulled out and tucked his flaccid cock into his pants.

Coming down from the high was like a free-fall through soapsuds. The group mostly sat in silence, watching re-runs of *Wild America*. Customers popped in, but left quickly. Matt itched to kick everyone out of his house. Hannah and Jared were sitting so close that they were almost snuggling. Jared—snuggling? Matt never thought he'd see such a thing, but it was part of the plan.

Hannah number two stood up. "I gotta go. It's getting late."

"Are you okay to drive?" Matt asked.

"Yeah, that's why I waited so long. I'm already late."

"Cool. Well, give me a call and we'll hang out again."

Matt stood up and kissed her. She laughed and smiled at Hannah and Jared sitting on the floor. "It's been fun. Maybe we can do this again sometime."

They mumbled goodbyes as she left. When the door closed, Hannah exhaled and stretched, moving away from Jared as much as she could in the process. It was obvious what she was doing, but Matt didn't fault her for it.

"I should go home, too," Hannah said.

"Early day tomorrow?" Matt interjected so Jared wouldn't invite himself to Hannah's house.

"Yeah. One more day until the weekend."

"Could you give me a ride home?" Jared asked.

"Sure." Hannah smiled, but Matt could tell she wasn't exactly comfortable with it.

In a matter of minutes, they were gone and Matt was pacing through his house. His thoughts were an eternal staircase—going up to yet another staircase. It was like he was caught between exhaustion and looking for the next trap. Jared's snare was inevitable. Maybe the subjugation of Hannah was something which wouldn't have bothered Matt a few years ago, but it reminded him of how he felt in kindergarten after eating too much paste because he was starving. It was something he couldn't vomit up.

Jared dangled the threat of exposing Matt as Danny's murderer. Matt chewed this threat like a piece of leather in his mouth. It pissed him off. Jared was smug when he mentioned he had left the information 'accessible' incase of his 'accidental' death. Jared understood Matt, and knew he'd consider getting rid of him. He was a smart cookie— but like all cookies hidden in pockets, they disintegrated back into sugar and flour crumbs.

CHAPTER 15
BLUEBIRD ON A SWING SET

Matt was the second man Jared had watched take a woman. The first was Harold, the county tax collector. Every Saturday morning he would kiss his wife goodbye, get a trimming and a shave from the local barber, and stop by Jared's house.

It was adult business, and Jared would not have cared, but the noises drew his attention. Crouching down and peering through the keyhole became a weekly treat for Jared—after his bowl of cereal, but before he watched cartoons. He tried to predict which position his mother would be in each weekend. It was a game he played in his head, by himself.

Jared's father worked as a line electrician. While at

work one day, his father's ladder tipped away from a telephone pole and he instinctively reached out for a wire—the wrong wire. Jared overheard his mother telling his aunt that they had to break his father's arm so it would fit into the coffin.

Breaking the arm of a dead man and the tax collector fucking his mother were two things he thought of everyday. The third was flying. His mother owned a pet bird—a yellow and green parakeet with clipped wings. The bird couldn't fly. His mother kept the cage near the large window in the living room and Jared would watch the bird observing the free birds outside flying.

Jared didn't even consider their cat, Apollo, when he let the parakeet out of the cage. He thought the cat was curled up on top of the laundry in the basement. He left the room for a minute and when he returned, Apollo held the bird under his paws, taking his time to give small bites to the terrified, ruffled mass of feathers. Jared rescued the bird and placed her back inside of the cage. The tiny puncture wounds from Apollo's teeth introduced enough bacteria into the bird to slowly kill it. Three days later, the bird was dead. Five days later, Apollo was dead. Seven days later, Jared's little brother took his first fall over the porch balcony. The circle of life was really a circle of flight.

*

Sneaking into Hannah's house when she was gone was easy. The key enabled him to slip in and out without anyone noticing. Exploring her belongings made her all the more fascinating to him. He knew what she ate, where she shopped, and he memorized the scratches written into her diary.

Saturday was his chance; he was going to visit Hannah while she was at home and attempt to spend the day with her. He woke up with an undefeatable confidence, a swelled ego, and an aura of power. Even the staff didn't bother him that morning; in his plan, they were insignificant—not even worthy of being called pawns. They doled his medicine out for the day, and he left for Hannah's house.

He knocked for several minutes, but she didn't answer. He worried she was gone, but he could hear Skye inside and her car was parked on the street. His lack of patience tore off pieces of his good mood, but she finally opened the door.

She looked surprised, but happy to see him. A towel held her hair in a turban and her robe was loosely tied.

"I'm sorry; did I catch you at a bad time?"

"No, I was in the shower—were you knocking long?"

"Not at all—can I come in?"

"Oh! Yes, sure, I forgot...sorry." Hannah stepped aside and let Jared in. She sat on the couch, but nervously at the end opposite of Jared. He could tell she still wasn't comfortable with him. "So, what brings you here?"

"Nothing special, I wanted to see if I could take you

out to dinner tonight."

"Dinner? Um…I can't."

"You can't?" His eye twitched.

"No, my parents are having a picnic this afternoon for my grandmother's birthday and I have to attend."

"Oh." Jared attempted to look sad. He never felt sad, but he thought he could fake it fairly well. "It's okay—I should have called you first. I assumed you'd be up for it and the group home is taking a trip today, so I'm locked out of the house until tonight."

"You're locked out?"

"Yeah, until tonight. I'm not sure where I'll be going then. Hmm…maybe I'll sit in the park or something."

"Sit in the park all day?"

"Umm…yes. Yeah, the park." Jared looked down and blinked several times.

"Well, I guess you could come with me."

"I could?" His head lifted and a smile broke out across his face.

"Yeah, just let me finish getting dressed and we'll leave. Here," she handed him the remote, "watch TV until I get back."

Hannah ran up the steps and Jared flipped through

channels. Normally he would snoop through her belongings, but he had done that all week, so he watched TV.

Skye stood at Jared's feet and growled at him. He snatched the dog up and twisted its neck a little bit. He threw the dog down and it ran off, trembling. *Your day will come, doggie.*

After several minutes, Hannah came down wearing her trademark long black sleeves and tights. Her wet hair was swirled into a loose bun on the top of her head.

"You ready?" she asked cheerily.

"Wow, Hannah, you look gorgeous."

"I do?" she smiled broadly.

"Yes, you're one of those classic beauties."

"I am?" she asked skeptically.

"I'm being serious, you are breathtaking."

"Um…okay…I am just going to my parents' house."

"Well, they must be proud to have such a gorgeous daughter."

Hannah laughed and picked Skye up on her way out of the door. "You're nuts, but, okay"

*

The ride to Hannah's parents' house took over twenty

156

minutes. The road was just as Matt had described it to him—secluded, farm-ridden, and with the cracked pavement ignored for the preference of the new highway.

Hannah parked her car in the yard and a little girl with dark hair came bounding out to them.

"Grandma's not here yet...ooh, ooh, give me Skye!!" After she noticed Jared, she said, "Who's that—your boyfriend?"

Jared got out of the car, "I'm Jared. I'm a friend of your sister's."

The girl gave him one look and ran into the house with Skye.

"That's my sister, Lorri...ignore her."

"Oh, she's cute." In her little blue skort and matching blue shirt with bows on the sleeves, Jared did think she was cute. Under his breath, he whispered, "Little bluebird."

Lorri came out of the house, followed by a woman carrying a bowl of cut watermelon.

"Hey, honey; who's your friend?"

Lorri answered first. "His name's Jared. He said he's Hannah's friend."

"Well, welcome, Jared. We'll be eating in about an hour."

"Thank you; it's a pleasure to meet you."

"Wanna see my new trick?" Lorri asked, putting Skye down. No one answered her, but she bound over to the swing set. "Hold onto Skye, I don't want to hurt her."

Hannah picked up Skye and they watched as Lorri climbed to the top of the sliding board.

"Okay, everyone watching me?"

"Lorri, get down from there!" her mother yelled.

"Watch me fly!"

Lorri jumped from the top of the sliding board, her arms spread out, and her little legs pointed towards the ground. Jared smiled in delight and began clapping. Lorri landed and looked at Jared with surprise

Their mother nodded towards Jared and laughed, "Oh, she's finally found someone who appreciates her trick!"

Lorri grinned at Jared, "Did you like that?"

"Yes! You're a little star. Can I see you do it again?"

Lorri bound up to the top of the slide again, "Okay, here I go!" and she fluttered downward. When she landed, she ran over to Jared. "I can't fly yet, but maybe if I keep practicing." Then she whispered, "Do you wanna see how high I can go on the swing?"

"Do you jump off of that, too?" Jared asked.

"Sometimes, I'll show you."

Lorri pumped on the swing set, her little legs urging her to go higher and higher. Her dark hair blew up and back with the motion of her swinging. When she was at the peak, she jumped out of the seat and arched into the air.

"Bravo, little bluebird," Jared clapped.

"Lorri, stop that! I don't want to take you to the emergency room on your grandmother's birthday," her mother yelled.

People arrived at the party and they started to eat. Jared sat next to Lorri, paying close attention to her ramblings about school and the neighbor's cat. Jared found it all fascinating, and listened intently to her. He had never experienced school the way she had, and he saw how special she was. Even after dinner, when he kept encouraging her to swing higher, or to jump further, and she complained her legs were tired, he still appreciated how much potential she'd have by the time she grew up.

At one point, he reached for Hannah's hand and squeezed it. He looked at her windswept hair and her faint pink lips. He had chosen the right girl; after all, these things had to be genetic.

CHAPTER 16
UNDER THE SEA

Hannah was glad she took Jared to her family picnic. He was charming and attentive, especially to her little sister, Lorri. She did think, at one point, he had an erection, which she worried about because he spent so much time with Lorri, but he squeezed her hand, and she knew it was for her.

He seemed happy on the ride home, chatting about how much fun he had at the picnic and how pretty he thought she was. His curfew was early, so she planned on dropping him off and driving past Matt's house to see if his lights were on.

Jared was late, so he startled Hannah by planting a quick kiss on her mouth and jumping from the car. She touched her lips and smiled as she pulled away, mindlessly licking the spot for several minutes. She traveled the few blocks to Matt's house and saw that the lights were on. Of course they were on. It was Saturday night and he had things to sell and customers to please.

As soon as Hannah climbed the last porch step, she could hear it—the sound of Matt fucking the other Hannah. Unsure of what to do, she stood for a moment. The last time she tried disturbing them, he ignored her knocking. She decided to keep her pride intact, and tip-toed down the steps.

Self-hate was a devil which flicked its tongue up and down her spine, treeing out to the rest of her. She cracked her neck. Tonight. It was time. She'd have to go to the twenty-four hour convenience store and grossly overpay for disposable razors, but she would show Matt what he had done to her. He had made her body into a canvas and she was only finishing the drawing.

The razors were in the last aisle with the other random and over-priced items: Six dollars for a quart of oil, three dollars for a can of dog food, and two dollars for two aspirins. The package of razors was dusty, as though they had been waiting for her for quite some time. She picked them up and grabbed something to drink so it didn't look as though she was there to buy self-harm paraphernalia.

She smiled with the satisfaction of a secret keeper as she confidently walked to the counter. Someone stepped in front of her and she looked up—it was Marcus.

"Hey, Hannah, what you doin'?"

"Ah, just stopped to get a few things." She noticed his

eyes moving up and down her as he chewed on a toothpick.

"You know if Matt's around? I stopped by and he didn't answer."

"Yeah, I just stopped by too; it seemed like he wasn't at home."

"Uh-huh. You lookin' or was you goin' to hang out?"

"Oh, I was lookin', you know."

"Yeah, me too. I know a place over in Prospect we can get somethin', but I would need a ride over there. It's a fuck of a long walk."

"Oh, cool. Yeah—Prospect is a long walk."

"What'd you think? You wanna give me a ride over there and we can gets some stuff?"

"Um…yeah, sure. I can give you a ride. I just gotta pay for my drink."

"Cool. I'll meet you outside; I'll just be a minute."

Hannah felt uncomfortable. The happiness she anticipated when she thought she was going home to make ribbons on her skin evaporated as she was unsure of what she was getting herself into. Marcus *was* attractive, but she didn't know him very well.

*

162

When they arrived outside of the house, Marcus waited for Hannah to open her door. "You gots to come in with me, girly-girl."

"I do?"

"Yeah, you can't sit outside of a drug dealer's house. You wanna be shot? Besides, you gonna hit it with me in there, right?"

"I thought I'd take it home and smoke it."

"Smoke it? Are you serious? You wanna waste your shit by smokin' it?

Hannah didn't respond. Veining it scared her; the risk of death, addiction, and repeating an act she had only done once and never expected to do again, made her heart race.

"You come in with me and I'll make sure you have fun." Marcus slapped his hand on Hannah's thigh and squeezed.

A flash of the sound she heard on Matt's porch invaded her thoughts and her body ached with devastation—vomit lurched up towards her throat and the urge to cry burned in her face. She smiled at him, got out of the car, and followed him up the sidewalk, through the rusty chain link fence gate which swung spastically because it was only attached at one hinge.

There were several people inside, and although Hannah wasn't the only girl, she was the only *conscious* girl.

Actually, she was the only normal-looking person—something she noticed three minutes before someone pointed it out to her when they asked her with a narc. She replied with a nervous smile and stayed close to Marcus as he answered for her. Not fitting in was something she'd become accustomed to over the years, but suspicion was new to her. Hannah considered herself so timid and harmless, she never expected anyone to think she might be any sort of threat. She quickly decided to tell them that she worked at the grocery store and to *not* mention City Hall, but they never asked.

The exchange was quick—money for buns and riggs. Hannah watched as Marcus pulled his kit out and prepared a hit for her.

"You first, babygirl?"

"Mmm-hmm," she nodded, acutely aware that she didn't want to be the second one to use the needle.

They were in the dining room, adjacent to the room everyone else was in.

"Where you want this?" He held the needle up, full of the brownish-liquid.

"In the ankle again? Can you do that?"

"Sure thing, hop up on the table."

"Sit on the table?"

"Yeah, they don't mind—trust me."

Hannah did trust Marcus—she had no reason not to.

"You little anyway."

Little. No one had ever called her that before. She was on a new diet...the three day diet. She was only allowed to eat every three days; it was working. All of her clothes hung off of her now and it made her happy to hide in them. *I'll never be as skinny as the other Hannah...*

He tied her up and smacked her ankle. "You got pretty feet, girly."

"Thanks," she giggled.

She didn't feel the needle go in, but she felt the plunger as it pushed into the barrel. He untied her and the wave was instant.

She inhaled, "Holy fuck. How much did you give me?"

"Don't you worry, you gotta trust me. You gonna be ohhh-kay."

Hannah was okay. After Marcus took his hit, he slid a hand under her shirt, grabbing her breasts as he kissed her. She felt good—too good. He pushed her back onto the table and she imagined she was lulling on a hammock under the sea. Jellyfish and stingrays swam around her as her tights came off and Marcus entered her. He was slow, and she was warm, like fire under the water.

I could live like this.

But then, her finger scraped the prickled tops of

starfish and the waves started raveling into themselves under the sea, curling so tightly, they crashed on top of her. She opened her eyes and Marcus was gone. The man who had let them into the house folded her in half as he worked his cock into her ass. Every drop of adrenaline her system could spurt out died by heroin's sword. There was no fight or flight in her, just acceptance of what she could not change.

Nothing hurt; it was only the pressure of the sea fighting its way into her body. He was pushed so far into her that she could feel him in her stomach. He asked her if she liked it. She said, "Yes" but meant to say, "Stop".

When they were all done with her—some of them twice, she rolled off of the table and onto the floor with a thud. Marcus gave her one more fix and left her alone. She knew they had run a train on her; the impatient ones edged in for an empty hole as someone else was busy with another. She opened her eyes as little as possible when it was happening. One time she looked into the face of an older man with shiny skin and only a few teeth. They asked her questions she didn't answer and moved her however they needed her. She was certain she was split open from one hole to the next.

She dreamt she was in a dandelion field, in the radiating sun, sitting in the new grass of spring time. She blew the seeds off of the stems and the white fuzzes took flight. Yellow flowers turned to seed as soon as she touched them, and her puckered lips cast swirls of delicate, feathered seeds into the air. Even though she couldn't see the butterflies, she could smell them.

*

The kick missed her face, but landed on her right shoulder. She opened her eyes and some girl was standing over her, spitting mad, kicking at her and screaming, "You white bitch, get the fuck outta my house. You fucking piece of shit drug slut. You fuck my man you whore?" Another kick landed on Hannah's ribs. Someone was giving a half-hearted attempt at holding the girl back.

Hannah scrambled to her feet, but kept slipping. The girl broke free and knocked her down before someone grabbed her again. Hannah pulled her pants on and stood up, holding onto the table.

"You come inta my house and spread your legs for my man? You fucking stupid bitch. Let me go, I'm tellin' you, let me go." She broke free from the man who was holding her as Hannah hurried past her. The girl swung her purse at her and missed, striking herself instead.

Hannah made it out of the house, but she could still hear the yelling as her anxious fingers searched frantically in her pocket for her keys. Her steps were crisscrossed and unbalanced. She made it inside of her car and locked the doors. The girl failed to open Hannah's locked car door, so she pounded the flat of her hand against the side window. With a running jump, she kicked in the side of Hannah's car door. Everything was still cloudy and spinning when Hannah started the car and pulled away. She wasn't sure she could drive home, but knew she had to at least make it down a few blocks and park.

She sobered up as she drove, certain she could make it home. The drive was blurry, but short, and she was relieved as she parked in front of her apartment. She tripped over her own feet and fell as she walked to her front door. Once inside, she crawled up the stairs to her bathroom. Skye yapped at her, wanting let outside, but she ignored her. She had stomach cramps, so she sat on the toilet, but could only shit cum and blood. A pile of dirty laundry on her bathroom floor softened her fall and became her makeshift mattress as she slipped into a deep sleep.

CHAPTER 17
MILK

Jared saw that the door panel of Hannah's car was pushed in. He wasn't worried—worrying would go against his nature—but he was curious. He knocked until it was tiresome; still, Hannah didn't answer. The old lady who lived next door kept peeking at him through her front screen door. Jared smiled and waved at her; she hesitated, but waved back. Even though it was Sunday, he decided to let himself in. The key slid in with silent cooperation, and he was inside within seconds.

The afternoon light was filtered through the blinds and the curtains. It was nearly dark inside. Skye came running to him, but did not bark; she just growled. He kicked at her and she ran up the stairs.

Jared took patient steps—agile like a cat, but far more lethal. He eased his weight onto his foot before shifting himself onto it entirely. He didn't want to be heard. Hannah was either not home, or she was upstairs. He decided to creep up the stairs and find out

He was quiet—like water seeping into cement crevices. Up-up-up the stairs...until...he saw...her. Long brown hair flowed away from her body in waves, except for the giant tangled mess of knots jutting out from the back of her scalp. Jared's mother used to get them. She called them rat's nests and she said they were from getting a restless sleep. Hannah wasn't sleeping—she was passed out. From the waist down she was naked, but she was lying on her side, so Jared couldn't see anything. With the tip of his shoe, he nudged her top leg until it flopped back and spread apart from the other one.

He crouched down beside her and could see her cunt. It was shaved, and without the hair to hide anything, he could see blood and something else—cum. It had been in his own palm enough times for him to recognize the smell.

Jared was angry. He had plans for Hannah and didn't want other men touching her. He stood up and went to the cabinet drawer. He knew where the scissors were— where everything was kept. He held them in his hand and knelt by her body.

How easy it would be to stab this into her throat. She'd open her eyes and gasp, but choke on the blood before she died.

He imagined her vacant eyes as he hollowed her soul out with the metal scissors.

No! You must find out if she can fly first, then use the scissors on her.

Jared opened the scissors, separated a long strand of Hannah's hair, and cut it off. He returned the scissors to the drawer and carefully wrapped the hair in a piece of tissue. After the hair was placed into his pocket, he crouched beside her again and looked closely at her leg scars. He twanged with jealousy that Matt had already had his chance to mar her.

It's my chance now.

He shook her, gently at first, but then more vigorously. She started to come to.

"Jared? What are you doing in here?"

"Hannah! Are you okay? I stopped by and saw what happened to your car. The door was open, and…I'm so sorry, but I was worried something happened to you, so I came in to see if you were okay."

"My door was open?"

"Yeah, and your car has this giant dent in it."

"Aw, fuck." Hannah sat up and realized she was partially naked. She hurried to cover herself with a towel. "This guy—Matt's friend—I ran into him at the store and he asked for a ride. Him and a bunch of his friends— they—." Hannah stopped. She moved a little bit and froze. "Fuck—I'm so fucking sore." Hannah sniffled back tears.

"Hannah—do you need to go to the hospital or should we call the police?"

"No. There'd be too many questions. I—I can't."

"I understand." It was all empty for Jared, but he was playing the part. He smiled, as he knew what Hannah's answer would be, and he was right.

"Could you please give me some privacy while I shower?"

"If you're sure you'll be all right."

"I'll be fine," she sniffled.

Jared went downstairs to wait for Hannah. He heard her footsteps and then the shower. He had lots of things to think about, but they all led back to the erection pushing against the resistance of his pants.

He didn't think about *people*, but rather *things*—the snapping sound a neck breaking made, the fleshy part of wounds, and open palms catching wind when someone fell. He tugged at his cock, squeezing out every drop of cum that he could onto his left hand. The noise of the shower stopped, and he heard Hannah moving around upstairs. Hair combing and dressing, all with sore parts, would take her a while. He walked over to the refrigerator, his flaccid cock still bobbing out of his zipper as he opened the door with one hand. He extracted the gallon of milk, removed the cap, and scraped the contents into the milk. When he was satisfied with the absence of fluid on his palm, he replaced the cap and shook the jug before placing it into the refrigerator.

Upon returning to the living room, he caught his reflection in the sliding glass door in the kitchen. He stopped to admire his cock and its length. He arched his back out like a couture model and placed a hand under its impressive weight. He thought about how Hannah would like it. She was a slut—there was no arguing that—but he would change her and she would love him.

He returned to the couch, tucked himself back in, and waited for Hannah.

When she came down the stairs, she was in her black tights under a black skirt, with a black shirt and a little black sweater. The air conditioning was kept high and Jared realized it was because Hannah's outfits weren't suitable for the summer. Her eyes were red and her skin looked freshly scrubbed. A hair brush was in her one hand and she moved slowly.

"I have a giant knot in my hair, but I can't seem to get it out," she said with a small voice.

"Would you like me to try?"

Hannah hesitated and looked down at the floor. "Could you? Please?"

She sat next to him on the couch with her back facing him, and handed him the brush. At first, he carefully ran it through her hair, but sometimes he would pull at the knot to watch her wince. Sitting this close to her allowed him to notice that she had a pretty neck and he admired her ears. Jared continued to take inventory of her details: she smelled like citrus, a faint blue vein ran down her chest from her right shoulder, and she had a small pimple at the top of her back.

Jared continued to brush her hair long after the knot was out. She closed her eyes and seemed to like it. After awhile, she turned to snuggle into the crook of his arm. He pet her hair as she wept.

"There, there, my little bird. Sshh, don't cry. Would you like me to take care of these people that hurt you?"

"Hannah nodded her head, but did not look up."

CHAPTER 18
SPRINKLE

Hannah had tears on her skin and tears in her skin. She found the irony in their identical spellings to be numbing. The water in the shower burned, but not as bad as the soap. When she was done, she threw the bar of soap and the washcloth away. She never wanted to use them again.

The knot was massive, and she tried to get it out of her hair, but her shoulder hurt too bad to keep using her arm. The only person to blame was herself. If stupidity were a cupcake, she had shoved the whole thing in her mouth the night before, icing and all.

At first, she found Jared's presence at her apartment awkward, but soon she realized he was exactly what she needed. He took care of her without her needing to ask. She hated herself even more now, and if she didn't hurt so badly, she'd do terrible things to prove it. Cutting wasn't the only thing she did, it was just her favorite. She'd hit herself with the back of her hairbrush, or she liked to 'fall' down the steps. The hairbrush was a consistent and easy method; the stairs satisfied her more. Today, she would do none of those things. Enough had been done to her, even by her own standards. She would spend the day crying.

Wanting the opiates made her itch, but after she had taken a few, she was felt sparkly and much more relaxed. The emotional fragility she was experiencing made her realize it wasn't the time to detox herself—she was scared. She wondered if Marcus knew she had liked him. She kept running through her head how she had acted towards him, searching through her memories of the brief moments they spent together, trying to figure out if she had made him think she wanted the sex. Yes, she had wanted it; she wanted him to want her—but not in front of others, and not to be shared. She concluded that it was, without a doubt, her fault.

Hannah wanted to go to the hospital and the police, but she knew it would only lead to questions about her scars and drug use if they tested her for it. As a rule, she avoided doctors and their questions.

*

Jared brushed long after the knot was out. He spoke softly and called her 'bird'. She liked it. In high school, they had a foreign exchange student from London who called girls birds—well, the pretty girls like Olivia and her friends. He never called Hannah 'bird', but Jared was doing it now. It made her smile. So few things made her happy anymore. Matt had the new Hannah, and she was only the old, fat Hannah. Her thighs still rubbed together and she had a little mound under her belly button which no amount of exercise or vomiting could melt away. Not only did she feel ugly, but she had abandoned herself.

Hannah fell asleep leaning on Jared as they watched a movie. When she woke up, she was startled for a minute and wasn't sure where she was at. Jared smelled clean when she nestled into his arm and the faintest hint of cologne lingered on his shirt. The pain ached and burned until she opened her eyes so she went upstairs to get more pills. She tossed them back in her throat and drank from the faucet.

Jared was standing in the doorway, watching her. He startled her. The odd look on his face gave her chills.

"How do you feel?"

"I hurt…in a lot of ways."

"Is there anything I can do for you?"

"No." She shook her head, folded her arms, and looked at her bright pink painted toes.

"What about the hospital? Are you sure you won't go?"

"Yes, I'm sure." She bit her bottom lip until she tasted blood, then she sucked on it, never looking up at Jared.

"You should really see a doctor—to you know—get tested and stuff."

"Yeah." She rocked sideways on her ankles, popping them out and back in. It hurt, but she needed the distraction.

"Listen, I'm not going to talk about it anymore, but if you want to, I'll listen…just ask. Okay?"

"Thanks." She smiled, but it disappeared as quickly as it crescented upwards.

"I gotta go soon. You know, curfew and all. But if you want, I'll stay on your couch tonight so you won't be alone."

"That's nice of you, but really, I'll be okay. I don't want you to get into trouble for not sleeping there tonight."

"I'd be glad to if it would make you feel better."

"No, I probably need to be alone for a bit as well."

"Okay, well, I'm gonna go then. I'll call you tomorrow or stop by to see how you're doing."

"Thanks." Hannah smiled at Jared, sincerely thankful for his kindness and that he strapped down his creepiness for the night.

*

In the morning, Hannah was still sore. She stood over

the ironing board, trying to press the wrinkles out of a white blouse. Her tears dropped onto the shirt, and the iron steamed them away. For a moment, she considered pressing the iron's hot plate against her cheek. The tear-shaped metal, dotted with little holes like insect eyes, stared back at her. She knew it would hurt—possibly stick to her skin, but she wanted to override her pain with something of her own doing.

With a sigh, she gave up on the idea and resumed ironing. At seven a.m., the thought to call off of work ticked in her head. At seven thirty, it seemed like a good idea. At seven forty-eight, she made the phone call. Terrible stomach cramps were her excuse. It wasn't a lie—the stress devoured her, as if it was trying to hollow her out to be like one of those chocolate Easter bunnies. Since she didn't have to work, she took more Percocets and went back to bed.

The pain killers made her drowsy, but she still couldn't sleep. Even the blood pumping through a vein in her neck was like a lullaby, but nothing soothed her. The feelings of panic were consuming her. Calling the women's clinic was inevitable; she knew she needed to be tested.

She swung both feet over the edge of the bed and placed them flat on the floor. With both hands, she gripped the edge of the mattress and breathed in and out as fast as she could in an attempt to calm herself. A psychologist she'd seen when she was sixteen had taught it to her. Largely ineffective, it was a last resort. She stood, retrieved the phone and the phone book, and did her breathing exercise one more time before she dialed.

It was easy—the receptionist was in a hurry and didn't ask a lot of questions. Hannah told her she was having a problem, needed seen as soon as possible and was offered an appointment for the following day. Hannah hesitated for a second—it would require missing work, but she agreed with the time, and hung up. After she did the calculated inhales again, she dialed her boss and left a message with the secretary that she'd be off work the next day because she needed to see her doctor.

Hannah was relieved to have taken care of scheduling the appointment. She bit her bottom lip and thought about calling Matt for a second, thinking he might be at home. She inhaled deeply, held her breath, and dialed. As soon as the phone rang, she exhaled. He answered.

"Hello."

"Hey, Matt. It's me, Hannah…um…Hannah Simmons," she added her last name because of the other Hannah.

"Oh, hey, what's up?"

"I was wondering if you had any H."

"Yeah, I have. Why? You know someone that's looking?"

"Um…yeah, me." Hannah didn't hesitate—she knew she wanted it.

"You?" Matt sounded surprised.

"Can I come by and get some?"

"Of course, just stop over."

"Actually, if I drive over in five minutes and park in the back, can you run it out to my car?"

"Err...sure. I have your money, too. You forgot to take it the other night."

"Cool."

"Hey—how much you want—of the H, I mean?"

"Two buns, just take the money out of what you're paying me back. I'll be there in five."

Hannah hung up. She wasn't looking to draw the conversation out with Matt. The itch wept from behind a bolted door and wanted to feel better.

The long robe her mother gave her for Christmas and her pink fluffy slippers would have to do. She wasn't in the mood to change. Without caring who saw her, she slipped outside, got in her car, and drove to Matt's. Working the pedals with her slippered feet felt odd, but she was intent on getting there as soon as possible.

She parked in his back driveway and within minutes, he came out and got into her car.

"Hey," he said.

"Hey." Hannah glanced at him, but then looked straight ahead.

"I put everything in the box." Matt held up a box of cake mix and shook it.

Hannah glanced at him. "Thanks, I really appreciate it."

"Are you doing this alone?" He seemed curious.

"Yeah, and I'm kind of in a hurry." Hannah arched both of her eyebrows and gave him a flat smile.

"Uh, sorry…but, um…thanks again for lending me the money."

"No problem."

Matt got out of the car, but leaned back inside, "Hey, call me sometime and we can hang out."

"I'll do that." Hannah nodded her head—anything to get Matt out of her car. The door was only shut for a few seconds before she drove away.

Once home, her fingers were anxious, but precise. Rip the foil. Cut the baggie. Sprinkle, sprinkle. Straw between lips. Flick the lighter. Inhale. Melt into an oblivion of bliss.

Behind tired, purple, closed eye lids, Hannah imagined pillows the size of swimming pools made of whipped marshmallow. She'd boing off of the top of one, onto another; and then bounce—weightless— free of her worries with and nothing to focus on except how she felt—like she could fly.

CHAPTER 19
HERE-ROWS

Hannah seemed in a dark place when she stopped by. The robe and slippers were another sign. Matt wondered if she was far along in addiction and tweaking, or if it was something else. The thought of Jared with her clenched in the bottom of his stomach. He tried to bite it back, but after pacing the length of his home, he knew the girl had him. He'd never been in love before, and it made him physically ill. The feelings were like foreign currency in the pocket of a traveler. He sat on the couch with his head in his hands.

He knew that if anyone could love the darkest parts of him, it would be Hannah—the girl he had destroyed, but now desired. Defenseless, she was so willing to give pieces of herself to him that he knew she could love him too. She was simple, and quiet, and had grown up to be one of the most striking women he'd ever seen. Of course he realized this might be the love clouding his thoughts, but he knew he wanted her.

He thought about putting an end to Jared's plan, but he didn't know how. As much as he wanted to save Hannah, he also didn't want to go to jail. All of the years in the state hospital taught him that he never wanted to be a caged rat again. The only thing it taught him was he needed to be a smarter criminal.

Jared said he had made sure that if anything happened to him, the secret would be disclosed. Matt didn't know if he should believe him or not, but knew he was crazy enough to be capable of anything. He would have to keep better tabs on Jared, maybe by reviving some of the relationships he had with people still living in the group home.

He felt like he was standing outside of a slaughterhouse, peering through the window at Hannah on the butchering table with a bloodied, mad Jared hovering over her. Matt wanted to save her—to be her hero—then, she would love him even more than he could imagine. He considered calling her, or walking over to check on her, but didn't want to alert Jared to anything in case he was there, watching.

*

Matt didn't expect Jared to come over after day treatment, and he frowned at being caught off guard. Jared was a flurry of high-pitched rants and flapping arms. Matt found it amusing until he started to understand what Jared was saying.

"Wait—Hannah was raped?"

"Yes, YOUR fucking friends did it."

"What do you mean, 'my friends'?" Matt retorted angrily.

"Marcus—you know, the junkie you introduced her to. You let him shoot Hannah up and now she's all fucked up on drugs and…"

"Stop. I've smoked and snorted with Hannah, but we've never shot up."

"I didn't say YOU, I said Marcus. You left him alone with Hannah and he shot her up."

"When did this happen?"

"Last week, here, in YOUR house. Hannah told me."

"Fucking Marcus." Matt shook his head.

"That's not even the worst part. He ran into Hannah at the convenience store and took her to some crack house where he shot her up and they all raped her."

Matt sat on his couch for a minute, again holding his head, before he jumped up and punched the wall. *Fucking Hannah, always getting herself into trouble.*

"Do you know where this house is that these friends

of yours hang out at?"

"No, I barely know Marcus. How the fuck—you need to get Hannah to show you where this house is. Can you do that?"

"Yeah, I'm going there as soon as I leave here. I want you to burn their fucking house down with me."

"What?" Matt laughed, "We can't just burn their house down. We can't even go over there with a couple of baseball bats. They'll probably outnumber us, two to one."

Jared breathed forcibly through his teeth, "I said, WE are going to burn that fucking house down."

"I'm done with your fucked up plans, Jared. I'm not playing games with you anymore. I'm not going to jail for arson," yelled Matt.

Jared smirked, "What about *murder*?"

Matt grabbed Jared by the throat and pinned him against the wall. "Listen, you creepy fuck, I'm not going to be your fucking bitch for the rest of my life over something that happened when I was a kid. Humans can't fly, you can't fly, and Hannah can't fly. Finish your freak plan with her and then leave both of us alone. Understand?"

Jared laughed. His face was all red and his arms dangled uselessly, but he laughed. "Touchy, touchy, Matt. Watch that anger, we both know how it gets the best of you." Then he screamed, "Now let me the fuck down." Matt released him. Jared's face was still flush as he straightened out his clothes. "You don't want to help me with this? Fine! I'll do it myself. You keep your end of the deal about Hannah and then I'll be done with you."

Jared walked out of the house, slamming the door behind him. Matt exhaled and sat down on the couch.

Just let him finish what he's doing and he'll be gone. I hope. And Hannah…letting Marcus shoot her up. That fucking Marcus—he's done. Watching his friends fuck Hannah—he probably got first dibs on her. I should have known. That time he was here, she was so high and he kept checking her out. Fuck! I'll just have to wait. Yeah, I'll wait this out. No wonder she looked like such shit today. She didn't fucking deserve this. I hope Jared does firebomb the house.

Matt picked up the phone and dialed Hannah number two. Only one thing could fix his mood, but since he couldn't have her, he'd settle for second best.

CHAPTER 20
HIGHLIGHTS

The amount of pills Hannah needed to swallow to make the trip to the women's health center bearable was lethal. She knew this, so she only took a few. A normal examination was hard enough without a rape confession, being tested for sexually transmitted diseases, and the inevitable questions about her scars.

The receptionist handed her a clipboard with forms to fill out while she copied her insurance cards. The basic information was easy, but as she flipped each page, the questions became harder:

Previous Surgeries: *Multiple/ orthopedic/ both legs*

Current Medications: *Percocet 10mg 1T TID; Zoloft*

100mg 1T BID; Xanax 2mg QID

Are you sexually active? *Yes*

Number of Pregnancies: *0*

Number of Sexual Partners in Past Year: *(left blank)*

Have you engaged in oral sex? *Yes (duh)*

Have you engaged in anal sex? *(left blank)*

Have you ever been raped? (left blank)

Are you a victim of domestic violence? *No*

Current Method of Birth Control: *None (Does hope count?)*

Reason for visit: *(left blank) (Fuck! Who writes these questions?)*

Hannah took the clipboard up to the receptionist and pushed it through the short glass opening. As soon as it was taken from her, she sat down. A few minutes later, the receptionist called her to come back up. With a blue pen she tapped the form Hannah had filled out.

"You didn't answer *all* of the questions. You have to *complete* the form." The woman took a highlighter and stroked it across the blank questions before handing it to Hannah.

Great. Not only did I want to avoid some of these questions, but now they're freakin' highlighted.

Hannah answered the questions and returned the clipboard. Festering anxiety punched the inside of her stomach, and she considered leaving before they called her name, but she didn't. Her feet danced over the carpet as her heart ran up-scales with its own beat until she was summoned by a young nurse dressed in pink scrubs.

"Hi, Hannah. C'mon back." The well practiced, welcoming smile was billboarded across her face as she held the door open. "Follow me into the second room on the right and we'll get your weight and blood pressure."

Getting her blood pressure taken was something which always led to problems. Nurses liked to roll sleeves up and the old scars, as well as the fresh, raised, red ones, always brought questions. This nurse didn't push Hannah's sleeve up, but she did try to turn her arm palm-up and Hannah's sleeve had slid up near the wrist, exposing horizontal and vertical embarrassments. The nurse kept trying to twist her arm, but Hannah resisted until finally the nurse left her arm as it was and finished taking her blood pressure.

"It's a bit high. Are you nervous?"

"Yes."

"Is this your first time? I was nervous my first time too."

"Yes." It was all the answer Hannah could mutter.

"You'll be fine. We all have to go through it." The nurse smiled and handed her a cup. "We need a urine sample. We give all of our patients pregnancy tests. The bathroom's the next door up. Leave the sample in the recessed cabinet and I'll be able to get it."

Hannah faked a smile and went into the bathroom. The walls were covered with posters encouraging women to get help for domestic violence and to report child abuse. It was an additional dose of education which she didn't want as she hovered over the toilet with her cup held between her legs. The urine splashed, leaving wet dots on the label. *Classy, Hannah.*

She placed the cup in the recessed area and washed her hands. There wasn't enough soap or running water to wash her anxiety away. She turned the cold water on and held her hands under it until they were painfully icy. In and out she breathed, trying to calm herself down. Again, she contemplated leaving, but she'd have to walk past the nurse and she was sure it would lead to questions.

When Hannah returned to the room, the nurse was waiting with her file. "All set?" She smiled an enormous, toothy smile. Hannah wondered if she peeked at her file, but she just nodded. "Great, follow me." The nurse led her down the hallway to an examination room. She stuffed the file into a holder on the door and breezed in, quickly taking out a gown and another item. "Okay, I need you to take everything off, including your bra and panties; put the gown on with the ties in the back, and sit on the examination table. You can use this to cover yourself." She handed the other item to Hannah, which was a blanket-sized paper towel. "I'll leave you alone so you can get undressed and the doctor will be in shortly."

She produced another obnoxiously happy smile, but this time Hannah could see her gums as well. It was a bit disgusting, but Hannah smiled back.

The nurse left and Hannah took inventory of what she'd have to hide as she undressed. There were scars on her thighs, her arms and her stomach. They were blades of grass compared to the tree-like scars from her leg surgeries. *It will have to do. She* will have to do.

Waiting naked, wearing a too-small gown, and being covered in a large napkin was humiliating. Hannah alternated between shivering and worrying about the sweat accumulating in her crevices.

The doctor knocked and opened the door without waiting for a response. She was engrossed in reading Hannah's chart. As she stepped closer, Hannah could see she was looking at the page where the secretary liberally stroked the questions with yellow highlighter. She was a short woman with a blonde pixie cut and masculine shoes. She shook Hannah's hand briefly, "Hi, Hannah, I'm Dr. Malvern."

"Hi." Hannah inhaled, but did not exhale.

The doctor sat on a stool and wheeled in closer to her. "So this is your first examination?"

Hannah responded quietly, "Yes."

"Well, don't worry, it doesn't hurt and before I do anything, I'll explain it to you." The doctor plunged her face back into the file. "What do you take the Percocet for?"

"Um…I've had a lot of surgeries on my legs and they hurt from time to time." Hannah began pinching her fingers into one another as a way to stop from crying nervous tears.

"And why did you have the surgeries? Were you in an accident or something?"

Hannah swallowed. "Yes, I had an accident."

The doctor was losing patience. "What kind of accident? A car accident? Did you fall?"

Hannah pinched her fingers harder. "Someone smashed my legs with a cinder block when I was thirteen."

The doctor looked at her with disbelief. "Someone smashed your legs with a cinder block? Who did that?"

"A boy who lived on my street." The doctor's look of surprise wasn't unfamiliar—it was the same look she'd been given before by many different people in her life.

The doctor glanced at the file again. "And you've been raped recently? This past weekend?"

"Yes."

"Were you seen at the hospital?"

"No."

"Did you file a police report?"

"No."

The doctor exhaled. "I'd like to use a rape kit on you. It's not much more than a normal exam.

Hannah paled and bit her lip as she pinched harder. "No police."

"It's just taking a few samples, and we'd be taking most of them anyway for your standard exam. It doesn't mean you have to file a police report or anything; we take samples, and pictures if necessary. Will that be okay with you?"

"Okay."

"Alright then. I'll get a nurse to assist me while I do your examination." The doctor stood up, stuck her head out of the door, and spoke, "Patty, can you come here for an assist?"

The gummy smiling nurse re-entered the room, but she was no longer smiling. Hannah didn't appreciate an additional witness to her humiliation, nor the extra pair of eyes scanning her scars and cuts. She didn't say no; she just cooperated with whatever the doctor did.

Dr. Malvern explained everything before she did it— the hand inside of her, the lubricant, the pressure, the cold metal speculum ratcheting her open, and all of the swabbing. She asked questions and marked down the answers as she went. The pictures were the worst—the thought of an image of her with her legs spread open mortified her. Hannah wondered what there was to photograph. She flinched with each snap of the camera.

When it was done, Hannah took her legs out of the stirrups and lay flat as the doctor unpeeled the napkin and gown to give her a breast exam. Her eyes darted across the cuts on Hannah's stomach, and then flashed to her arm, as the scars she had seen on her thighs must have suddenly made sense. Hannah concentrated on the divots in the ceiling tiles. She considered slowing her breathing down, but didn't want to do anything obvious. She could feel the lubricant melting out of her, onto the examination table. The fluorescent lights were yellow, running in sunny tubes above her. If she floated above the table and rose to the ceiling, she could press against the lights. She imagined them burning her skin. These were the things she tried to concentrate on.

The doctor finished the breast exam and helped Hannah to cover herself.

"We'll give you a few minutes to get dressed and then we can talk in my office about the exam." Dr. Malvern was business-like as she excused herself and frowning-Patty.

These were the times when Hannah most regretted cutting herself—as long as it was a secret, she appreciated the dive into her bloody serenity, but when others found out, she was angry. She dressed and exited the room. Nurse Patty directed her to Dr. Malvern's office, who sat at a large desk, waiting for her.

Once they were alone, the doctor spoke. "We're testing for all STD's as well as checking for the presence of semen and hair. It will take a few days to get the results back. You can call the office on Friday and see if they have come in yet. Here's a pamphlet explaining everything we're testing for." Dr. Malvern handed Hannah a yellow pamphlet and a white pamphlet. "You have bruising on your thighs and some slight tearing at your rectum. This is what I took pictures of. The tears don't need stitches, but you should watch for any signs of infection—redness, swelling or if the area starts to feel hot. I'll give you a pamphlet on that as well."

The doctor dug in her desk as Hannah arched an eyebrow— *monitor a red, swollen, warm spot for redness, swelling, and heat?* She almost rolled her eyes. The doctor handed her another pamphlet.

"We have tested you for pregnancy—it was negative, but if you miss your next period, you should come in and be retested. We'll need some blood work from you, and we can draw it here…if you'd like?" Dr. Malvern locked eyes with Hannah.

"Sure, here is fine."

"Now, what about birth control?"

Hannah shrugged.

"Are you interested in it?"

"I—I thought about getting on the pill."

"Okay, I can write you a prescription for that as well." Dr. Malvern started scribbling on a prescription pad. "Now, about your cuts…"

Hannah could almost feel her spine flinch. She stared at the carpet—variegated strands of green and tan in no particular pattern.

"Do you see a counselor or a psychiatrist?"

Hannah started counting the carpet loops. She shook her head.

"I see you take an anti-depressant and medication for anxiety. Who prescribes them for you? Your family doctor?"

Hannah continued to count the carpet loops, but nodded her head.

"Hannah, after all you've been through, I'd like to suggest you see a counselor. We have one in-house here who specializes in working with rape victims. Her name is Iris. Would you like to set up an appointment to speak with her? She's in her office on Thursdays."

Hannah nodded again.

Hannah took the papers and followed the doctor to the room where she was to get her blood drawn. Dr. Malvern patted her arm and said, "Good luck," before scurrying away.

The blood work was quick, and the nurse was content to use Hannah's left arm instead of her butchered right arm. Hannah scheduled her appointment to see Iris, paid her co-pay, and left with eager steps. Once in her car, she started crying and shaking, swallowing two pain killers for the ride home.

CHAPTER 21
LUNCH

Matt did the shit labor at his job. He carried the shingles up to the roof, loaded and unloaded the tools, and if something needed dug, he was the one to do it. He liked the crew he worked with, and most of them were his customers as well. Bob treated him like a younger brother, and gave him rides to work most days, so it was convenient.

Matt never bothered to wash the dirt off of his hands before he ate lunch. He sat on a bucket of joint compound and unwrapped his sandwich, leaving black fingerprints on the white bread. His soda was warm, but it was another thing he didn't care about. One by one, he popped cheese crackers into his mouth and thought about Hannah—the *real* Hannah. He missed her. Despite all she'd lived through, despite all of the angry cuts on her skin, she helped him. If he could bottle her essence, he'd drink it. It would be swirled with dysfunction, but it would only make it easier for him to digest. He simply thirsted for her.

Hannah number two stopped by the work site with a hot lunch for him. She stood before him, offering it to him like some sort of Stepford wife with a plastic smile and vacant eyes.

"What the fuck am I supposed to do with that?"

"I brought you lunch." She smiled.

"Lunch is over, princess."

She walked over to the garbage dumpster and tossed the food in.

"Hey!" Bob yelled, "I would have eaten that."

She ignored him and stood in front of Matt again, smoothing down her skirt. "How about dessert?"

Matt chewed his last cheese cracker and took a drink of his soda. He didn't answer her; he stood up and pulled her between the two work trucks.

"You wanna fuck? I didn't wear panties," she said, lifting her little pink skirt up a few inches.

"Nah, I'm tired, just suck me off."

She hesitated before getting on her knees, and even

more so when she saw how sweaty he was. Matt's face was partially shaded from the sun. A shadow from one of the trucks cast a rectangle over his left eye while the right side of his face reflected the high noon sun. He closed both eyes and lost himself in memories, like flickering through pages in a magazine—colorful pictures and stark typesetter articles about the night skies he had slept under and the shooting stars that arched over him. Something kept startling him—pictures were out of place—a girl with bloody legs and eviscerated kneecaps.

Matt pushed Hannah number two off of him and returned to the joint compound bucket next to Bob.

Bob laughed. "I only saw one head sticking up over the bed of the pickup, so I figure someone needs to brush their teeth, huh?"

Matt didn't answer. He stared ahead, waiting for Hannah to leave. She did so without even approaching him, and he knew why—animals can smell fear and she sensed she had made a momentary slip down the food chain to 'prey' instead of equal. He *could* hurt her, and he wanted to. He *chose* not to.

Some things never left Matt. As he returned to the ditch he was sketching into the soil, he abandoned the shovel for a pick axe, and drove the end into the earth with his thoughts.

Four different men had raised children with his mother, so it made no difference to her which one was around. When Matt was six, she settled in with the one who raised him until he was arrested—Vince.

Vince had a minion which helped him raise the children—a three-foot piece of a broken shovel handle with the words "Board of Education" scrawled on it with permanent black marker. The Board of Education's wood grain was imbedded with Matt's genetic code via blood, skin, hair, and body pulp matter.

There were scratches rutted into the painted walls of the hallway. Vince would run his stick along the wall as he made his way back to Matt's bedroom. The first bump-slide was the stick sliding across the bathroom door. The second bump-slide was the laundry room door. Next was a long slide to Matt's room. It would stop at his door before Vince's boot found the familiar spot on the bottom right hand corner to kick.

Matt knew not to fight it. Fighting meant extra swings, kicks, broken ribs, black eyes, and bloody knots on his skull. Whatever was wrong with Vince, The Board of Education tried to exercise out of Matt. There were other tortures. Talking back meant digesting a bar of soap and subsequent days of vomiting. A missed curfew equaled two days of no food.

Soap-induced vomiting spells and weeks of welted faces were days off of school for Matt to avoid questions. Whenever the school counselor did asked questions, he lied. When Children and Youth Services came, he lied to them, too. He knew none of the people would rescue him from Vince, so he made the best of it by lying to them. He hated them anyway—the concerned outsiders who had all of the evidence but never acted. Even with a silent witness, they had to know. Matt was a product of an abusive home and a system which failed him.

Vince thought of alternative punishments that didn't leave evidence. Once Matt forgot to shovel the dog shit out of the back yard and Vince produced two slices of white bread with week old dog shit between them. Matt was forced to eat the dog shit sandwich. The second bite made him vomit on the kitchen table. He was told he would have to eat that too, but his vomiting became so violent, Vince gave up on the ill-planned torture. Matt was pushed out the back door, into the yard, where he finished his puking into the grass, bent in half, while he learned from The Board of Education anyway. It was one of the lowest moments of his life, and he looked across the street and saw Hannah standing at the edge of her yard, watching dumbly with her blossom mouth perched into an 'o' shape. She ran inside after she had witnessed enough of his humiliation.

Matt shit psychologists and ran Everglade circles around counselors. He was the danger lurking in the tall grasses, and they knew it. They couldn't break what needed to be fixed and they couldn't fix what was broken. He lived on an infinitely looping drive belt of abuse and consequences. If he hadn't been so intelligent, he would have spent his life being examined. The system wasn't equipped to handle a "probably". Matt would never be caught again. With this satisfaction, he left the work site without a word and walked towards the nearest bus stop.

Thirteen stops until the bus deposited Matt in

Prospect. Three blocks to Marcus's cousin's house. Two knocks until they let him in. Each person who fought Matt had a line they wouldn't cross. Matt's lines were non-existent. There were only two of them, including Marcus, and no one pulled a gun. If Matt's gun was with him, he would have shot them clean and quick. He won the fight because he tried to kill them with his hands and he failed. Rage gave him the advantage.

His knuckles were split and his left eye swelled shut. He was glad he didn't have a broken nose because the blood would have been hard to hide as he walked home. He held his ribs—several knees had met with his right side during the fight. It made breathing difficult. A few miles down the hill, he stopped and sat on a curb. Across the street was a pay phone. Even though it was the middle of the day, in the middle of the week, he called City Hall and asked to speak to Hannah.

*

Hannah left work and drove to meet Matt. She pulled up by the sidewalk near the pay phone from which he had called her.

"What happened to you?"

"Fuck, Hannah. I got into a fight. What does it look like?" Matt did not have patience for her questions; he felt hot and was in pain.

"I'm sorry." Matt thought she apologized too much. Hannah dug in her purse with one hand while she drove and emerged with a pill bottle in her hand. "Take these."

"What are they?" Matt reached for the bottle with one hand while the other arm was still wrapped around his waist, holding his ribs.

"Percocets. Do you want me to take you to the hospital?"

"Fuck, no. I'll be fine." Matt swallowed the pills without anything to drink, making a face as they disappeared. "I've looked worse than this before."

"What happened? Weren't you at work today?"

Matt's head drooped back against the seat and he looked at Hannah with swelling eyes. "I was in Prospect."

Hannah glanced at Matt, and then looked ahead. She drew the back of her wrist up against her mouth and grimaced as she fought back tears. She inhaled in steps, like a ratchet clicking. Her arm lowered and she sighed deeply. Matt realized Hannah did not know he knew about her rape.

They arrived at Matt's house after a few minutes. Neither one spoke. Hannah stayed in the car as Matt went inside. From the small window at the top of his door, he watched as her head bobbed against the steering wheel—her sobs hysterical, but silent due to the distance between them.

CHAPTER 22
LOCKS

There was freedom and there was free dumb. The group home had little of the first and an excess of the second. The time Jared spent there was not by his choice. He either wanted to be with Hannah, or to be sorting through her belongings. That wasn't possible at the moment. He was sitting on the couch, waiting for the mandatory weekly house meeting to begin. On the cushion to his right, he placed his backpack so none of the other residents would sit next to him. There was a giant pear-shaped woman named Dana who often sat too close to him. She was in her sixties, sported a grayish-white flat-top hairstyle, and she wore a diaper for a 'nervous bowel'. The first time Jared heard her empty herself into her diaper with splurts and sighs, he screamed at her for being too lazy to get up and run to the bathroom. Her only reply was an emotionless, "Hehheh."

Dana was a disgusting housemate, but the rest were of the same variety which he grew up with in the state hospital. Many of their fingers were stained yellow from excessive chain smoking. They gathered on the front porch, sitting in plastic chairs, going through a constant rotation of cigarettes. Davey looked like a Bolshevik. His staunch face and curled moustache only needed a fur hat with earflaps to complete the look. Davey never had money for cigarettes, so he smoked other people's butts out of the ashtray.

The other female residents were middle-aged women with severe depression. They avoided everyone, as if they were busy planning their next suicide attempt. At least once a week, one would agree to do Jared's chore so he could be away from the house longer. The residents were expected to take turns cooking the dinner each night and to keep the house clean. The older women didn't trust someone as young as Jared to cook anything edible and were happy to take on his cooking chore. No one had the extra money to spend on food, so they made sure whatever was cooked would be something they'd eat.

The staff ran the house meetings and wanted them to end as quickly as the residents did. They passed out menus so the grocery list could be planned, and they listened to complaints they did nothing about. Asking for things to change, or confronting a housemate was disregarded and discouraged.

Sandwiched between dinner and curfew, a house meeting deftly ruined everyone's evening. A thunderstorm shook the house, and rain pounded the panes. Jared decided that rather than arrive soaking wet at Hannah's house, he would stay at home for the evening. The meeting ended and he retreated to his bedroom. His roommate stayed downstairs to watch television, so he shut the door and sat on his bed. He pulled a wooden box from his backpack. Inside were the things he had taken from Hannah—pictures, the hair clipping, two pages carefully torn out of her diary, and a clean pair of her underwear.

He ran his fingers over the piece of hair, twirling it and rubbing it. The softness was as compelling as the sheen. Holding it under his nose, he tried to smell the last remnants of her shampoo from the strand. He returned the lock of hair to his box and gathered his items to shower.

Normally he'd masturbate in the shower, but because he believed Hannah was so close to being his, he resisted—saving it all for her. Due to the lack of privacy, after his shower, he dressed fully, and finished by putting on his shoes. A nice breeze blew through the partially ajar window, and he opened it fully to let the steam escape. Taking paper towels, he dried off the mirror so he could see himself. His blonde hair looked almost brown when it was wet. Blue eyes accentuated his good looks. Turning one way, then the other, Jared examined himself. He was impressed with how good looking he was. His pointed face reminded him of the French explorers he'd seen pictures of in his history books in school. Even though he wasn't French, he told people he was. He collected his shower items and returned to his room across the hallway.

His body seized and halted when he saw Dana sitting on his bed, looking through his box of things he'd collected from Hannah. Between her fingers, she examined the lock of hair.

"WHAT are you doing?" Jared bellowed. Dana flinched from being startled and she jumped at the same time, releasing the hair as it sprinkled into the air, falling to the floor.

"No!" Jared dropped his shower items and dove at the falling hair. He grabbed the wooden box and held it above his head, as though he were about to bludgeon Dana with it.

Dana smiled and nervously laughed her flat "Heheh." Just as she did in all bad situations, Dana's intestines began gurgling into her adult diaper.

Jared lowered the box and yelled, "Get the fuck out of my room. Get out you stupid fucking cow. Get. Out. Now." He followed her, yelling, as she waddled out quickly. One kick with his foot and the door slammed shut. He rushed over to the fallen hair, trying to pick it up. It was useless. His insides were like a lit cremation oven. Panic seared his bones. He needed to get another piece of hair—what was sprinkled on the floor was lost.

Carla came into his room without knocking, as the staff often did. "Did you threaten to hit Dana?"

"She was in my room going through my stuff." His voice was deep and growling.

"And did you have your door locked like you're supposed to?"

"I was in the bathroom." His tone was fierce but calm. It seemed to startle Carla.

"Well, try to remember to lock it so we don't have any more incidents and I'll talk to Dana about going into other people's rooms."

Jared knew his mood made her uncomfortable and he used it to his advantage. "All these talks about locks, Carla, but what good are they if the staff have the key and come in whenever they want to?"

Carla dropped her hands as though she was exasperated. "Jared, I'm not arguing with you. You cannot threaten other housemates, no matter what they do to you, and the best way to prevent this from happening again is for you to lock your door. Can you agree to that?"

Jared did not speak to Carla; he slowly approached her, starring at her until she started backing out of his room. When she was in the hallway, he slammed the door and locked it.

CHAPTER 23
WALK

Iris was a tall, thin woman with a bayou twang. She looked like a classic movie star from the 1920's with a wispy short hair cut and gorgeous creamy skin. Casual clothes draped softly over her frame and seemed to emulate the Leonard Cohen that caressed from her stereo. After she briefly introduced herself, she told Hannah to just relax and that there was no time limit— they could stay there until she was done talking. She skipped the usual get-to-know-you questions and breezed into the conversation.

"I want to hear you talk about what you've gone through, how you feel, and what's your take on your situation and behaviors."

Hannah chose to sit on an enormous, poofed white leather chair. It almost felt like it was holding her. "Where should I start?"

"When things started to go wrong."

Hannah's buzz hadn't worn off from the heroin she smoked earlier in the day. She took half of a day off of work so she could smoke, relax, and then go to the appointment. She felt like she was weaving in and out—frayed fibers and loose strings between lucidity and awareness. Once she started talking, she didn't stop for neither breath nor tears:

I can't tell you if I was happy before it happened. I'm not sure what happiness is, really. I think, if anything, I was just okay. I don't remember hating myself, but I did wish I was different— better. Every girl wants to be prettier, right?

And my parents—it's not their fault. They did a good job; I was the one who messed it all up. I know everyone likes to think it might have been how I was raised, but it wasn't...it wasn't.

That's when it happened—in the summer—the bad things, or when things started to go wrong. Wait. What if I was born wrong and it was my destiny to be like this no matter if something had happened to me or not? Hmm.

There was a group of us that were friends. We all lived on the dead end street. Olivia was my best friend. Well, she was the only other girl, and she played with me when we were kids and as we got older, I was convenient—just down the street. I guess you could say I was the outcast of the group, but still in the group, if that makes sense. Olivia was the pretty one. All of the boys wanted to go out with her. And rightly so—she was perfect, really.

Matt wanted her the most. He lived across the street from me. He was poor. I mean like more poor than regular poor people. There were so many kids, I'm not sure how they fed them all, but then again, I guess they didn't. His mother lived with her boyfriend and that's who made things worse. I could always hear the yelling— everyone in my house could. A couple of times my mother wanted to call the police—she said it sounded like one of the kids was getting killed, but she never did. I'd see Matt getting beat. I saw it a lot of times. It made me feel bad for him and I liked him. He didn't like me though. He called me names—fat, ugly, stupid—it was the only constant between us.

Olivia went away on vacation. Matt was really mad at me because he had asked Olivia out and she turned him down. She told him things I had told her—things I had witnessed happen in his house. He thought it was my fault because she mentioned that he made fun of me and she didn't like it. Ha. Little did he know, Olivia didn't really give a shit about me. At first, I stayed away from all of them. They all treated me nicer when Olivia was around—but with her gone, I also saw an opportunity to get some of the attention they usually gave to her. It was my fault for wanting attention.

I rode my bike up to the end of the road—that's where we all gathered. We played this game—the fainting game—where you hold your breath until you pass out. We were stupid kids...and bored— we were really bored. But when it was my turn and I passed out, I remember waking up and all of the pain. My body was bouncing with each hit. I didn't even realize what was happening at first. Matt was standing over me with a cinder block—over and over again; he smashed it down on my legs.

I couldn't see anything. It was like I had lost my vision—everything turned white and I was screaming. I know they tried to help me—the other boys that were there, but there was nothing they could do. The ambulance came and I was fighting them. I kept pulling the mask off and they kept putting it back on. Have you ever tried to scream with a mask on? It's hard.

They took very good care of me at the Children's Hospital. Everyone was so kind to me and my mom stayed with me almost all of the time. It almost seems odd now that I was at a Children's Hospital, but I guess I was—a child, I mean.

I missed that entire school year—between the surgeries and therapy. And Matt. Matt went away.

When I went back to school, I was even more of an outcast. I got a boost of attention when I first returned, but after that, I was a freak. The kids said horrible things to me—asking me if Matt had smashed my face because I was so ugly—and they called me fat. It's not easy being a fat kid.

But, I graduated and got a job as a clerk as City Hall. I make decent enough money and was able to move out of my parents' house within a few months. I work with a woman named Donna. She's always acted like a good friend to me. I guess I should tell you, when she was out of town a couple of weeks ago, I gave her husband head. I didn't want to; I didn't know how to say no. I think that's one of my problems—I don't know how to say no to people. I just did it and now I wish I hadn't. I don't think she'll find out, but I hope she doesn't.

And there's another problem. Matt works with Donna's husband. Yeah, I know—what's the chance of that? So I ran into

Matt at this party Donna had. I was scared. He still scares me. But I wanted him to like me. And you know, I'm nice to everyone, really. He asked me for a ride home—we don't live that far apart now. And I took him home. I passed out and I think he had sex with me. I wasn't sure. I know you're wondering how can you not know, but I didn't.

So now Matt and I hang out sometimes—well, he used to hang out with me—he has a girlfriend now, so he doesn't really spend much time with me. But he showed me things. Sometimes we do drugs together. Not that I'm an addict or anything, just smoking weed and other stuff here and there. But there was this other night, I'm sure of it—I was nearly passed out and he had sex with me. It's not rape. I didn't tell him no. I wanted it. I wanted Matt to like me—finally. I mean, I know it's fucked up, and if my parents even knew I talked to him—they'd freak out. I don't tell them anything. I guess I don't tell anyone anything. Well, I'm telling you now.

Matt has this friend—Marcus he would stop by sometimes when we were hanging out. I dropped by Matt's house one night and I was standing on his porch and I could hear him fucking his girlfriend. I could hear things I don't even want to think about. I didn't knock—I mean, who would? I left and went to the convenience store. Marcus was there. He asked me for a ride. That's it. And why wouldn't I give him a ride? So, I did.

A ride started all of this. No. My stupidity did. Honestly, I was high, so I don't really remember it. Maybe that's the worst part—not knowing, so I imagine the worst. I can't tell you much about it. Did you ever go to the ocean and get pulled under by the rip tide? That happened to me once, when I was a kid. I ended up a few miles down the shore. It was like that. I woke up on a different patch of sand. I didn't know what had happened—exactly, but I figured it out. You can forget the questions, I won't answer them. I'll never go to the police—I know that. I'll be okay—if okay is a destination. It would be nice if I could walk down the shore instead of almost drowning to get there. Maybe that's why I'm here. I want to learn how to walk instead of drown.

CHAPTER 24
PLOTS

Matt knew it was Jared waiting on his porch—he knocked like a girl—light and urgent. Jared had a different definition of emergency than Matt did. The two were polar opposites except for the girl they made communal—they shared Hannah in acts of attraction and repulsion.

He opened the door and Jared burst in. Matt could smell his desperation. It amused Matt to see Jared so flustered, but this was a more maniacal variety—one Matt had seen before when they were cheeking and spitting. Matt knew how unstable Jared was while he was un-medicated.

"You have to help me." Jared dropped his back pack

and began waving his arms up and down in frustration. We have to get Hannah to pass out."

Matt closed the door and stifled a laugh, "You ready to fuck her, then?"

Jared ran up to him and got into his face, "No, I would NEVER do that to Hannah. I need to cut a piece of her hair off."

A chuckle escaped from Matt. "Have you switched from fire bombs to witch craft?"

"This isn't fucking funny. I need some of her hair for my own reasons. I had a piece and that fucking cow Dana got a hold of it, now it's gone."

"Dana from the group home?" Matt laughed, "What did the Mad Pooper do now?"

"She went through my stuff when I was in the shower and took Hannah's hair."

Matt shook his head. "Yeah, she likes to steal stuff. If you're ever missing anything, have a look in her room. Why don't you ask Hannah for one more piece? I'm sure she'd give it to you."

"I didn't ask her for the first one. I don't want her to know." Jared sat on the couch, but continued to flap his hands.

"Oh. I see. You have a crush on the girl, huh?"

"This isn't a fucking crush. She's the one."

"The *one*?" Matt raised his eyebrows. "Wow, you gonna marry her or something?"

Jared erupted, "Will you stop fucking with me and just help me?"

Matt smiled and laughed, "I'm sorry man, look, I can tell you aren't feeling so good. Have you been taking your meds?"

"Fuck the meds!"

Laughing, Matt blurted, "Fuck the meds! Yeah!" Jared's insanity was like watching the three stooges wrapped into one tumultuous package with butcher's paper and twine. "You can't just go around cutting chunks of Hannah's hair off. Girls notice that kind of shit."

"I don't care. I *need* it. And stop fucking laughing at me."

"No, man, it's all good. It's that there's a difference between want and need. You gotta understand that."

"I get it. Okay, I want it. Are you going to help me?"

"What do you want me to do?" Matt sat in a chair and watched Jared contemplatively.

"When she gets off of work, I need you to go over to her house and get her high."

"That's it?" Matt said sarcastically, but Jared missed it.

"Yessss," he hissed.

"Hannah's not at work."

Jared's eyes both twitched inward. "How do you know?"

Matt's tone was flat, "I work with some guy who's married to one of her coworkers—he told me." He leaned back onto his bent arm, his hand under his chin as he looked at Jared. "But I'm having a party tonight, so bring her over then."

"Can't you go over to her house now?"

"No time, man. Just bring her over tonight and you'll get your hair."

Jared rubbed his palms together in criss-crosses, like he was wiping something off. "I'm sick of the fucking group home."

"Yeah? I remember what it was like. How much longer you got?"

"They haven't told me yet." Jared rubbed his hair. "What do you think would happen if I didn't go back for awhile? Do you think they'd recommit me to Oakmont?"

Matt knew the answer. He wouldn't be sent back to Oakmont. Addicts had gone on benders and left for weeks at a time. It was almost like the staff expected you to fail. Everyone who eloped from the program was accepted back into the house. "When I was there, no one was dumb enough to do it. Someone told me that the last person who did it got shipped right back to Oakmont and they stayed there for years." Matt considered this lie his weekly act of community service.

"Really?"

Matt raised his eyebrows, "Yeah, man, I wouldn't risk it." He shook his head and sighed. "So what's going on with your firebomb plan? Still heading up to Prospect for payback?"

"I can't do that now. I need more time. It wasn't part of the original plan. I have to follow the original plan."

"The original plan?" Matt nodded, mostly at the thoughts he was having about how insane Jared was. "What's your original plan? You gonna steal more puppies?"

Jared's head snapped towards him. "Stop fucking with me. This isn't a game—it's a plan and telling you what I'm going to do isn't part of the plan."

Matt was losing patience. "Then maybe stop asking me for help."

Jared smiled sarcastically, "Not liking the hole you've dug for yourself?"

"I'm in no hole." Matt was stoic, his face locked on Jared's.

Jared laughed. Matt knew it was to break the tension.

"Plots and presents. I have them all."

Matt continued to stare. "Good for you." He paused and took note of Jared's flinching face. "So, are you going to tell me about this plan?"

"No, you'll just be told as you need to know things. Don't assume I'm stupid, Matt. I know you like Hannah and it eats your fucking insides out that I'm with her."

"I never said I liked her." Matt said flatly, refusing to give Jared any sort of reaction.

"I can almost hear the maggots in your gut chewing away at you when you see us together."

"Good luck with her. You might want to make sure you get her before she gets you."

"And what is that supposed to mean?"

"You'll find out. Now how about leaving here? I got shit to do. Bring Hannah to the party tonight, if you want. I'll help you get your hair."

"Wait. I need another favor."

"*Another* favor? What now?"

"I need you to send your Hannah to the group home to pick me up and show me where this house is in Prospect."

"Ah, so you are going through with your f-f-f-firebomb. Okay, 6:30, after dinner and chores, she'll park out front. And Jared—try not to creep her out, too."

Jared left without answering, but nodded once. Matt could see things getting worse. Jared was dangerous while medicated—un-medicated? He was lethal. And Hannah—he could see her being given a cup of poisoned juice. The image jerked at him. She was, after all, the only person, in the middle of an ordinary day, in the middle of an ordinary week, to do anything kind for him.

CHAPTER 25
KINDERGARTEN SCISSORS

Jared knew where Hannah kept her hairbrush, which seemed to surprise her. He told her it was a very 'girl' thing to keep it in the top drawer and it was just a good guess. Hannah didn't know better. She was like a leaf dropped from a tree into a mud puddle—spinning in the wind. She sat on the bed with him and let him brush her hair. He had asked to do so and he knew she would agree. If she thought it was an odd request, she never made her feelings known.

He was very attentive—always asking how she was, and if there was anything he could do for her. She seemed to like it, so he kept doing it. They sat on her bed—her in front of him—and he brushed small sections at a time so he could relish each special portion. The under-section had some curl to it, which he thought was cute. He twirled them around his finger, but didn't linger, or else she might think something was off.

He was impressed at how meticulous her routine was for getting ready to go to Matt's party. She planned her outfit, showered, applied makeup, did her hair, and dressed—he watched it all except the shower. She seemed amused that he wanted to watch. He thought she enjoyed the attention. Jared brushing her hair was an added bonus. According to his plan, he was short on time, but stealing those extra moments with her were worth it.

While they drove, she held his hand. It was cold, so he rubbed it. He smiled at her. He hadn't asked her for anything yet—but he would.

The vacant spots on Matt's street were taken, so they parked a block over and walked. Hannah wore a little muted pink cotton dress with her black tights and shirt underneath. She carried her black sweater with one hand, and held Jared's as they walked.

When they entered the house, Hannah looked like she was going to panic. There were a lot of people and Jared knew she was more likely to be worried about the people she knew, than didn't know.

He leaned in to whisper to her, "Don't worry, no one is here that you don't want to run into. I made sure of it." He hadn't made sure of it, but he wanted her to think he was the person who would do such things for her.

Jared watched for Matt's reaction to Hannah arriving. He showed nothing, but Jared knew better. Matt was able to hide things. Matt nodded to them from the living room and pointed into the kitchen, "Help yourselves to a beer."

They did—they both had a beer and mingled. Hannah talked to people, despite her tendency to pull herself inward. The lights made her skin glow. She smiled when Jared smoothed her hair back. He kissed her and called her his little bird. He couldn't remember feeling so happy before. It was a child-like emotion—something close to the anticipation of Christmas.

He didn't need to look to see if Matt had been watching them. They were both watchers—it was to be expected. Matt played along with Hannah number two, as though they were seriously dating. Jared knew better. Matt didn't give a shit about the other girl. He was using her. It was part of the *plan*, and luckily for Matt, he could enjoy the perks of the lascivious Hannah number two.

Jared needed to make his eleven o'clock curfew and at nine o'clock, he was starting to worry he would run out of time to get the hair. He caught Matt's attention and nodded his head at him.

Within a few minutes, Matt made his way over to them. "I'm gonna go upstairs to smoke, do you guys wanna come?"

Hannah looked at Jared before answering. "Can we?" He smiled, pet her hair, and nodded at her.

Snaking between people and precariously positioned

cups half full of liquor, the three started to climb the stairs. Hannah number two saw them and bounced like a little gazelle towards the stairs. She whispered, "Me too," into Hannah's ear.

The upstairs bedroom remained empty except for garbage bags full of clothes, unpacked boxes, and a patched together coffee table. They all sat around it as Matt poured a pile of Xanax onto the table. Under the cellophane removed from his pack of cigarettes, he slid the Xanax and crushed them with the bottom of his lighter. He used the edge of his cigarette box to cut the pile into thick lines of white powder.

He tossed a cut off straw onto the table. "Okay, girls, you're up. I want those lines gone by the time I'm done getting the H ready."

Hannah number two jumped forward to go first. She tucked her hair back and bent over the coffee table with her ass poking out. Matt gave it a quick smack as she held the straw to her nose and then trailed it up a line as it disappeared. She handed Hannah the straw. "You're next."

Hannah did it the exact same way, but Jared held her hair back and encouraged her to do two lines in a row. She listened, like a good girl. Jared was pleased. She rubbed her nose, "Fuck! That goes right between my legs." Only the Xanax made her talk like that. Matt smiled, and Jared noticed.

"Okay, who wants to go first?" Matt asked. "Actually,

fuck it. We can all have straws." He pulled two more out of his pocket and handed each girl their own. "You in, Jared?"

Jared scowled at him. "No."

Matt shrugged, "Let's go, girls." He held the flame under the foil and as soon as the smoke started rising, the three of them greedily inhaled it.

Matt kept producing the powder-filled wax stamp bags and liquefying it for them, until the girls were droopy-eyed.

"I'm so high," Hannah said. She leaned against the wall and took sips of her beer. She had the metabolism of a kitten.

"I need to fuck." Hannah number two said, laughing. She kissed Matt and they began making out. He stopped and crushed up another line of Xanax.

"This is for you." He pointed at Hannah. She didn't move. She had a distant look in her eyes. "Hannah, c'mon. Do it."

Without changing her expression, she crawled to the table and inhaled the line. When she was done, she licked the top of the table, and rocked back on her knees while she held Matt's gaze. She slid beside Jared and kissed him deeply before leaning against the wall and reacquiring her blank look.

"What are you thinking about?" Jared whispered to

her.

She laughed faintly and smiled for a second. "A bathtub."

"A bathtub?"

"Yes, full to the top with lots of bubble piled high— just leaning back in the tub and letting it swallow me so I can listen to the crackle as the bubbles pop."

"That's pretty." Jared pushed a piece of her hair off of her cheek, but she didn't hear him. Her eyes were closed and he imagined she was in the bathtub.

"Happy?" Matt asked, pushing Hannah number two off of his lap.

"You didn't give her too much, did you?" Jared asked.

"She'll be fine. She's taken more than that before."

"How long will she be out?" Jared leaned her head against his shoulder.

"A couple of hours, I dunno. It's late, maybe she'll sleep all night."

"All night?" Jared shrieked. "I can't leave her here all night."

"Why not? She'll be fine. We'll keep an eye on her." Matt nodded towards Hannah number two. "If she pisses herself, Hannah will help her."

"Pisses herself?" Jared sounded disgusted.

"Yeah, that shit happens. She's got a fuckload of benzo's pumping through her. I'll go downstairs and find someone to give you a ride home before curfew. You need scissors or anything?" Matt asked.

"Scissors? What for?" Hannah number two was suddenly interested in their conversation.

"Go downstairs." Matt instructed her.

"But…"

"Now."

Jared was impressed with how well the girl listened to Matt. She didn't utter another word, but staggered to her feet and found the door.

"No, I have scissors." Jared pulled a pair of small scissors out of his pocket.

"Kindergarten scissors? You're going to cut her hair with kindergarten scissors?"

"What's wrong with that?" Jared looked at the small plastic and metal scissors.

"They cut like shit. Do you want another pair?"

Jared set the scissors down. "No, I'll be fine."

"Okay, I'll be back in a few minutes after I find you a ride, so hurry up and cut before someone walks in on you doing something incredibly creepy to a passed out girl."

Jared's scowl was lost on the back of the door as Matt closed it behind him. He lifted Hannah off of his shoulder and carefully laid her down. He knew exactly which piece he wanted—he had found it earlier while he was brushing her hair. He turned her head, located the section, and separated it with his fingers. It was in the back, but a nice sized chunk, so he wasn't sure if she would notice it.

He pushed the scissor blades as close to her scalp as he could and snipped. The cheap blades bowed outward at the pivot point as he snipped. He had nicked her scalp and it started to bleed a little bit. Leaning down, he kissed the bloody spot.

Wrapping the hair in a piece of tissue, he folded it neatly and slipped it inside a baggie which he then tucked inside his pocket. He stretched Hannah out, methodically lifted her arms from her sides, straightened her legs, and smoothed out all of the wrinkles in her clothes. He brushed her hair with his fingers until it fanned out perfectly from her head. She looked like a little bird-doll to him. He wanted to peek at her secrets under the clothes, but did not want to disrupt the image he had created. Crouched over her body, he was startled when Matt opened the door. He stepped inside the room, dousing Hannah's body with yellow light from the hallway.

"God, you're a creepy fuck. I got you a ride—they're waiting."

"Have you ever seen anything so beautiful?" Matt didn't answer Jared and there was a long pause. "Just one more minute."

"If you smack one off over her body, she'll know when she wakes up and there's no way I'm taking the blame for that one."

Jared was still crouched over her, almost as though he was guarding her and coveting her at the same time. "Fuck off. I'd never do that to her. She's not some whore, you know."

"Yes," Matt said, "I know."

CHAPTER 26
MASON JAR

Matt heard Hannah wake up and walk to the bathroom before coming down the stairs. Everyone had left besides Hannah number two. They were about to smoke before going to bed.

Hannah paused on the second from last step. "Where's Jared?"

"He left." Matt said.

"What time is it?"

"Just after five."

"It's Saturday?" her voice was small, like a little girl's.

"Yeah—Saturday."

Hannah number two lifted her head from Matt's shoulder. "Come sit down, we're going to smoke."

"I—I should probably go."

"Sit, Hannah." Matt pointed to the couch. "It's the weekend. You need more fun in your life."

Hannah listened to Matt. He tried not to look at her. He didn't care what either of the two girls would think if he stared at her, but he had a time and a purpose for everything.

He slit the bags open, carefully, and prepared to smoke with the girls. It was a mindless action for him now—he'd done it so many times. He had a plan, and he was saturated in the electricity of it.

The three huddled together with their straws, chasing smoke wisps with pressed smiles and squinted eyes. They pulled away, laughing. Matt's imagination was cottony and luminescent. He smiled because Hannah smiled. He wanted her to stop—he did. He knew her habit had crossed over into her pill stash when she wasn't with him. She walked the glass rim carelessly if she'd allowed Marcus to shoot her up more than once. He'd have to talk to her about it. Later.

"Kiss." Matt's dazed smile was drowning in want. "You two—kiss—for me. I want to see it."

Hannah number two was as predictable as monsoon

rains. She cupped Hannah's face between her hands and kissed her softly. Hannah took the kiss and then sat back on her legs, wiping her mouth with the back of her hand.

"Kiss more."

They listened, both of them—as he told them what to do. They undressed each other and explored under his direction, putting rosebud mouths on each other's breasts and fingers where they became lost. He watched, as he liked to do.

"Make her cum." Both girls looked at him, not sure who he was speaking to. "The other Hannah, you," he said, pointing to his girlfriend. "Make her cum."

With her face buried between two scarred thighs, she carefully explored her with her mouth. Matt rearranged his erection. Only one of the girls was still new to this— he could tell—and she was lost somewhere on her carpet of dreams, smiling. She kept her eyes closed and he wondered if it was the drugs, or if she was pretending it wasn't a girl making her feel so good.

When she started to orgasm, her legs closed around Hannah number two's head, who just increased her speed. Her voice cracked in small gasps. She was ready. Matt moved Hannah number two aside and lifted Hannah's legs up over his shoulders. He missed the weight of her legs on him.

She opened her eyes when he entered her, inhaling as he plunged to her very bottom. Hannah number two moved above her and started to position herself on

Hannah's face.

"No, she's not eating you out, just kiss her."

Obedient—both of them; he was pleased. He withdrew from Hannah and stood.

"Both of you, on your knees, like last time."

They were both eager, fighting over him like two hungry kittens. Matt arched his head back. He had fantasized about it for so long. They were both beautiful and willing with their outstretched tongues and open mouths.

"Enough, on your knees, side by side."

He took time with both of them, switching back and forth, pushing their hips back into him, grinding furiously as he sampled the girls. When he was ready, he stood and pulled them both by their hair so they were once upon him with anticipation of which he would empty his load into. When it was time, he evenly spread it across the faces and lips of both girls.

He stepped back, "Clean each other's faces off."

Hannah looked around for something to use, but Hannah number two came at her with a lapping tongue. Cute licks were exchanged between the two girls as they laughed and kissed.

When they were done, everyone dressed and Matt prepared more heroin for them to smoke. The two Hannah's seemed to like each other more now, but if it wasn't for the drugs, he would have expected some sort of tension.

After they smoked, Hannah number two relaxed on the couch until she fell asleep. Hannah lay on the carpet, with her eyes closed, making carpet angels like she usually did.

"Where are you at, Angel?"

"I'm in a Mason jar with holes poked in the lid. Someone stuck a dandelion in with me. I tried to climb out, but the glass was too slippery. I'm okay though—I see the world and the world sees me, but the world sees something I want to see. I'll be safe in the jar."

"That's beautiful, Angel."

Matt stood up from the couch and curled next to Hannah on the floor. She stopped sliding her arms and legs against the carpet and let him cradle her. He could tell she was holding her breath.

"Breathe, Hannah."

She exhaled, and then inhaled.

"You don't have to be afraid of me," he said.

"I know," she whispered.

"Things would be different if you'd only let them."

Tears escaped out of the corners of her eyes, down her temples, and became lost in the spirals of her ears.

CHAPTER 27
DOLL HEART

Hannah woke up alone and sore on Matt's living room carpet. On the couch were Matt and the other Hannah, quietly sleeping. She tried to remember what happened, but she decided she'd do that later. She tiptoed as she gathered her things and snuck out of the house.

The walk up the block to her car was shameful. She smelled liked cum and beer and the back of her hair tangled into a cascade of knots. She hurt and wanted to hurry home to swallow some pills. As she reached her car door, she noticed her dress was on backwards. She sighed and slid the key into the lock. Shaking her head, she realized she couldn't count on herself for much of anything.

Part of the way home, Hannah recalled everything— the threesome, and the things Matt said to her. He watched her too—all night—she kept catching him, but he was unapologetic and did not look away. During the sex—he favored her—he did! How he kissed her, fucking her first, and not letting the other Hannah sit on her. Ironed into the fabric of her mind, she knew these things were true and not hopes she shabbily pieced together with an agenda.

It panged in her gut—whatever it was, and she felt ready for it. Matt was her paradox. It did not make sense that she should feel this way about him. His fascination with her was part of it, but not entirely what was making her organs collapse inward onto their own walls. She wanted him.

Stupid! You're trying to fix things in your past by being with him. You are fucking nuts. And when you woke up, who was he sleeping beside? Remember that.

Hannah did think about it—all morning after she arrived at home. She thought about how the other Hannah was prettier than she was, thinner, and more outgoing. It was an easy choice—why have the broken version when you could have the shiny one?

Hating herself was getting easier. One therapist had told her she'd outgrow the self-destruction and the cutting—as if it was child's play. *Ha! Silly woman.* Time will tell, and tales of time were both cataclysmic facets of Hannah's life.

A cutter finding themselves in emergency rooms was the equivalent of a drug addict showing up, complaining of pain, and requesting opiates. The doctors expected all of her roads to be well signed—manipulative, attention seeking, and a false desire to die. They were wrong. What they saw as manipulation were her poor attempts at grappling with her anxiety. She never learned how to manage the overwhelming waterfall of her feelings. Desperate to feel better, she did the most primal of all remedies—injure herself. And the attention seeking behaviors they labeled her with? She never wanted attention, positive or negative. When someone became interested in her, her first reaction was to become scared—the next was to run.

Jared and Matt's recent attentiveness confused Hannah, and she didn't like it. She wanted them to like her, but when they did, it was difficult for her to process—and they frightened her. Everything was two-sided for her, but with Jared and Matt, she wondered what they wanted from her.

Still…it hurt. The other Hannah replaced her so quickly and she could not help but compare herself to her. The smooth, unmarred skin, the defined stomach, and perky breasts—she was stunning. She would have picked her, too. The desire to punish herself for not being good enough was intense when these thoughts playing in constant rotation in her head.

The crazy things she did—like drive too fast, take too many drugs, have promiscuous sex, and put herself in dangerous situations—they were all veiled ways to hurt herself. Once, she attended a therapy group for girls like her. Sitting in a circle, hearing all the different ways people found to hurt themselves only gave her ideas. It did nothing for her self-discovery except in terms of her pain threshold. After a month and a pocketful of new ideas, Hannah quit the group.

Her parents blamed the incident with Matt for her behavior. They were grossly uninformed of the extent to which she hurt herself. Despite this, she was carted between therapists and doctors who spent the majority of the time either telling her she needed to follow their suggestions and 'be normal'—as if it was a choice, or she lied to them, playing games with their inability to circumvent a mind-fucking from a teenage girl. Once she spent an entire hour telling the therapist how successful and happy she was. The therapist jotted notes and smiled along pleasantly. At the end, pleased with it all, she asked Hannah, "Well then, why are you here?"

Hannah said, "Because I cut myself."

The therapist lowered her eyes and let the smile fall from her mouth as she made a note on her tablet. The previous attempts might have failed, but Iris seemed different. Hannah liked her. She knew she'd go back.

*

She didn't use the cold water, only the hot. The nail brush went into the shower with her instead of the washcloth. Scrubbing *that girl* off of her skin took time. The brush tore at the skin on her body, but it was necessary. Matt didn't love what was on top, so maybe if she took it away, she would be good enough. All of the times she couldn't say no to him—she wore the things she did for and said to him under her skin—they crawled around, moving when she tried to cut them out. She lost herself years ago and the only way to get her back was to escape out of her skin.

The hot water tank was empty and the water ran cold. The self-loathing she felt remained. A lesson would be taught. Preparation took time. Hannah dressed, dried her hair, and applied make-up. In her head she reviewed the different scenarios—cutting would not suffice. The feelings etching her skin achieved echoed throughout her body with a much greater intensity. It was a calming sensation. Most people didn't understand it, and she failed at explaining it. For Hannah, self-harm was simple: she hated herself, so she dealt the punishment she thought she deserved; or her anxiety was so bad, it could only be lessened by physical pain.

Snapping her make-up case, she walked to the top of the stairs.

It's decided then.

The worst thing that could happen to her was nothing. Suicide wasn't her intention, but she wasn't afraid to die. Being paralyzed would keep her from herself—on the outside. No courage was needed, just hate—and that is what she concentrated on. When she jumped from the top step, she thought things would be better in a few seconds.

Tumbling downward in a tangle of legs and arms, Hannah landed in the middle of the staircase, not even making it to the bottom. She looked at a new scrape on her elbow which burned as the troughed skin exposed the lower layers to the air. The failure left her feeling defeated, but she climbed the stairs again, intent on improving her technique.

The landing was very small—barely two steps in any direction. She stood in her bedroom doorway and started off with a slight run. Springing off from the top step, Hannah soared into the air. For the fraction of a second she was airborne, she was happy—thinking it might work.

Hannah landed hard, on the outside of her right thigh. Her arm instinctively reached out to grab something and she could hear it snap as her body twisted on top of it. Sliding down, she settled at the bottom of the stairs. Good intentions to do bad things to herself didn't always end in satisfaction. Trembling, the pain was welcome, but a trip to the emergency room was not. Her arm was definitely broken, and they would undoubtedly see her scars. Her mood wouldn't be helped by uncomfortable questions and raised eyebrows.

Hannah cradled her broken arm on her lap, wincing at the pain. A large sigh escaped her lips. She was tired of herself. Getting to the emergency room on her own would be difficult. She considered calling someone, but she wasn't sure who. No matter what, she'd never admit to throwing herself down the stairs, but just as before, she knew they'd figure it out.

Broken parts—arms, legs, skin, head—like a fragmented baby doll. One day she'd be whole, with a doll heart that was stronger than her flesh. Hannah was a mess. It seemed like Jared, Matt, and Marcus only wanted to play with her so they could feel her break. Letting them fracture her only made her want to do so herself. Existing in overlapping circles of dysfunction, she couldn't remember the way out.

CHAPTER 28
RESTORATION

Hannah's wing was broken. Standing in her living room as she cradled it, Jared worried about his little blackbird and how this might affect her flying. He drove her to the emergency room, even though he didn't have a driver's license. Muttering something about him knowing how to drive anyhow, she said she was too exhausted to not believe him. The hospital was only two miles away, so the ride was short. Parking near the doors, he walked around to her side of the car and helped her out. She moved like more than just her arm hurt. A pink tongue poked from behind his lips to lick them as he imagined seeing her bruises.

Once inside, Hannah insisted that she go back to the triage on her own. Jared paced after she first left. The snack machine's inventory didn't appeal to him, nor did he have enough change to purchase a soda. There was a fish tank where he spent fifteen minutes tracing the glass with his index finger, following the same fish as it swam back and forth. When he realized it might take a long time for Hannah to return, he gathered the golfing magazines and the Watchtower booklets, and stacked them in a pile which he placed at one end of the bench seating. He lay down on the bench and used the magazine pile as a pillow.

This could take forever. I might as well sleep.

The waiting room filled in with people as Jared slept. He didn't wake up until a puddle of drool had dripped from his partially open lips onto the magazines. He knew people had watched him snore. Hannah entered the waiting room; her arm was in a cast and a sling. She walked slowly and carried yellow and white papers. She nodded at Jared and they exited the hospital together.

"What did they say?"

Hannah's head hung and her hair flopped downward over her cheeks. "Can I tell you in the car?"

Jared put his arms across her shoulders and pulled her close to him as they walked to the vehicle. "Of course."

Jared drove again, as Hannah sat solemnly. She complained that the ride from the hospital made her car sick from all of the weaving on and off of the road.

"Now are you going to tell me?"

"They saw all of my scars on my arm and asked if I had broken my arm on purpose." Hannah sniffed. Jared didn't look to see if she had been crying or not, but it sounded like she was.

Little bird's broken on the inside. "Well, did you?" Jared sounded shocked that someone would do that, or even ask Hannah if she had done so.

Her voice was small—he almost couldn't hear her. "Yes," she said.

"Hannah! Why did you do it?" Jared began swerving even more as he drove the car.

"Just watch where you are going or we're going to wreck." Hannah panicked, holding her broken arm to her chest.

Jared exaggerated his breathing. "Fine. We can talk about it later. What did the doctor say about your arm?"

"I fractured my ulna. I have to follow up with my orthopedic surgeon in a few days. That's it."

"Did he give you any other directions?"

"Just stupid ones like keep it elevated and he gave me pain killers—not that I didn't already have some."

"Yeah, that's another thing we need to talk about." Jared had staunchness to his voice.

Hannah leaned her head back against the seat and closed her eyes. "Let's not talk at all until we safely get back to my house."

"Deal." Jared laughed at her uneasiness.

After arriving at the house, there was an uncomfortable silence. Jared didn't want to bring up the things the doctor had asked Hannah about, but he needed to know. Watching her wasn't good enough anymore.

"How about I make you comfortable in your bed and we can talk there?"

"Okay."

He hadn't yet discovered anything which Hannah refused to do.

She sat on the edge of her bed and he took her shoes off for her. Rubbing his hands over her small feet excited him. He pulled back the covers and helped her to lift her legs onto the bed.

Jared savored fussing over Hannah. "I'll fluff your pillow...okay...we can stick one under your arm...that's right...I am about to cover you up. Yes. Now how about I get you your pills and a glass of ice water?"

Hannah nodded, "Thank you...that would be nice."

Jared ran downstairs for the water and her purse. When he came back, he eased onto the bed with her, petting her hair as she swallowed pills. "Why did you throw yourself down the stairs? Did you think you could fly?"

Hannah laughed, "I can't fly."

Soon. Jared stroked her hair. "Then why did you jump?"

"Sometimes I feel like it's the only thing I can do to stop from thinking about the bad things. What do normal people do to forget things?"

"We just push them out of our minds."

"I don't know how to do that. Maybe that's why I hurt myself."

Jared moved next to Hannah, slid her head onto his chest, and put his arm gently around her shoulder. "I think you're amazing and beautiful."

"You do?"

"Uh-huh...since I first met you."

Hannah snuggled closer to him.

"In fact, I need to ask you two questions. This is embarrassing for me, but I was wondering if you'd be my first?"

"First what?" She turned her head to look at him.

Jared took Hannah's uncast hand. "I mean my first time to be with someone. I think it's awkward to ask, but I feel a special connection with you and I want to share this with you."

"That's sweet. You're so nice to me and I don't know how I would have made it through these past few days without you. It's been really hard, you know?"

The prey takes the bait. "I always want to be here for you. But I also want to take care of what happened to you— erase the memory in a sort of way."

"How can you do that?" Hannah's face scrunched in confusion and she repositioned her hand in his so their fingers intertwined more.

"If you let me borrow your car for a little while, when I come back, I'll explain everything."

Hannah shrugged. "You can borrow it; I don't mind."

Jared smiled and kissed her forehead, "Thank you. I need to leave now—will you be alright?"

"Of course, take my keys and lock the door on your way out."

"I will." Jared leaned in to kiss her mouth and Hannah returned the kiss.

*

Without a car, Jared couldn't make the preparations previously, so he had a lot of work to do. In his backpack he had hidden an empty beer bottle, rags, and a brick. He stopped at the convenience store, purchased a gas can, and filled it. He forgot a lighter, so he went back into the store and bought one. He remembered where the house was and before he arrived, he filled the beer bottles with the gasoline and stuffed the tops with shredded rags.

Parking in front of the house would only have been a problem if they expected him, or if he was slow—he was neither. There was no thought behind the act. The brick in one hand, the Molotov cocktail in the other, Jared stood on the sidewalk, put both items down, and lit the rag coming out of the bottle. He quickly grabbed both items, took three running steps, threw the brick through the front window, and immediately tossed the bottle inside.

There was yelling, but it ceased as soon as he shut himself into the car. For someone who didn't know how to drive, he left the scene stealthily. Towards the bottom of the hill, he was laughing so hard, he almost jumped the curb, but he regained control and cut across town to a bar two blocks from Hannah's house. Pulling in next to their dumpster, he jumped out of the car and tossed the gas can and extra rags in with the bar's garbage.

Jared was proud of himself. He knew Matt doubted he'd do it, so he looked forward to seeing Matt's expression when he told him. *Such a fitting act of revenge and it happened so quickly.* Jared tried to calculate how long it took him—maybe fifteen minutes, total—*if that!* Time meant something to Jared which few people could understand. He'd lost years of his life in the institution. Some things were never recovered, and he knew this. Going back to the state hospital wasn't an option for him.

Jared parked Hannah's car about three feet from the curb. Parking was not a skill he had mastered. Inside the house, Hannah was sleeping. As he crawled onto the bed, Jared studied her. Leaving her to rest was an option he didn't have the patience for, but there were many things he could do while she was asleep. After twirling some of her hair through his fingers, he kissed her gently. She stirred and emitted a soft moan. His erection moved in his pants. He sported a stiff cock since he had thrown the brick. Pyromania wasn't his usual style, but he enjoyed the rush nonetheless.

The thought of exploring her body as she slept appealed to his lurid curiosity. She would not sleep through this—she hadn't taken very many pills, so he chose not to wake her in such an uncivilized manner. Waking up with her was something he looked forward to. There were parts of her which she hadn't given to anyone else. These would be the things he would take, savoring moments that lay across other moments like a pile of discarded pictures.

Jared was not a virgin, but he would not tell Hannah. In fact, no one knew but Jacqueline Spelding. She was the night nurse on the solitary confinement unit. At first, she let Jared out of his room at night, chatting and eating sponge cakes with him. After three months of stuffing his greedy mouth with her sponge cakes, she proposed an arrangement with him: They would have sex as an opportunity for mutual pleasure, and nothing else. Lifting the awkwardness of being in a relationship would allow them to get each other off without an unnecessary complication. Jared agreed. Jacqueline was not attractive. She was in her mid forties with a short, dark, graying, curly hair style suitable for a woman twenty years older than her. Long black hair grew on her arms which disgusted Jared. She was overweight with joints which cracked when she either stood up or sat down. Despite this, Jared looked forward to having sex with her. She taught him how to be attentive to a woman's body and what it meant to give pleasure as well as to receive it. These would be the things he would show his little bird...*soon.*

Hannah was still asleep when he left. Fresh ice water, her bottle of pills, and a note saying he'd stop by the next day, sat beside her on the nightstand. Using his key, he locked her door behind him and walked to Matt's house. Time expanded for Jared that day—he regained a portion of his lost years by making some of the moments worth twice as much.

CHAPTER 29
THE RIVER OF HANNAH

Jared knocked like a girl, with a faint pounding on the wood with a closed fist. The knock startled Matt, who wasn't expecting visitors. He opened the door; Jared sauntered in and plopped himself on the couch with both arms extended outwards on top of the cushions. The stroll was feminine, so any respect he gained by the surprise visit, he lost with the walk.

"Guess what I did?" Jared smiled.

Matt closed the door and internally stuttered, waiting for Jared to say he had slept with Hannah. "I don't know. What did you do?"

"I burned that house to the ground."

"Really? What house?" Matt tried to stifle Jared's glee by pretending not to know.

"You know which one—the one where those men did that shit to Hannah."

"You've been busy."

Jared clapped his hands and rocked as he laughed. "You should have seen it. I threw the brick at the window...it shattered—glass everywhere...and then in went the Molotov."

"Was there anyone in the house?"

"I don't know." Jared laughed as only someone lost in the whirlpool of their own joke could.

"Did anyone come out?"

"I didn't stick around to find out; I drove away."

"You were in a car? Who was driving?"

Jared wrinkled out a flat, smug smile. "Hannah let me take her car."

"You used Hannah's car? Are you kidding me? Why would you do something so stupid?"

"What do you mean?"

What if someone saw her car? They'll go after her for revenge."

"Relax, relax—no one saw me."

"Did you use gloves?"

"What for?"

"So you don't leave your fingerprints on the bottle."

"Why would I worry about it? All of the evidence is burned."

"Yeah, I'm sure it is." Matt didn't want to share in Jared's pleasure, but he was not indifferent to his stupidity. Carelessness could be a carefully crafted key to Jared's downfall. Matt did not offer advice, but sat and listened.

Fascination with fire was something neither Jared nor Matt had. These things were explored between them, at length, during their stay at Oakmont. They had swam in all areas of deviancy, exchanging what they enjoyed and what they couldn't be bothered with. Matt knew Jared as well as he knew himself. He didn't need to tell him what his intentions were—the story was a well worn path they'd both traveled together—one as the story teller, the other as witness. What Jared had in store for Hannah wasn't pretty unless one liked a canvas of crushed bones and internal injuries. She would not live if she could not fly. Matt knew this; Jared did not. A large part of Jared believed she *would* fly. Matt understood that Hannah, like every other human, could not fly.

The most important unasked question was: Would Matt help Hannah? He could not answer this. Part of him wanted to be a hero—Hannah's hero, but another part was indifferent. Lover and love-her were two different words. What panged beneath him, where a soul should have rested, was a need for her which no other could fill.

Matt cut Jared off, "So are you telling Hannah what you've done?"

"Pfft, of course I am. She'll be mine before the week is out."

"You firebombed a house to get laid?" Matt asked in disbelief.

"No. It's all part of my agenda." Jared's voice was clear and confident.

Matt entertained Jared with such questions so he wouldn't suspect he knew him as well as he did. "Cool."

Cool as grass under a dead body. Cool as an unused cook spoon. Cool as Jared. Matt had heard enough. "Listen, man. The other Hannah's coming over, so do you mind leaving? She went home to shower and when she gets back, we're going out."

Jared looked at Matt, but didn't indicate that the last sentence registered with him. "You've acted like a good friend, Matt. I want you to know that after this is all over with, you'll have nothing to worry about—I mean in terms of the stuff that happened at the hospital."

This was a test Matt intended to pass. "Thanks. I appreciate this. Anything you need, just ask."

"She's the one, Matt. I can feel it this time. I was drawn to her—even from your stories—and honestly, you weren't too nice about her. But, she's special. There's something about her. I couldn't stay away from her, even if I tried. Do you know what I mean?"

He did. Matt and Jared were twins of a sort—like two wings of a butterfly, opposite mirrors with their contrasting dark and light appearances and both with paradoxical loves of a girl they persistently destroyed. The river of Hannah penetrated both of them. He kept denying it, but it was there. "I kind of know what you mean."

"You don't hide it very well." Jared shook his head and smiled, looking up at Matt. "Who do you think you're fooling?"

Matt squinted his eyes. "What?"

"You heard me. You think I don't know? You take pieces of her every chance you get. You know the deal—you need to stay away from her. I'm not giving you any opportunity to fuck with the plan. And if you fuck with me…" Jared laughed. "…and if you fuck with me, I will gut you on the middle of your fucking living room carpet while you sleep." Jared was stoic and solid when he spoke. "I know you as well as I know myself. If I find out you're interfering, I'll make you wish you hadn't."

Matt didn't speak. He held his gaze on Jared. He was a crazy fuck, and very, very clever, but Matt would not let him have Hannah simply because he thought she could fly, and he would not keep her because he liked to watch her break.

"Do you know I was at the emergency room with her?"

Matt sat up, "You were? What the fuck happened?" His brow was furrowed and his stomach contracted from being anxious.

"She broke her arm."

"How did she break her arm?" Matt shook his head in confusion.

"She threw herself down the stairs. I found her just after she had done it."

"Why the fuck did she do that?"

"Think about it, Matt. You've done a hell of a job fucking her up."

"What the fuck are you talking about?"

Jared stood and picked up his backpack. "We are different, you know. You tried to destroy her. You put drugs up her nose and into her veins. I love her. I want to set her free. You could never do that. You aren't capable."

In the quiet after Jared left, Matt considered the truth in what he had said. Saving Hannah might mean the end of him, but their story would come full circle.

CHAPTER 30
HAPPY PLACES

Hannah had chosen a black arm cast. Everything she wore was black anyway, so it only made sense to her. Jared told her he was pleased with her color choice since she was his little blackbird. She liked the nickname he had given her, but once in awhile, his mannerisms and the things he said creeped her out. She tried to go back over it in her head, but it was no use; she had trouble remembering things lately. Her pill habit had become a constant, but she was functionally high as long as she didn't overdo it.

After some thought, Hannah knew she was content with her broken arm. The unrelenting throbbing and aching was a nice chiming reminder of what a bad person she was. If they weren't lessons to be learned, at least they were lessons to be taught. She would seal herself in an envelope if she could, but even then, she'd find a cooperative seam she could maneuver paper cuts out of.

Nothing satisfied her like punishing herself. Just as people escaped to their happy place, Hannah escaped to her safe place. Visualizing it made her cut less and it tucked her need into bed when it was necessary to keep it contained. Closing her eyes in the fragility of quietness, Hannah pictured herself sitting on the floor in a barren padded room. The walls, floor, and ceiling offered the same cushy white sterility. Before her was a brown cloth tool roll tied closed. Once she untied it, she unrolled the cloth to show a yard of pockets with treasures tucked inside—hand saws, scalpels, butcher knives, boning knives, scissors, a small hand axe—everything a girl like her might need. She would choose her tool and begin her work.

In her mind, the skin split smoothly; peach flesh erupted into red fissures with the slightest touch from the sharpest of her tools. All of them were sharp, and all of them sang to her. Their allure was shiny and offered her a peace she only knew in their presence. Hannah was much bolder in her fantasy. She took great liberties at trying to hack off her leg in her mind. In real life, she was not so eager to remove a limb. Her imagination held her hand like a childhood friend and led her down gruesome paths. It helped. Hannah didn't cut herself when she concentrated on these things in her head; it filled the need.

*

Jared kept a newspaper tucked up under his arm for the first few minutes he was inside of Hannah's apartment. After they sat down, he uncurled it and offered her a view of the front page. Her face scrunched up in confusion as she read the first story...a home...a fire...a total loss. She never smiled so broadly—with complete and utter happiness.

"Is that—ahh..."

"Yes...it is," Jared said with a hint of craziness.

"And did you..."

Jared smiled, "Mmmhmm..."

Hannah threw her arms around his neck, cautious not to hit him with her cast. "No one's ever done anything like this for me before."

She buried her face into his chest. It was the first time she realized he was an entire head taller than her. Hannah enjoyed him holding her. This was one of the few moments in her life that she was held without having to exchange it for the things her body could do to another's. It made her flush—almost as if champagne bubbles traveled up her spine. Hannah was a celebration inside the walls of her skin. Jared made her very happy—a feeling she was only just beginning to explore.

Jared pulled back from Hannah a few inches so he could look at her face while he stroked her hair downward alongside her cheek. With the softest movement, his cautious lips moved in and kissed her mouth. Hannah began to feel as though she would liquefy. Jared trembled, as if he was scared, but kissed her skillfully.

When he pulled away, she spoke; her voice cracked at the edges, "I think we should do something special to mark the occasion."

Jared's eyes were intent on Hannah's mouth, "You do?"

Her left eyebrow arched and she bit her bottom lip as she shook her head. "Tomorrow; it will be special." Hannah felt Jared move against her leg. She smiled at him and giggled. "I promise it is a proper thank you." Leaning to meet his partially open lips, she kissed him again before pulling back, "We have to get going— remember—my parents are having us over for dinner?"

Jared's words were a loosely formed whisper, "I remember."

*

Jared kept his palm down on the top of Hannah's thigh as she drove. Every few miles, he'd softly rub one of his fingers over the fabric of her skirt and Hannah would smile. It took nearly twenty five minutes to get to Hannah's parents' house. Jared told Hannah about his own mother, and how he adored her. This made Hannah feel more at ease with him. Disclosing his past made her solidify him more as a normal person than she had before—questions which had formed in her mind began to dissolve as he spoke of his pet cat and his favorite places to walk in the woods.

"Hey—do you think you can take me for a walk around your parents' house today? I'd like to explore a little bit."

"I'd love to. We can even take bikes and ride up the road. I used to do it nearly every day when I was a kid."

"It sounds perfect."

Hannah hadn't fully parked the car when Lorri ran up to them, "Guess what mom and dad bought me? It's in the back yard. You have to come see. C'mon! Come see...hurry!" Lorri grabbed Jared's hand and pulled as he laughed, shrugging at Hannah before following Lorri.

Lorri ran ahead, disappearing around the corner of the house. When they caught up to her, she was already jumping on a large, round, blue and black trampoline in the back yard.

"Look at me!" Lorri fluttered into the air with her toes pointed down and her little arms out at her sides. She sprang back into the air after each time she landed. " C'mon, Hannah, you have to try."

Hannah moved her arm from behind her back as she approached, waving her cast in the air, "Can't, kiddo."

Lorri stopped jumping, coming to a bouncy stop. "What happened?"

"Oh, I just slipped getting out of the shower."

Lorri frowned and wrinkled her forehead downward. "That's what you said last time."

Hannah laughed it off, "Okay, I'll jump with you if you show me how."

The smile returned to Lorri's face and she began jumping again, only pausing for Hannah to cautiously climb onto the bowing surface. "I won't jump until you're ready."

"Thanks." Hannah rose on shaky legs. "I'm glad mom made you put shorts on under your dress—it flies up when you're airborne."

"It was my idea, not hers."

"Good thinking, sis." Hannah bounced slightly on the trampoline's surface. "Now what?"

"At the count of three, we'll jump together; just don't jump too hard because of your arm. Ready? Wait—Jared, are you going to watch us?"

"I'm beside myself with excitement. I won't move from this spot—I promise you." Jared beamed.

Lorri smiled, "Good! Okay. Ready? One—two—three! Jump!"

Hannah and Lorri laughed at their first jump, but as their pushing propelled them upward, they locked their hands together for stability and jumped higher. Hannah peeked at Jared—he had an expression of awe on his face. She smiled at him, but to her, it seemed as though he was lost in the depths of an untouchable, happy thought.

Their mother emerged from the house and waved. Her smile fell as she approached the trampoline, "Hannah, what happened to your arm?"

"It's a small break—no big deal." The smile dropped from Hannah's face and she stopped jumping. "Do you need help with dinner?"

"No, everything's nearly ready; your father is lighting the grill in a few minutes." She looked at Jared, "Nice of you to come! Can I get you anything to drink?"

Hannah climbed down off of the trampoline, "Nah, we're going to go for a quick bike ride up the road."

"Can you do that with your arm in a cast?" Her mother frowned.

"Yes! I can ride with one hand, I think."

"Okay, but we'll be eating in about half an hour, so make sure you're back or it'll be cold."

"We will!" Hannah started walking towards the garage.

"Hey, can I come?" Lorri called after them.

"Not this time, but the next ride we take you can."

Hannah opened the side door, stepped into the garage, reached around the corner, and hit the button so the garage door rose. She got on her sister's bike—although slightly too small for her, and told Jared he could ride hers. After he mounted the bike, the two kicked off down the driveway, traveling up the nearly abandoned road where Hannah used to ride her bike with her childhood playmates. As they passed Olivia's house, Hannah noticed they had erected a swing set already, anticipating the need for one in a few years.

Jared didn't speak, but crisscrossed in front of Hannah's bike, weaving in and out of her path. It was almost hypnotic and Hannah, carefully balanced with her one good arm, watched him with interest. Their biking patterns were like a tapestry-song; she thought it was lovely. When they reached the salvage yard, she could see Jared's eyes darting over the building and she wondered if he knew what had happened to her there. They were both quiet as Hannah peddled faster, entering the graveyard.

"This place is kind of cool. The headstones are mostly for little kids. We think it must have been from the Spanish Flu."

"Wow. That is interesting." Jared stopped and put his bike down and leaned over a headstone to read the washed out lettering.

"I used to come here to play with the neighbor kids when I was young."

"You didn't mind hanging out in a graveyard?"

"Nah, we played hide and seek a lot here."

"But there's no place to hide."

"Sure, there are lots of places. All of the trees at the border of the graveyard were up for grabs. See the big oak tree in the corner?" Hannah pointed to the far corner of the clearing. "I used to climb that tree and watch everyone. No one ever found me there."

"Huh," Jared said lazily, "you don't say. What if I chased you now? Would you let me catch you?" His voice was smooth, almost in a drawl.

"You can try." Hannah took off running in the cemetery, dodging head stones and divots in the ground. Jared started pursuing her. Within a few seconds, he caught up with her and looped an arm around her waist, sweeping her against him as he spun her around, her feet bent upwards into an angle.

"Try?" He laughed and kissed her while his panting chest sighed in and out quickly. Hannah kissed him back. It was the single best moment she'd ever had in the graveyard.

CHAPTER 31
VESSEL

Jared reminded Hannah he was a virgin and she seemed to like that. She chirped up a shy giggle as she said she'd take care of him. They discussed it, and agreed to wait until her arm healed more. They filled two weeks with intense make-out sessions and dates, but all of that time, he was consumed with learning her. He wasn't nervous about being a good lover because the nurse had taught him well. Years before, he had watched his mother brought to orgasm enough times that he knew what to do. Someone like Jared made imitation an art. He laughed when others laughed and he smiled when they smiled. He thought he pulled off 'normal' better than most crazy people.

That night, he had dinner with his housemates at the

group home. They served green beans and he ate each one singularly, relishing the squish and the buttery flavor. He chewed them with his front teeth in a peculiar way while his thoughts drifted to Hannah. Over and over again, his mind reran the plan of what he was going to do to her.

After dinner, he gladly completed his chore— sweeping the kitchen floor—before taking a shower and departing for her house. For days, the two had flirted about the night. Hannah listened to the specific details of what Jared wanted her to do as he fucked her. Through repetition and charm, he convinced her that his plan must be followed specifically in order to ensure the best experience for them both. She shyly agreed, but he expected nothing less from her. Hannah liked to please, and consenting to follow his plan was the easiest way for her to do so.

When she answered the door, he knew she was ready. Hanging loosely, her hair was as he had requested. She wore her white silk robe with pink piping. Faint lipstick and sparingly applied mascara were the only things on her face. Jared hadn't instructed her on what make-up to wear, but he didn't like it. He smeared her lipstick across her face with his palm and told her to scrub it all off with very hot water and bar soap. Skye stared at him as he waited outside of the bathroom door for her to finish. Emerging with pink, scrubbed skin, he led her into the bedroom.

His little bird lit candles on her dresser and one small lamp illuminated her bedroom from the far corner, leaving it fairly dark. Jared smiled because he knew she had probably done so intentionally to make her scars harder to see. Lighting was one of the few details he hadn't outlined for her; instead, he gave her the freedom to be predictable.

The last hint of summer blew through her partially opened window, fluttering her robe as she lay on the bed and waited for him. Serious lines etched across Jared's face—the shadows seemed to age him and his blonde hair looked silver. Each of his movements tocked in quiet meters as he removed his pants, folded them, and placed them on the dresser. Jared's fingers moved with a symphonic grace when he slowly untied the bow of her robe and spread it open. Hannah wore the simple underwear he had chosen from her drawer the day before. He could see all of her and the things she kept hidden.

A large moth was stuck in between the light bulb and the lampshade. It beat its wings against the shade, casting a shadow of itself onto Hannah's skin. The giant flickering movement made Hannah all the more beautiful to Jared. The meaning was not lost with him. It was another bead on the string the universe had given him. He kissed the inside of her left arm, the raised surfaces on her stomach, the scars on her thighs, and the red river scar map on her leg's flesh.

She was still, but trembled like a frightened animal trapped in a box. Jared did not know if she shook because she was scared, or cold. When he began to slowly remove her underwear, she started to help by lifting her hips, but he pushed them back down...he knew the difference between taking her and having her, and he wanted the former. The underwear crumpled into a small ball in his palm that he squeezed in pulses as he climbed onto the bed with Hannah. The flesh on her body was a portrait of rage—but he would force a different sort of surrender from it. He drove his fingers down deep inside of her, keeping his face hovered over hers without allowing them to touch. She gasped and her eyes flickered as he began working an orgasm out of her—he was trying to observe a flash of her soul. When her head started rolling slightly from side to side, he used his free hand to grasp her face from underneath her chin and hold it still. He didn't care if he was hurting her; he couldn't lose the chance to see what might only appear for a slice of a second.

Her throat cracked and she inhaled deeply as he moved his fingers faster and pressed deeper inside of her. He could feel her releasing all over his hand and he smiled. She exhaled and seemed to sigh into the bed. He had seen it—a glimmer in her eye—which he took as a sign of her soul.

When he stood up and removed the rest of his clothes, her legs were still quivering and her skin was flushed red. His thin frame mounted Hannah, pushing her legs up and outward as he rolled a finger across her clitoris. He knew he was pleasing her and before he was done, he would own her.

By the time he twisted her onto her side and placed her leg over his shoulder, she was no longer shivering, but grinding back into him. He was as delighted with her response as he was with his own, but she hadn't taken all of him yet. When he pushed the full length of his cock inside of her, she cried out in pain and tried to push him back with the flats of her little palms on his stomach, but failed. Jared was glad it hurt, and expected that she'd never taken a cock as large as his inside of her. Beneath his body, hers look small and flat, and he enjoyed watching her hurt as each thrust pounded her so forcefully that her entire body flinched. When he finally erupted inside of her, he bent down and kissed her, biting her tongue slightly hard.

He stretched out beside her and ran a fingertip over her scars. "I'd like to count these."

Hannah nodded and cuddled closer to him. The curls at the end of her hair felt like silk between his fingers and he thought the smell of her skin was a cross between sunshine and a windy day. Jared planned on sleeping there—with her, all night, petting her hair, fucking her, and kissing her scars. He discovered the scar tissue was slightly warmer than the surrounding skin. He kept testing the temperature with his cheek until he was sure he wasn't imagining it. It was one of his favorite things which he learned about her that night. He was satisfied and even more certain that she was special enough to fly.

Hanging above Hannah's bed was a blue dream catcher. Jared pulled out one of the dyed feathers from the suede tie. He ran it over Hannah's body—up the peaks, down the mountains, and across her scars as though they were plotted trails waiting for the first person to follow them.

Jared knew he'd lose privileges at the group home for not coming home, but he didn't care. He would also miss medication time, but he had stopped taking those weeks ago. Since he started cheeking and spitting the pills, things had become very clear.

CHAPTER 32
RULES OF RULERS

Jared returned to the group home Monday morning after having spent the entire night with Hannah. Sleep would have been a waste of time. When she wasn't awake receiving him, he watched her sleep and explored her body. The futility he felt in counting her scars was because even her scars had scars, or he could not determine where one ended and another began. Jared didn't mind them. He didn't see the ugliness behind the result, only the tension of oppression and freedom trying to occupy the same space.

Even if she was the first girl his age to have sex with him, their lovemaking was more of a melting experience. Where Hannah stopped, Jared began until their outlines smeared into one entity. Being with her was an exploration of his soul and the depths of feelings she had awakened in him. He didn't doubt she was destined to be his little bird and he put aside planning what to do if she was not. In the end, before it happened, he would decide her fate if she did not fly.

*

The last block of sidewalk cement caught the sunlight in pixelating gleams, mesmerizing him. He was nearly to the group home when he noticed his mother's Lincoln parked in front. The thought of his monthly allowance coming early made him smile. Bounding up the stairs two at a time, he first encountered Pamela, the house supervisor.

"Where have you been? You've been gone all night." She whispered it so forcibly between clenched teeth that spit sprayed into the air.

Jared ignored her and breezed into the house with the confidence of a thoroughly fucked man about to receive a lump sum of money. Taking his coat off in the foyer, he contemplated telling his mother about Hannah. The remains of this idea kept the corners of his mouth turned upwards as he entered the living room.

His mother sat on the couch and beside her was her lawyer, Mr. Davis. A woman in a short gray dress suit stood up from a corner chair when he entered the room. "Hello, Jared. My name is MaryAnn. I'm with the county crisis intervention unit. We're all here because we'd like to talk to you."

"What is this shit?" he blurted. His mother looked frail, her blonde hair pinned into a neat twist and her thin frame seemed bony. Even in the summer, she wore sweaters to ward off her eternal chills. "You too? You're in on this?" She began to cry, choking into an overused tissue.

Mr. Davis gave one smart pat to Jared's mother's left knee before he stood and spoke. "I'm afraid we can't let you leave. I'm here because the police have a warrant for your arrest. They'll arrive shortly. I'm sure Miss Pamela has already called them."

"Police?" Jared guffawed. "What for?"

"They recovered your fingerprints from an arson scene which occurred a few weeks ago. They want to ask you some questions." Jared started to speak, but Mr. Davis raised his index finger into the air and continued to speak. "As your lawyer, I advise you not to comment on the incident. We are all here to help you. I want you to talk to MaryAnn so we can find out if she can improve your predicament or not."

"This is bullshit. I didn't do anything." Jared yelled. The seriousness of the scene was starting to creep upon him, as well as the unfamiliar choke of panic.

MaryAnn took a step forward, "Jared, can we please talk?"

His backpack slid to the floor and he sat beside it. With closed eyes, he spoke, "What do you want?"

Social workers were the most uninteresting creatures to Jared. His mind ran circles around their predictable thoughts and lists of ulterior motive-stuffed questions. Digging information out of him only went as far as he wanted it to. Murdering Danny at the State Hospital remained a felony on his record, despite his age when it happened. Because of this, the state police had a record of his fingerprints. As soon as Jared remembered this and started thinking back to what Matt had mentioned, the fear of charred fingerprints being likely evidence clicked in Jared's head and he began answering the questions in ways which would benefit him. He wore his mask of insanity as more than a label—it was a part of him and he saw it as something that walked a path for the greater good. It took him parallel to destiny's trail and smelled like the hair of a girl who could fly.

Amidst the blur of questions, Jared pulled out of his own thoughts. "You're right; I haven't been taking my medication. In fact, I don't even remember the last time I took them."

Everyone sighed and sat back in their seats with a "that explains it all" attitude. Some of the group home staff allowed smug smiles to sneak upon their faces as the police walked up the porch stairs. The two officers squeaked in the confinement of their polyester uniforms and leather accessories when they entered the living room.

The larger officer nodded towards Jared. "You Jared?"

"Yeah."

"Okay, stand up." The officer wagged his fingertips at him as Jared got up from the floor. "Turn around...put your hands behind your back...you're under arrest for arson..."

Jared cooperated, but allowed a laugh to run scales up and down—out from his chest. Everyone played their role well. The police were indifferent and business-like. MaryAnn was quick to give her recommendation for immediate transport to the local emergency room. Jared's mother kneaded her thin fingers around the tattered tissue they held, and Mr. Davis stood at his lawyer-sentinel post, awaiting the next step.

It wasn't the first time Jared was in the backseat of a police cruiser. The plastic seats offered no resistance as he slid from side to side with the motion of the car. The hospital came into sight and Jared laughed more, shaking his head. After spending most of his childhood in a state hospital, he knew a local hospital would not be prepared to deal with him.

CHAPTER 33
CLEAN

Hannah rode the elevator at City Hall for the third time since she arrived. Going downstairs to face Donna still wasn't an option until the drugs swept everything aside for her. They had worked together many times since the incident with Bob, but Hannah wasn't one to hide her feelings very well and she didn't want Donna to read about Bob's infidelity in the twitches of her face. Since she missed the past two weeks because of her broken arm, seeing Donna after such a long time was like starting at the beginning again.

The elevator's certificate of operation had smeared dates behind its display of foggy plastic. Hannah squinted at it as the cables coughed and sneezed her up to the roof. She rolled her eyes at the thought of the elevator cable snapping; she wasn't afraid to die. There was no better way to relax in a building packed with disgruntled employees and tax payers. Each corner of the building was adorned by a medium sized, carved stone gargoyle. In her head, Hannah had named each one—Pernaticus, Hector, Salazar, and Frank. As she walked around on the roof, she would rub their heads and wonder out loud to them about things they didn't remark upon. This ritual, like others Hannah performed, seemed to calm her. Eventually, she was able to descend the stairs into the basement and greet Donna.

"Oh my God! Your poor arm. And that happened from a slip in the shower? You need to be more careful!" Donna gushed.

To maintain her calm, Hannah fixated on Donna's overbite and her semi-yellowing teeth. "I know—I can be so clumsy."

"Oh, honey, I feel so bad for you. How are you even able to work with a broken arm?" Donna shook her head. Hannah wondered if she did so in expectation that she would explain how she couldn't really work.

"Well, what we do isn't hard. I'm sure I can manage. The doctor told me the two weeks off was enough and the swelling's gone down."

"I don't want you lifting anything! Just work with the boxes you have over on your side and if you need more, I'll move them over for you."

"Thanks…" Hannah started to talk, but Donna threw her arms around her in an unexpected hug.

"I've been so worried about you, Hannah." Hannah returned the hug with a reluctant pat on the back with her good arm.

"Thank you." Hannah pulled away. "I really appreciate the help you always give me. I do have to get a jump on all of this filing I've fallen behind on. I've missed a lot of work these past few weeks." Hannah froze her face in a slight smile.

Most of the time they worked in silence, but kept a radio playing. Sometimes a song would come on and Donna would sing along, but Hannah kept to herself in her quiet section, sorting files folders. Anytime Donna wanted to make small-talk, she yelled across the room to Hannah. The only time they whispered was when they gossiped.

"Hey—I almost forgot because I haven't seen you in so long—Bob and I are having another party this Saturday. We both plan on you being there."

Hannah stopped her sorting and focused on the label of the manila folder, 'Zone 23-1489 Water Permit'. "Oh really?" she called across the room.

"Yeah, a barbeque in the afternoon, then we'll have a bonfire—you comin', right?"

"I wouldn't miss it." Hannah mustered up a fake smile which Donna returned with a real one.

"Great, Bob will be so happy to see you. He keeps asking when you're going out to lunch with us again."

Hannah continued to focus on the label. "I'm sorry, really I am. I have a doctor's appointment on Friday, so I can't go."

"That's okay; Bob is coming to take us today."

Hannah froze. "Uhh…I didn't plan on eating lunch today. I have to go home to make a few phone calls to my doctor over our break."

"Aww…Bob will be disappointed. But why don't you make the phone calls from here?"

"I guess I could, but…well, you know what the lack of privacy is like around here."

"Just call from my desk. I'll be gone and no one ever comes down."

"Maybe I will."

Footsteps slowly came down to their level. Hannah assumed it was one of the other secretaries with a list of files they needed. She should have known by the heavy footfalls—it was Bob.

"Bob! What are you doing here?" Donna jumped up from her work area.

"I finished sooner than I expected so I thought I'd pick you girls up for an early lunch." Bob smiled at Hannah. She sat in a corner of her section on a rolling stool with a stack of files on her lap.

"Oh! Hannah can't come. But let me run and go pee real quick and then we'll go. I didn't expect you this early!"

Bob swatted Donna on her ass as she ran past him in her high heeled-shuffle run. He watched her go up the steps and as soon as she cleared the landing, his head turned towards Hannah.

"Where 'ya been?" He took two steps towards her.

Hannah froze; there wasn't even an expression on her face. "I've been here and there." Bob came three steps closer. Hannah stood up. Bob kept approaching. She stepped backwards into the wall and Bob was upon her.

"Did Donna tell you about the cookout we're havin'?" Hannah nodded. Bob reached his hand out and slid it under the fabric of Hannah's skirt. His fingers walked to her crotch as he struggled against the pulled fabric of her tights. He groped her hard, grabbing in the same rhythm as her kettle-drum heart. "Maybe we can pick up where things left off...sneak away during the picnic and have some real fun in the woods."

Bob gave up playing on the outside of her tights and dove his hand between her waistband and her hip bone, working sideways until his greedy fingers plunged into her so fiercely, it was as though he was trying to lift her off of the ground with one hand. The sound of Donna's wooden heels descended the stairs, and Hannah pushed Bob away from her, the elastic on her tights making a loud snap as she scrambled to move quickly.

Donna hit the bottom step and smiled at Bob, "Ya ready?" He nodded and started walking towards Donna. "See ya, Hannah. Do you want me to bring anything back?"

The crack in her voice came first, and then she cleared her throat, "No thanks."

Alone. Always alone. Hannah paced, choking back garbled phlegm and tears as her hands held her head, and then smacked to her sides repeatedly. She ran up the steps to the elevator and hit the button for the top floor over and over again until she rose inside of the stone building's belly.

The gargoyle brothers waited for her, and so did the edge. Jumping was a temptation she didn't trust herself with. Half way through her climb up to it, she gave up and slid down, crying against the stone wall for several minutes until she finally dried her eyes on her skirt and returned to the basement of City Hall.

Sitting at Donna's desk, she removed a white business card from her purse. The number of the women's clinic was printed on the front. Just as she had done when she was a teenager, Hannah inhaled quickly several times, but this was only to calm herself down. After her last breath in, she held it and dialed the number, exhaling after she heard the phone ring. Hannah anticipated the same annoying receptionist to answer, but she had been patched through to the nurse who retrieved her chart.

The weight of her head rested on the closed fist of the arm she had propped on the desk. The wait slapped against the tears in her stomach like it contained a fish out of water. She bit her lower lip and smiled as the nurse spoke. Hannah did not test positive for any of the sexually transmitted diseases. She was *clean*.

CHAPTER 34
DOGS

With a palm on the back of Jared's neck, the policeman pushed him into his holding cell. Jared cooperated, yet he couldn't help but remark upon the excessive time the officer had taken when searching his crotch during the pat-down. Pissing off the officer resulted in Jared being mishandled and he hit the side of the wall. A bruise waited to seep through his skin tissue on his face. Such a thing was an asset when you were in Jared's position. The cell door slammed and the officer walked out of sight.

Jared raised his cuffed wrists in frustration. "Great! How the fuck am I supposed to take a piss?" Hysterical laughter echoed out of his chest, down through the other cells. Someone yelled at him to shut up. "No, YOU shut up," he screamed back as he laughed, pacing his cell.

Jail did not bother him, nor did the hospital. The only thing etching regret into his anxiety was the thought of not seeing Hannah fulfill her destiny. Everything was going as he had planned—better actually—and then he was finding himself, "Chained like a fucking dog!" he screamed.

The cement bench formed outward from the wall and was freckled with areas of darker gray stains. Jared gave up and sat on it. Nothing was of any use until his lawyer could get him out of there.

*

Jared was digging up a garden of Hannah in his head—going through what it was like to be with her and explore her body when an officer began unlocking the cell door. The interruption annoyed him; he was just about to gather his fingers around her leafy crown and extract her roots.

"Let's go."

Jared smiled. A few inches made a world of difference to him and he slipped past the iron cell door with the movements much like a house cat who knew the contents of every cupboard in the home in which he slept. He could have skipped down the hallway, but he chose to walk with confidence instead. Festering in the system's guts had only taught him which knotty ropes he could climb, and which would leave him trapped. The lawyer and the law would set him free—nothing else.

The private consultation with his lawyer was short. A brief insistence when Jared exercised his right to remain silent during the questioning was all the lawyer needed to say. Jared rolled his eyes and squeezed out a tight smile. "I *know*."

The green indicator light illuminated on the mounted camera in the corner of the room. An ordinary man with an ordinary build, wearing an ordinary, but slightly wrinkled, gray suit, entered the room with a cardboard box in his hands. He nodded his head once at them and sat the box on the table. Jared fidgeted with the sole arm handcuffed to the table.

"Jared, I'm Detective Lewis. I'm going to ask you some questions."

Jared replied with a narrowing of his eyes. The detective removed an overstuffed manila file from the box and began reading it. "You're no stranger to this, I see. Third time familiar, first time arson." The detective flipped a few pages. "Oakmont, eh? And you just got out. How did you like it there?"

Jared ignored him. Detective Lewis closed the file and slid it to the side. "You want to tell me about the fire?" Jared fiddled with his handcuffed wrist again, twisting it back and forth. "I guess that's a no, then?" The detective sighed and leaned back in his chair, his fingertips tethering him to the table as he rocked his chair backwards on two legs—like a boat tied in a dock.

"Listen, I'm not going to mess around here. We have your fingerprints on the bottle you threw." Jared didn't flinch, but he stopped fidgeting and listened carefully.

"Crisis intervention, your lawyer here, and the District Attorney have all agreed to let the hospital sort you out for the time being—get you back on your medication." Jared still didn't respond. Detective Lewis's attitude shifted. "I thought you might like to talk to me about Hannah." Jared's attention flickered, and so did his eyes.

"I sent some officers over to City Hall to pick her up and bring her here to be interviewed. I assume she won't have a lawyer with her, so maybe you can save some trouble and tell me about her before she arrives."

Jared's voice was succinct and on the verge of hissing, "Hannah has nothing to do with this. Hannah knows nothing and you aren't worthy of even speaking her name," he spat.

The Detective was quiet, studying Jared. "Heh. You don't say. Okay, maybe we can talk about something else." The detective reached into the cardboard box and withdrew Jared's backpack. He set it on the table and unzipped it. "I guess you can recognize this as your backpack. We've already searched it. I found the most interesting box in it."

Jared's head turned and his eyes widened with fury as the detective extracted the treasure box full of Hannah's stuff from the backpack. Carefully, he placed it before him and opened the lid. Pictures of Hannah, a pair of her underwear, and pages torn from her diary were set aside on the table top. The detective unwrapped, and then lifted the section of Hannah's hair, holding it under his nose. He smiled at Jared. "Pretty. Does she know you took this?"

Gestating rage birthed into something Jared could not control. In one quick movement, he stood, knocked his chair backwards, and climbed the table, kicking his feet at the detective. His foot caught the detective's arm and the long strand of Hannah's hair was released into the air. Horror dealt an uppercut and a kidney shot to Jared as his inner monster crept out from the closet in his mind. Tethered to the table by one arm, his other three limbs flailed as the detective and the lawyer sought safety out of Jared's range. Jared howled and screamed, thrashing about, painfully pulling at his captive arm. If time belonged to him, he would have chewed his own arm off to be free to gather Hannah's hair.

Two uniformed officers came in and restrained Jared by cuffing his hands behind his back. Each one took a side and dragged him out by the loops of his arms. His feet scuffled and sought the ability to snag his body to a halt. Jared was reintroduced to his cell, face first.

He lay on his stomach, crying, snorting, screaming, and drooling until a large, wet puddle gathered under his face. He calmed down and rested his cheek in the spittle, whispering, *"Little bird, little bird."*

CHAPTER 35
HALVES

Hannah stretched on Iris's couch and ran her hands over the material. "I feel like this couch could swallow me, rinse all of the problems out of me, and spit me back out, freshly laundered—kind of like when Dorothy arrives at Oz and they take the time to clean her up and solve all of her problems. Perhaps I should reach my hand between the cushions to see if I feel a bunch of munchkins running around down there." Hannah looked at Iris and chuckled. "Okay, I'll start:

I have to think of Jared in two sections—almost like cutting an apple apart. I know it's my black and white thinking. I know that. I can't have him be gray, or whatever color he is, I have to think of him as good Jared and bad Jared—not coexisting in the same body. It doesn't make sense to me. We made love before he went away.

And I know it was love. I've never had it that way before—he was gentle and sweet with me. Like he wanted to be with me, and not just for sex. He was kind to me, all of the time…always concerned how I was and he kept saying he adored me and that I was his little bird—sometimes he'd call me his little blackbird. It makes me smile to even think about it.

But there's the other Jared—the one Matt tried to tell me about and the one that did all of those things this week. The fire in town last week? He did that. He had told me as much. But is he really sick, or just misunderstood? And the police have him painted as some sort of sociopath. They said he had a lock of my hair and a key to my house

He does have to pay for setting the fire. He's lucky no one was hurt and I'm lucky there were witnesses. I was humiliated when they came to my work. Can you imagine? I could have died. But thank God they didn't haul me out of there or anything. They just asked me a bunch of questions. He had taken my car and they wanted to know why he had picked that house. I told them about being attacked in there. They never even flinched or tried to take my police report—can you believe it? If they would have asked, I probably would have filed charges. I think my arm cemented it for them; they knew I couldn't have set the fire with a freshly broken arm. Like the self-harm fairy had finally delivered and made me hurt myself to keep me safe. Ha. Not likely, I know.

Yeah, the arm. I guess there's no hiding it from you—normal people are suspicious, I can imagine you'd see right through the 'slipping out of the shower' lie. Hate builds up inside of me. It gathers between the boroughs of self-loathe, punishment, and the need to feel better. I know it's sick. I regretted it a couple of times. After it first snapped, it hurt worse on the outside than I did on the inside.

That almost never happens.

I did it because of Matt. He treats me like a whore, even after all I've done with him. And his girlfriend? The other Hannah? She's prettier than I'll ever be. I can see how he's not only attracted to her, but he's comfortable with her—something he never was with me. It makes me feel like a fool for ever thinking there would be anything between us. Besides, could you imagine my parents if they found out I've been fucking him? Jesus! They'd kill me.

I don't know why I seek his approval so much. It's almost like I need to validate why he did this to me. If he keeps rejecting me, it must be because I am bad; therefore, I deserved everything he did to me. It's like I need that from him. I can't even see living life without getting some sort of acknowledgement from him as to why he hit me with the cinder block.

I went back, you know, back to the cemetery with Jared over the weekend when we went to my mum and dad's house for a cookout. It was like I was a child again. We rode bikes down to the end of the road to the cemetery and…well, it is kind of a beautiful place now. Maybe in my head it can stay like that. Sometimes it is almost like a shape shifter, switching between the good times and the bad times there. It was my first time back there since the incident with the cinder block. I was nervous at first, but then, it was peaceful. It's hard to think of a cemetery as such—all of those dead bodies of children beneath my feet—but it was.

I was trying to block the rape out of my mind, well until Bob came. He was picking Donna up for lunch and when she left to go to the bathroom, he shoved his hand down my pants and stuck three fingers inside of me. I didn't move or even say anything. I was terrified that Donna would find out. I didn't want to suck his dick the first time, but I had done it. I didn't say no, I just did it. I could never tell her what I've done. I could never face her if she knew I did that to her husband. She's been such a good friend to me. Maybe she's the only friend I've ever really had and look what I did to her. I don't know how to even keep simple boundaries with people—who I should fuck and who I should not fuck. Inside of my head, things are so messed up, I don't know if I'll ever set them straight with her again, but I can't let her know.

Tomorrow they're having another cookout. Bob asked me if I'd sneak off and fuck him. I didn't answer him. I don't want to. I know I don't want to…but if I'm put in that position, I might. I can see that—just sneaking off with him. It's not the sex for me. It's the need to have someone think I'm good enough to fuck. That's how I view sex—a confirmation of something I can't feel on my own. I equivocate sex with love. Sometimes having it multiple times with one guy isn't enough, I need approval from many men. And there's something else—this desire to make a mess of everything. I know I'm self-destructive. There isn't a star in the sky I wouldn't rearrange if I could, no matter the consequences. I'm impulsive to begin with and the urge to ruin it all for myself? Humph. It runs deep and wide within me.

And Matt will be there. I don't even need to wonder if he will for sure or not; I know he will be. I wouldn't be surprised if he brought the other Hannah. It's hard for me to see them together. I know he never made a commitment to me, but after all we had done together, I felt like there was something more there that would stop him from passing me aside so he could be with someone better.

I did have Jared to help me through it. Honestly, even after everything, I'd take him back. I'm lonely and he filled up a spot beside me where no one had ever sat before. It was nice while it *lasted. Oh, I did find the place where he had cut a chunk of my hair away. That does piss me off. But besides that, I feel alone. Empty too—like I swing between being overwhelmed with how I feel and complete numbing emptiness. Both extremes hurt.*

God, the past two weeks have been so crazy—the drugs, the rape, the fire, Jared messing with me, and now the police stuff. One more week like this and I really will crack—right down the center, like a halved-Hannah—the good parts and the bad parts separated by a peach seed.

CHAPTER 36
TRAP DOORS

The revenge arsonist's capture made the local news. Matt had been watching in case information about the incident was released. Jared's mug shot flashed on the screen in-between interviews with people who were happy with the police department's success. Matt's plan had trumped Jared's. By Matt remaining a passive player, Jared destroyed himself. His insanity and desire for Hannah made him carelessly confident. Matt was relieved he was gone and immediately began preparing to lure Hannah back. He broke up with Hannah number two and planned to be at Bob's barbeque.

Missing Hannah pulled at his gut, but wanting her pulled everywhere else. Once, while she was sleeping at his house a few weeks before, she started talking in her

sleep about a revolution. This is how he saw her—
eternally battling herself. Matt blamed himself in part, but
he also wanted to save her from herself. The parts of her
that were fucked up could be fixed and he wanted to try.

Matt sensed that with him, Hannah would never know
when bad things might happen. She'd never understand
what segregated her life from safe and unsafe. It would be
as though she was always sitting on the cracked bench at
the park, waiting for the wood to split. As selfish as it
was, he still wanted to be with her. Too much of his time
was spent figuring out whether or not this was because he
was looking for redemption, so he gave up and submitted
to his desire to be with her. To do this, he understood
that he would have to undo a towering stack of
dysfunction. Like pages in books randomly filled with
parchment pressed flowers, he would have to sort and
learn the stack as he disassembled *it*—disassembling
Hannah—with his mind and fingers instead of a cinder
block.

*

Bob picked Matt up early so he could help him arrange
the tables, move chairs, and stack the wood for the
bonfire. Matt wanted to be there when Hannah arrived,
so helping with the party preparations worked well. Bob
talked a lot, but Matt never listened. As both men loaded
wood from the pile along the edge of the woods onto the
trailer, Bob was able to chat without the fear of Donna
hearing.

"Once Donna gets drunk, she'll be in the house

playing cards with her sisters. I'm gonna take her behind the wood pile and fuck the shit out of her."

Matt shook his head. "What are you talking about? Why would you fuck Donna behind your woodpile?"

Bob laughed, "Weren't you listening to me? I didn't say Donna, I meant that little whore she works with—you know—the girl you went to high school with—Hannah."

"You were talking about fucking Hannah behind your woodpile?" Matt's grip tightened on the quartered piece of log he was holding.

"Yeah," Bob laughed so heartily that he had to take one step backwards to keep his balance.

Matt focused on the piece of wood in his hand and considered striking Bob across the face with it. "Does she want to fuck you?" He started shaking from his anger.

"I doubt she *wants* to, her being friends with Donna and all. But if I get her drunk, I know getting her back here will be easy. Plus, with her, that's half of the fun part. She's all scared and shy. I don't think she'd say no to anyone, so why shouldn't I try her?"

By knowing this, Matt could stop it. "Yeah, Bob, why not?" He shrugged and went back to loading the wood.

Eventually guests began to arrive so Matt sat at a table where he'd have a full view of the driveway. Some square shaped woman in her late twenties talked to Matt the entire time, despite him ignoring her. She smelled like cheap cigarettes and the faint odor of shit lingered from her. When she started to annoy him, he responded to her for the first time, "You know, you kind of smell like shit."

The woman did a half snarl, "Excuse me?"

"Shit. Feces. Manure. Whatever it is that comes out of you, I can smell it. Didn't you wipe your ass very well, or is that your breath?"

"Fuck off." The woman stood up and walked off, leaving Matt alone at the table with a bowl of potato chips and a half-empty bottle of beer. He kept doing what he did best—watching.

The gravel popped under tires and Matt strained to see if it was Hannah's car. So many vehicles were parked in the driveway; he no longer had a clear view. He stood and watched as Hannah's car came to a stop. She got out and shut her door—a large silver pan was carefully held in her one good arm while her casted arm balanced it. Matt ran up to her.

"Here, let me carry that." As he took the pan from her, they smiled at one another, but Hannah quickly looked at the ground. "What is it?"

"Strawberry pretzel salad."

"No shit. Did you make it?"

"Yeah, that's why I'm so late." Hannah held up her broken arm.

"Oh…yeah…how is your arm?"

"Um…still broken…but it doesn't hurt as much." She nodded her head, raised her eyebrows and looked at the ground.

"How about we take this into Donna and then we can go sit and have a beer together?"

"Sure." Hannah smiled with uncertainty, but followed Matt inside the house.

When Donna saw Hannah, she did a drunken trot over to her and gave her a hug. "Hannah! You made it! Oh, and you didn't have to bring anything."

"It's strawberry pretzel salad. I'm sorry, it probably should be cut up but I didn't want to try to do it before I brought it in the car."

"No, no, that's fine. I'll cut it now and put it out for everyone. There's food out there—Bob's been at the grill for the past few hours, and help yourself to a drink. I'll be out in a few minutes."

"Okay." Hannah nervously exited the house into the backyard crowd while Matt followed closely behind.

"It's been getting pretty crowded, but I was sitting over by the one pine tree at an empty table. I'll grab us beers and you can follow me."

Hannah wrinkled her forehead, but followed Matt. As he stopped to grab the beer, Bob winked at him and pointed at Hannah. Matt nodded and led Hannah to the table.

"Why did you get four?" she asked.

"Four beers?" Hannah nodded. "You'll see." Matt opened two of the beers. "Okay, get ready to drink fast. You won't be picking your bottle up, so slide in closer to the table." Hannah slid in. "Ready?" Hannah nodded. "When I tell you, drink it, but you can only touch the bottle with your mouth." Matt slammed the beer down on the table and it started erupting like a volcano—beer foam frothed out of the top and down the sides, "Suck it down, quick!"

Hannah put her mouth over the top of her beer and drank it as it gurgled out the top. When it stopped overflowing, she sat back and wiped her mouth on the back of her hand.

"See? You drank half of your beer already. Now chug the rest with me." Matt raised his beer and waited for Hannah to do the same. "Ready...on the count of three...one...two...drink!"

Matt kept watching Hannah even though his beer was raised upwards as he chugged it. Drinking so fast seemed like a struggle for her, but it made an even more enjoyable sight for him.

She set her beer down and swallowed hard. "Are you trying to get me drunk?"

"I'm not. Someone else might though." Matt lowered his eyes to meet hers. Hannah quickly threw a glance at Bob.

"Will you tell me what you mean?"

"I think you know Bob has plans for you."

Hannah stopped watching Bob cooking at the grill and bit her bottom lip. She turned on the bench so she was facing Matt. "He thinks he does." Her left eyebrow arched up for a second.

"Hannah Simmons…there's fight in you after all."

"Yeah, well, I've had enough." Hannah turned back in her seat and continued to watch Bob.

"Careful with all of that staring—Bob's gonna think you want him."

Hannah took a drink of her beer. "It's not a want. It's a dare."

"Trouble like that isn't a Frisbee; it's more of a boomerang. Maybe you should be careful."

Hannah tilted her head to the side and rested her eyes on Matt. She looked him up and down—once. "Where's your girlfriend?"

Matt could tell Hannah was mad. He'd never seen her like this, and it seemed out of character. Instincts told him that if he pushed back, she'd return to her timid self. "I broke up with her because I want to be with you."

Hannah's façade began to collapse. "What do you mean, 'be with me'? Do you mean fuck me?" Rolling her eyes, she took another drink of her beer.

"No. I mean I like you."

As she shook her head, Hannah's chest bobbed with stifled laughs. Her tone was sarcastic, "Yeah—I like you too."

"No, I mean I love you."

The beer in her hand slid down in her grasp a few centimeters until she tightened her grip. She wouldn't look at him. "Stop fucking with me."

"I'm not. I'll show you."

"How can you do that?"

"Go tell Donna your arm hurts and you're leaving. Tell her I'm driving you home. Leave out their front door and meet me at the car."

Hannah paused her breathing. Matt reached across the table and lightly touched her fingers. "Breathe, Hannah. There are no more surprises, I promise. Just do what I said and I'll show you, okay?"

Hannah didn't respond to Matt. She stood up and began walking towards the house, her hurt arm pressed across her stomach. Matt waited until she opened the front door, and then he started walking towards her car. Nervousness was an unfamiliar feeling for him, but it cast a scant beam of happiness through the shadows in his mind.

CHAPTER 37
NESTS

"Can you lie stomach down on the couch? Will your arm be okay?" Matt asked Hannah and he undressed her as he kissed her. The black tights she normally wore were crumpled in a ball on the floor next to her shirt. Both of her arms were folded upwards, covering her breasts. Careful not to hurt her arm, Hannah stretched out onto the couch.

Gathering her hair, he moved it over her shoulder and knelt beside her. Armies of men could be lost moving across the softness of her skin. It was intoxicating in both smell and texture. Matt had never experienced anything like it in his life. She trembled, and he wondered if she had always shaken before when he touched her and he didn't notice it, or if she was just cold and nervous with him at the moment. One hand petted her hair while the other slid down the dent of her spine. Repeating these strokes seemed to calm her and she stopped quivering. Matt leaned in and inhaled her hair. His lips moved to her neck and trailed down to the soft dip of her lower back. She was halved by her spine, and he enjoyed both sides equally. The loveliness of her offered body was no longer something he sought to destroy. He saw her now...as Hannah...the girl who had always been more than she was that day, as her chirality—her mirrored self— had changed with each attempt at obliterating or possessing her.

Four words breathed alongside her cheek caused her to open her eyes, "I love you best." Matt gently rolled Hannah over, cradling her in his arms like a doll. She still held her arms over her breasts. The scars on her arms...her legs...her stomach—they were all there for him to see, but each one was something he had to undo—work ahead of him—to put the disjointed figure back together.

"Don't you want me to smoke first?" Her tiny voice was nearly a whisper.

"No." He softly shook his head.

"Do you want to smoke first?"

"You are my heroin."

Between her raised legs, he hovered. Drawing one ankle to his mouth, he kissed it fully. Two wide, round brown eyes watched him as he continued down her leg, kissing the branches of the lightening strike-scattered scar.

"You're beautiful."

The gasp she made when he entered her made him push deeper until her lips formed a perfect open pout. Hannah wasn't bottomless and this view was something no one had seen before—she belonged to him.

Hidden inside of her, Matt swam in her abyss and swirled with her beating soul. Hannah had always been his destination, and he, her fate. He finished with her and kept her still, slowly lowering her legs.

"Don't move. I want you to keep what I put inside of you."

Hannah didn't move. Her eyes followed him, and he cast a blanket over her naked body. Patches of red flushed across her skin. A smile began to upturn the corners of her mouth, so he leaned down and kissed her forehead. Pulling his pants on, he sat on the floor beside her. To the left of him was the coffee table with the heroin, foil, straw, and lighter. The preparations began.

"We'll smoke now. Okay?"

Hannah nodded.

"How is your arm?"

"It hurts a little."

"A little?"

"Just a little."

"Well, it won't in a minute."

Matt let her smoke first. Absolute peace blessed her face after her first hit. They smoked until it was gone and both were high. Hannah began dancing her arms slightly.

"Do you want me to put you on the floor so you can make carpet angels?"

"No, I'm okay."

"Where are you?"

Hannah's eyes were closed and she smiled, "I'm throwing rocks at swans and clouds are spitting snowflakes down a wishing well."

"Are you in the snow making snow angels?"

"No, I'm one of the snowflakes now," she sighed.

Matt smiled. "Yes, you are, Angel."

*

Six days passed, and Hannah hadn't returned home yet. On her first day with him, Matt retrieved Skye and some things she'd need. He took care of her so she wouldn't want for anything. In some ways, he treated her like a child—stripping her down to her bare self so he could attempt to build her back up again. They smiled at each other over cold breakfast cereal and held hands as they watched television. During the week they went to work, but she returned to Matt's house afterwards. Life was good—for both of them.

Matt still sold drugs out of his house and Hannah number two was one of his more frequent customers. It seemed liked they had sorted most things out between them and Hannah number two never stayed long and only called Matt outside to talk once. Hannah watched, and because of this, Matt was careful. It was one thing to make money off of the other Hannah, but he didn't want to make his Hannah feel uncomfortable. Occasionally, she tried to pick a fight with him about this. Matt blamed himself—and for this reason, he controlled his temper.

Maybe it was the couch—how it sighed in the middle, or the constraint of huddling two people on it—but Hannah never slept well. One night, Matt found her sitting on the floor in the dark in the dining room. She discovered an old box of Christmas decorations someone had given to Matt. There was a mob of tangled light strands and she plugged them in. The illuminated nest rested in her lap. Dots of red, yellow, blue, and green brightened spots on her skin with their colors.

"What are you doing?"

Hannah jumped from being startled, "Oh! I was just playing with the lights."

"They look beautiful on your skin."

She arranged them on her lap like a blanket, "I

suppose they do. It's not so easy to see my scars in this light."

"I don't mind your scars."

"I hope not…you put some of them there."

Matt crouched down so he could see her face. "I'm sorry."

"I'm okay."

"I didn't ask if you were okay, I said I was sorry."

"It's okay," Hannah whispered.

Matt inhaled "Can't you quit?"

"Could you quit heroin?"

"I could quit everything but you."

Hannah looked into his eyes. "That's lovely."

"So are you."

She smiled. "No, I don't think I can quit."

"Well, what do you do when you're somewhere you can't cut, like work?"

Hannah sighed. "I go to the roof of the building and think about jumping off."

Matt's face winced. "What? You think about killing yourself?"

"Mmmhmm. Or, there are four stone gargoyles on the roof. I talk to them."

"You talk to rocks?" Matt's tone adopted a skeptical tone.

"Not rocks, gargoyles. I even named them."

"And this makes you feel better?"

"It clears my mind."

"Maybe you should keep one of those gargoyles with you?"

"They aren't likely to fit in my purse." Hannah laughed and repositioned the lights.

"You should move in here with me."

Her head snapped upward, "What?"

"You're here all of the time anyway."

"I...I don't know," she stammered.

"What's stopping you?"

"My parents would kill me."

"Hannah..." Matt sang, "...you keep bigger secrets than me." He reached for her arm and pulled it to his mouth, kissing the scars on her wrists.

CHAPTER 38
SHOWERS

Hannah lay on the couch with Matt, his arm slung over her as he slept. She did not sleep, instead, she thought about dead skin cells and body fluids from the other Hannah being irrevocably part of the couch. In her mind, there were still three people on the couch; Hannah could not escape this. It placed her somewhere between repulsion and wanting to die. The blankets and sheets they used were washed since she came to stay, but she still couldn't shake the obsession with the remains of Hannah number two.

Sliding out from Matt's arm, Hannah went upstairs to take a shower. In her backpack were her nail brush and other items. Retrieving them, she wrapped her cast up in a plastic bag and began her methodical shower. First the hands—they were the easiest place to start as she adjusted to the pain. As she moved up her arms, she flinched when the bristles scrubbed over new wounds. Plastic hairs ripped at healing cuts and reopened old wounds. Anytime Hannah did this, there was blood flowing down the drain like a faint smoky red stream.

Spots of blood were left on the white towel after she dried off. Her skin was bright pink and raw, but she only felt marginally better. After dressing, she crept down the stairs and was surprised to see Matt awake.

He looked at her and shook his head. "Jesus, Hannah. Did you give yourself one of those Silkwood showers again?" Matt pulled a cigarette out of the pack, lit it, and then tossed the lighter onto the coffee table. It bounced like a neat V, into the air, and fell to the floor. Hannah went over and picked the lighter up, setting it down next to the pack of smokes. "Why do you do that shit—the showers, the cutting, and your fucking arm?"

"I don't know. I start to think about bad stuff and it's the only thing that makes me think less."

"Well, what are you thinking about?"

"Lots of things."

Hannah could hear Matt started to lose patience. "What did you think about today?"

Hannah fidgeted. She never imagined she'd tell anyone any of the bad things she thought of. "The other Hannah and how much you fucked her." It came out in almost a whisper.

"What about it?"

"I think about how you fucked her on the couch and every time I sit on it, I wonder what bits of her or her body fluids I'm touching."

"Oh, for fuck's sake, Hannah; we've been over this a hundred times. I only dated her because of Jared. Look— as soon as he went to jail, I told her to fuck off."

"Did you really though?"

"Of course—why are you asking me that?"

"Because I found a pair of underwear under the couch the other day and I wondered if they were hers."

"Fuck if I know. Stop being so paranoid. You're the only one I'm fucking. Those panties were probably left here by some junkie tying herself off with them in my living room."

"And how do I know you didn't fuck the junkie, too? I don't even think I can trust you."

"Will you shut your fat fucking mouth?" Matt yelled. "I have a fucking migraine and I'm dope sick."

The tears immediately started dripping from Hannah's eyes, as much from anger as from hurt.

Matt shook his head, got up from the couch, approached Hannah, bent down, and gave her an apprehensive hug.

Hannah pushed him off of her with both her good arm and her cast arm. "Get away from me."

Matt staggered backwards for a step. "Calm down!"

"Leave me alone!" she screamed at him with a shrill voice. "You're white trash."

He spit into Hannah's face. She kicked and squirmed, but could not move with him on top of her. He slid up and trapped her arms under his knees. As she tried to wheeze in air, her stuttering chest kept seizing. Slowly, Matt placed a pillow over her face and pressed it into her scream.

The shrieks were stifled, but so was her breathing. Hannah was able to inhale one time before the fabric sealed around her mouth. Struggling only made it worse, so she intuitively stopped. Everything was static-like and fuzzy. There were no paisley trees...there were no moss covered carpets...Hannah just faded out.

First came a giant breath in, then her eyes flicked open. Matt was no longer on top of her. Scrambling backwards along the floor on all fours, she scurried like a frightened crab, Hannah's eyes darted until she found Matt.

"Hannah, stop."

Hannah jumped up and ran up the stairs, but Matt pursued her. She ran into the bathroom and slammed the door shut, just as Matt reached her. Throwing her body weight against the door with her hip, Hannah managed to push back enough to get the door lock clicked. The wooden door bulged inward as Matt rammed it repeatedly with his body. It didn't give.

"Open the fucking door, Hannah." Matt pleaded, "C'mon, I just want to talk to you."

"You tried to kill me!" Hannah screamed and cried as she frantically occupied all of the space in the bathroom in one blur of a constant movement within its confines.

"You'd be dead if I was trying to kill you, now calm down and let me in."

"Fuck you! Fuck you!" she screamed over and over until her voice was hoarse.

The lock on the door broke through the frame, splintering the wood, and Matt was deposited into the bathroom. Hannah came at him, screeching—a tornado of arms and legs as she tried to beat him back out of the room. Her cast came down on the bridge of Matt's nose and stunned him, causing him to stumble backwards, out of the bathroom. Desperate, Hannah slammed the door shut and braced it with her body—her shoulder pressed firmly into the wood. Her desperate fingers tried to push the wood back into the door frame so the lock would hold once again.

Matt's footsteps traveled across the hallway, but returned. One sharp kick and the door flew open, scattering Hannah backwards for a second before she retreated to the far corner of the bathroom, trying to melt her body into the wall as Matt approached her slowly. In his hand was an old plastic soda bottle. It held a rust-colored liquid and Hannah recognized what it was. Sometimes they smoked heroin in the empty upstairs bedroom. If Matt was too high to walk across the hallway to the bathroom, he would piss in old bottles. There had been several old bottles in the bedroom he hadn't dumped out yet. The urine was turning cloudy and orange from age.

Matt raised his arm up and dumped the urine on Hannah. She tried to push his arm away, but he was stronger and she squeezed her eyes tightly closed as the old piss showered over her head. Humiliated and helpless, she shivered as she stood in a puddle of Matt's foul piss.

Cracking an eye open, she saw Matt standing before her, sneering. He leaned forward and spit in her face. "I didn't try to kill you, you fucking cunt." Whipping the empty bottle at her feet, he stormed out of the room. "Clean that shit up," he yelled as he stomped down the stairs.

Hannah had never felt so embarrassed in her entire life. Tears gurgled from her eyes as she struggled to remove her wet clothing. She dropped each item where she stood and tiptoed to the shower, gently pushing the bathroom door shut on her way there.

The hot water felt nice. Hannah continued to cry as she soaped and scrubbed every crevice which might have been a reservoir for Matt's piss. There was no point in her trying to keep her cast from getting wet in the shower—the soft gauze inside was saturated with urine.

The hot water ran out before Hannah shut the shower off and dried herself off. She was glad the mirror was fogged; she couldn't even look herself in the eye. There was only one incomplete set of clothes in her bag, but it had to do, despite that meaning she'd be wearing a pair of shorts without black tights under them.

Taking the pissy clothes home wasn't an option. Hannah didn't have anything to put them in, so she said goodbye to her favorite pair of pants and a nearly new black shirt. She sprayed cleaner all over the floor and walls where she had been standing and wiped the entire mess up with paper towels. They were the paper towels she had bought for Matt, trying to make his house homier.

With her backpack slung over her shoulder, Hannah descended the stairs. Skye was still curled up, sleeping on the one chair. Matt sat on the couch, watching TV. When Hannah picked Skye up, he shut the TV off and repositioned himself on the couch.

"Hannah, I'm sorry. That was so fucked up and wrong of me."

Hannah did not look at Matt. She stood before him, her bare legs glaring back at him. It was the first time she had let anyone see her bare legs in the sunlight. Matt stared at them, but Hannah did not care; she wanted him to see what he had done.

"I'm gonna go now," she all but whispered. He did not stop her.

Hannah drove home and took four Percocets as soon as she poured something to drink. She kept old newspaper under her kitchen sink. Carefully arranging it, she retrieved scissors and a pair of needle-nose pliers. The process was tedious, but she pulled all of the cotton pads out of her cast and then snipped out the gauze. The swelling had significantly decreased since her fall, and the cast was already loose. Once Hanna removed all of the padding, she was able to slide the cast off of her arm. Doing so made her wince from the pain. She cradled her arm, took it to the kitchen sink, and scrubbed the last of the piss evidence from it.

The orthopedic surgeon's office would open the next day. Until she could have the arm recast, she wrapped it in an elastic bandage and used her sling. The pills had kicked in by the time she was done, and she lay on her bed, her hurt arm rested on her stomach. In all terms and meanings, she was broken.

CHAPTER 39
LATCHES & CATCHES

The nurses called them restraints; Jared called them a reason to scream at night when everyone was asleep. No one on the sixth floor of St. Agnes's Regional Hospital slept for the first four days he was there. On the fifth day, he changed. It might have been the medicine, or it might have been the dreams he started having about Hannah. It was almost as if he could see her as he stood below her in the dark field. The stars twinkled through the kaleidoscoping leaves of the trees, but he could still see Hannah—flying above him—her little black covered arms and legs stretched out as she soared.

"Why do you adore her, but not me?" asked Jared.

The doctor shifted in his seat. "Excuse me? Who are

you talking about?"

Jared narrowed his eyes and looked at the doctor. "Sorry, haven't you ever been lost in a thought? Now you know I'm not schizophrenic."

"I never suspected you were. What diagnosis would you give yourself?" The doctor was calm. Jared liked this, but he would still play with him.

"Special interests with a dollop of wishful thinking and little bird shaped sprinkles on top made out of marzipan."

"You have quite the imagination."

"I'm bored. Get on with it...or, allow me. I am not, nor have I ever, experienced auditory or visual hallucinations. I've never experienced a manic episode; I do not have an extraordinary fascination with fire—although it is pretty; and you can't categorize my thoughts as either suicidal or homicidal. That Bible all of you read—The Diagnostic and Statistical Manual—whatever I am, I'm not in there, so you can stop injecting me with the antipsychotics."

"Jared, whether or not you think you're beyond any diagnosis, I still have one for you."

Jared laughed. "You're all the same. Fucks like you give people like me a label so you can separate yourselves from us. The thing is, we're all alike. The way I figure it is, the shit you got tucked away in your head could get you tied to this bed just as fast as mine did me."

The doctor held his stare on Jared for a full minute before he scribbled on the chart. "I'm increasing your doses. I'll keep you here for a few more days and see how it settles out for you. If I write an order to get the restraints off, do you think you can control your behavior?"

"Yeah, doc. I never was the violent type." He smiled.

"Okay." The doctor continued to write. "Anything else you want to talk about? The girl?"

"Nah, doc." Jared let his head rock back on his pillow so he was staring ahead. "Are you going to send me back to Oakmont?"

Sighing loudly, he closed Jared's chart. "I don't foresee that. I don't know what will come of your legal issues, but I'm willing to release you to the group home. In the meantime, I'll get someone in here to untie you." The doctor lightly tapped his chart on the bed as he stood and then walked out of the room.

*

As the doctor promised, Jared was no longer restrained. He took a shower and called his mother—he needed to see his lawyer before he was arraigned—he had plans which needed his immediate attention. The hospital's patients had a different flavor to them. Jared watched the bony anorexic girls who were confined to wheel chairs so they'd conserve energy. They'd move two pushes forward and then sit, waiting for someone to take pity on them. No one did, and they sat in a still herd of dull hair and bumping wheel chairs.

Most of the people were there because of threatening suicide. Jared was bored with wrist stitches and horror stories about charcoal. These were the fluffs of the mental health system. Revealing in group therapy that he had grown up in the locked ward of a state hospital gave him more than credibility; it guaranteed that the other patients would fear him enough to leave him alone. Being criminally insane put you at the top of the mental health food chain. Even the nurses avoided Jared. The binder with his name on the spine was never on the shelf in the nurse's glassed in office. Someone was always *curious* about him.

The day of his arraignment before the district magistrate, Jared woke up feeling lucky. The police arrived to transport him, as his mother and his lawyer waited for him to arrive at the courthouse. It was simple enough—a few questions, the opening of Jared's medical records, the setting of bond, and the case was passed onto the higher court system. Jared's mother was more than able to post the bond with the collateral from her home. Had she been a gambling woman, she would have cashed out before the dealer had the best of her, but Jared was her son.

*

Jared returned to the group home two weeks after his arrest. It was long enough that the doctors considered him 'safe', but short enough that he was guaranteed his old room with his stuffed animal-fucking roommate and a quiet slide back into the chore rotation where he was, once again, scrubbing other people's shit freckles off of the shared toilet.

Three days passed before he had enough privileges restored so he was able to walk to Hannah's house after day treatment without causing too much suspicion. He knew she was still at work, so he slid one of the many duplicates he had made of her house key into her front door lock. The familiarity was missing, and subsequent tries didn't cause the comforting click he longed for. She had changed the locks.

Jared slipped through the alley to her back yard, quietly tugging on the handle to her back sliding door. It was locked. Skye eyed him curiously from the other side of the glass, her pink little tongue panting with anticipation of the door opening.

Soon enough Skye, soon enough. Jared left Hannah's house and walked home.

CHAPTER 40
HOME

"Did you have a fight with your boyfriend?" Mrs. Oberlin peeked around the threshold of her door at Hannah. Mrs. Oberlin lived in the apartment to the right of Hannah's.

"I'm sorry, Mrs. Oberlin, I don't have a boyfriend."

"Oh, well whatever you kids call them these days. That boy—he stopped by."

Hannah's heart fluttered; she had been hoping Matt would come to apologize. "When was he here?"

"Oh, about an hour ago. He's nice looking; I always did like blonde men."

Hannah tilted her head and her right cheek flinched

under her eye. "What blonde man?"

"Your friend, the one you gave a key to. He stopped by, but his key didn't work, so he left."

"Are you sure?"

"Well, of course I am! I saw him."

"Thank you, Mrs. Oberlin. He's not allowed here anymore. If you see him…next time, just stay inside and call the police, okay?"

Mrs. Oberlin looked frightened. "Why, I'll do that if you think it's best. Maybe you should get some mace to carry with you if he's that much trouble."

"Thank you, I think I will. I have to hurry now, but I appreciate you telling me."

"Certainly, my dear."

Hannah rushed to put the key in her lock and get inside. She let Skye out the back door, locking it behind her. Racing up the stairs, Hannah grabbed her large overnight bag from her closet. When she pulled it out, things fell on top of her, but she kicked them aside and began packing. Her mind raced with a list which she wrote as she went along: clothes, toothbrush, make-up, hair stuff, drugs, food for Skye, and extra shoes.

Skye wore her leash since Hannah only had one good arm, and the two of them left her apartment quickly.

"Hannah!" Mrs. Oberlin was poking out of her

doorway once more.

Hannah whirled around and saw her neighbor's liver spotted arm extended.

"Take this with you. I have two. Maybe it will help you."

Hannah reached for the item and took it. It was pepper spray. "Thank you, Mrs. Oberlin."

"You're welcome, dear. Are you going someplace where you won't be alone?"

"Well, I'm going to my parents' house. They're away, so I will be by myself, but they live in New Florence, so at least I'll be far away from here."

Mrs. Oberlin smiled. "Be safe and I'll watch over your place."

"Thank you." Hannah paused to sigh and smile genuinely before putting her bag and Skye into her car.

Donna's house was always an option, but Bob had ruined that. Keeping secrets meant she was alone, so Hannah drove to her parents' house. They had taken her little sister to Hershey Park for the long weekend. Being alone frightened her, but she took comfort in the distance between her and Jared.

Skye curled up on the seat beside her and she navigated the busy streets in town until she was on Haw's Pike. For several miles, the road followed a deep gorge which cut through the Laurel Mountains. Summer was ending and a few trees dotted the mountainside with yellow and orange. Hannah rolled her window down so she could smell the forest. Stretching her arm out, she caught the breeze. Skye jumped on her lap and gingerly allowed his face to catch some of the wind current.

*

The house was eerily quiet. Usually old farm houses shifted and sighed occasionally. Hannah took her bag upstairs and unpacked it in her old bedroom. Lorri had taken over the small bathroom they shared. Hannah went in to find something to pull her hair back out of her eyes. Like most young girls, Lorri owned a lot of hair accessories. Hannah opted for brushing her hair into a ponytail, and then added one of Lorri's pink ribbons around it.

In Hannah's old bedroom closet were clothes her mother bought her that she'd never worn—colorful items that would leave her arms and legs bare. For the first time in years, Hannah wore a sleeveless sundress without tights or a long shirt underneath. She felt naked, but the freedom exhilarated her.

It was dusk and before the house would be totally encapsulated in the night, Hannah checked all of the doors and windows to make sure they were locked. She had rarely ever been alone in her parents' house while she was growing up. If both of her parents left, she was usually stuck babysitting Lorri. She looked at photos of her little sister hanging in the foyer. Her school pictures were cute—with her dark hair and bright eyes. She always seemed so happy, and Hannah wondered how two daughters could take such different paths in life. It was unlikely that Lorri secretly hurt herself—Hannah watched for the signs or the scars, but neither appeared. If it had to be one of them, she was glad it was her. She loved her sister.

Skye's toenails clicked on the hardwood floors as she followed Hannah around. She seemed comfortable at the house, but she also had adjusted to Hannah's home as well, and she now knew it wasn't his first. Lorri loved Skye so much; Hannah often considered allowing her to have the dog. The house and yard at her parents' home was so much larger, and Lorri enjoyed combing the dog's long fur. Hannah liked Skye, but wanted to shed as many things about the past month and a half as she could. Jared had been a mistake, as had Matt. Whatever feelings she had for Matt were starting to fade away. She realized they were deep rooted, but she wanted to plant flowers in her mental garden instead of razor blades and dysfunction.

Healing inside was harder than it was on the outside. Maybe that is why she tried to replace her inner pain with outer pain. She hadn't been to therapy with Iris in weeks, but she knew she needed to go back. Iris could help her. So far, it had only been Hannah talking, but it was helping her to become comfortable. In time, she could see herself giving Iris the questions and answers she needed to help her unravel the mess she had become.

Her scars meant a lot of different things. Hannah used to be able to look at a scar and remember why she created it. Now, there were so many, she wasn't able to. Also, she had reopened dozens so that they were more like a collection of short stories rather than a single sad vignette. At times, it was easier to live in the shadows of her head, but what she really wanted to do was feel the heat of the sun on her skin. Hannah still had hope, and it hadn't yet been bled from her like a lamb, so she would search for whatever would make her right.

CHAPTER 41
PAWS

The earth had been overturned. It was a bird's grave—shallow with a mixture of dirt and the duff composite of the forest floor. If Hannah did not fly, she would have her place in the belly of the ground. The recent rains had left the soil soft and velvety. Along the edge of the forest and the cemetery, lavender was blooming in soft purple plumes. Jared picked some and lined the bottom of the grave. Surely, if her body would not take flight, it might have been because of her broken wing and she deserved a proper grave. Jared was pleased. He left the spade propped against an oak tree and walked back to the house where Hannah had grown up.

A growl rumbled in his stomach. Jared hadn't thought he'd be executing his plan that night, but fate intervened and instead of walking back to the group home, he hovered nearby to catch a glance of Hannah. Overhearing the conversation between her and the old woman neighbor meant the time was right—he had to seize the opportunity.

Hannah might have had a heightened awareness of the danger which waited for her, but with all the lights illuminating the home, Jared could easily observe her as she moved from room to room, her black clothes discarded for a little summer dress. He sat on top of the picnic table and dusted the dirt and leaves from his socks as he waited.

Hannah stared at the television, her legs pulled up under her, and a bowl of popcorn on her lap. Even though her hair was pulled back into a ponytail, stray strands kept falling in her face. Jared longed to be sitting next to her, brushing the hair back, holding her hand, and laughing at the movie. Choices were like quarters slipped into bubble gum machines—lost when you cranked the handle. Hannah was locked inside of her parents' house like a little bird in a glowing glass cage, and Jared was on the picnic bench, watching her for a reason.

She should have loved me. He saw her outstretched wing click the remote control. *And her little broken wing—so sad. But even birds with broken wings can fly.*

Jared's time had run out. It was tonight or never. They were coming for him, and they would find him. Going back to Oakmont was inevitable, but this time it would be the adult ward and the games would be very different.

The only option he had was to fulfill his dream and fall back into a system which punished people like him. He was convinced that sometime in the future, the systematic imprisonment of the mentally ill would be seen for what it was—an easy solution for a society which didn't have answers and were too frightened to explore all of the possibilities. Life may have failed Hannah, but so did the system. She spoke freely about all of the psychiatrist she had seen in her life. They knew about her cutting, yet they responded with phrases such as "manipulative", "attention seeking", and "childish behavior". Not one had simply taught her how to say 'no'.

The sun had nearly set and Jared retrieved a machete from the wall of the garage. It had been hanging there the day he and Hannah rode the bikes, and he had a use for it now. Sitting outside of the house, so close to her, he marveled at how she did not notice him watching her, but the earth had drank up most of the sun's rays and the orange-ish hue left scattering the scene was disappearing. The last thing to do was to wait. In the meantime, Jared focused on Hannah and her little oddities through the glass windows.

Time wasn't predictable, but humans and animals were. Eventually Skye began running in circles, jumping, and barking. Hannah leaned forward to place the bowl of popcorn on the coffee table. She stretched her arms upward, and stood up. Jared did the same—standing and following on the outside as she walked through the house. She opened the door a crack to allow Skye outside. Once the door closed, Jared stepped from the shadow and approached Skye, who was squatting in the grass. As soon as the dog was done, Jared whispered her name and Skye came to him. He scooped her up and walked into the shadows.

The dog trembled in his hands, as though it knew its time as a dog was coming to an end, just as its time as a lamb was about to begin. Jared stroked the animal's soft fur as he grabbed her skull in his palm and twisted until he heard a crack.

Skye was limp in his hands, yet Jared continued to pet the dog until he laid her body at the base of a tree. Hannah was in the kitchen, opening the cupboards when Jared removed the cover from the box mounted to the corner of the house and cut the phone wires.

Returning to where he had left Skye's dead body, Jared pulled the dog into a small burp of light from one of the house windows and looked into its empty eyes, and then held the dog near his face and whispered into its fur.

It was time. Jared used the paws of the lifeless dog to scratch at the rear door and then ducked into the shadows. Hannah opened the door, but when Skye did not come inside, she closed the door. Jared watched as she returned to the kitchen, pulling items in the refrigerator. Staying in the shadows, he ran to the front door and scratched as well. Hannah set a bowl of grapes on the kitchen counter and walked around to the front door, opening it.

"Skye. Skye!" She sighed loudly. "Don't make me come out and find you…stupid dog!"

Through the oval glass door pane, Jared could see Hannah as she stood in the foyer by the front door and slipped her shoes on. Jared used the paws to scratch once again. She flung the door open and there stood Jared, a machete in one hand, and a dead Pomeranian in the other.

"Hello, my little bird."

Hannah paled. Her attempt to slam the door shut failed as Jared's foot returned the swing with a powerful kick. Hannah ran into the kitchen, her arms out at her sides as she bolted from the room. She grabbed the cordless phone, pressed the on button, and held it to her ear. She dropped the phone and ran out the back door. Jared followed.

The clouds had rearranged in the sky, uncovering a bright, nearly full moon. The darkness, which had cooperated with Jared's plan, was now unforgiving for Hannah's fleeing escape. Jared stayed close behind Hannah as she ran down the main road. He was too near for her to dash to one of the neighbor's homes; surely she thought he'd slaughter her as she waited for them to answer their door, so she ran.

Not a particularly fast runner, her feet kept finding pot holes which threw off her balance. Jared learned from her footing and did not make the same mistakes. He could hear Hannah crying and suddenly, his medication-induced erectile dysfunction lifted, and he found it difficult to run with such an engorged cock.

It was almost too easy to close in on her. He never knew how slow she ran. His hand stretched out, as he considered touching her hair, but he stopped as he raised the machete above his head. With the blade pointed away from her, he brought the unsharpened side of the weapon down across the back of her knee quickly.

Hannah fell. Her palms pressed down into the dirt and her head hung as a string of spit inched from her lips. Jared stopped because she stopped. The purpose in striking her was to slow her down. He did not follow her as she got up and commenced running, although now she did so with an obvious limp. They had come to the edge of the cemetery, and Jared knew where she was going.

CHAPTER 42
DIRT

Hannah's thoughts were very simple, but repetitive: *run* and *I'm going to die.* The whack to the back of her leg hurt and it made the already pointless task of running even harder. When she had fallen, she expected the machete to come down across her body, but it did not. She knew this could only mean one thing: Jared was playing with her. It was impossible to outrun him, even though he now kept a distance behind her, but she thought if she could hide until daylight, she had a chance.

Her feet sought the familiarity of the graveyard, where she had spent so many days playing hide and go seek. She knew the dips and divots in the ground there; she still had them memorized since childhood, and if she could make it to the giant oak tree, she could climb so high, she would not be found. Even if he looked for her there, the branches fingered out in such multitudes, she would be safe.

Counting headstones, she raced onward. There were twenty-six white headstones in the last aisle and she checked them off as she passed them. The wind was starting to blow and the clouds were drifting back over the face of the moon. If she wanted to be able to find the tree quickly, she had to move fast. Jared was no longer in sight, but she suspected he was close behind.

By the time Hannah reached the great oak, her shoes were wet from running through the dewy grass. It had been many years since she last climbed the tree, but like a fingerprint, her feet fit into the wood's knot swirls that she had learned as a child. Because of her cast, her arm kept slipping and she struggled to find a secure grasp. The cast sloughed bark off of the trunk and the sound echoed through the maze of trees as her desperate climb upwards took her under the leafy canopy.

The branch she settled on was as high as she dared go without fearing her weight would snap one of the tree's generous arms off. As soon as she settled, with her legs wrapped around the branch, she began shivering. Human eyes weren't meant to see in such light, but she strained as she searched for signs of Jared. After a few minutes, the clouds parted and even in the forest, Hannah could see things, but she was better off in the dark, because below her stood Jared, the machete in his hand, glistening in the silver light.

"I see Hannah..." he sang. "I see a little blackbird in a

tree."

Hannah did not move. She did not breathe. She did not think. Everything about her that was alive froze, pathetically hoping to blend in with the bark of the tree.

Jared spoke in a calm, even tone, "Didn't you know I knew you'd come here? Silly little bird...you think you hide everything, but you wear it all on your skin. Now I know you're probably scared. Am I right? You are scared, aren't you?" His voice was caught between pleading and a cocky assertiveness. His arms waved emphatically as he spoke. Hannah did not answer him. "I don't want to scare you, Hannah. I *love* you. I want you to be the best that you can be. I know you don't see your potential—but it is there. I'm going to help. I'm *here* to help. People don't understand us, and they never will. You'll spend your entire life going to doctors who will try to fix you, but ultimately, Hannah—you're already fixed and you don't even know it. What you need is inside of you. You need one event to set you free. And what Matt did to you? That just bound you to this earth. You deserve better. I'm going to give you better. But you have to listen to me. Can you do that? Will you do that?" Hannah was silent.

"Hannah, answer me or I'll get mad. I don't want to hurt you, but I will if you don't listen. For the last time, will you listen to me?"

"Yee—yes," Hannah stuttered.

"Well we have an understanding then. And you know...no one's coming to rescue you. No one's going to hear you scream. I know that has already passed through your head. So, there's only two ways out of the tree for you...in pieces..." Jared struck the tree trunk twice with the machete, "...or you jump. So what's it going to be? You want to jump, or do you want me to come up and get you?"

Her voice was small and crackled with tears and fear. "I want to stay here."

There was a pause, and then Jared screeched, "Weren't you listening? That's not an option. What will it be...the machete, or will you jump?"

Hannah did not answer. Her tears, snot, and spit gushed onto the tree bark. She could have done so many things differently and not have ended up in an ordinary tree, in an ordinary forest, in the middle of an ordinary night. It was too late for that. Things were about to end, and she knew it.

"I'll help you make up your mind. I'll start coming up the tree. If you want me to bring you down in pieces, stay on that branch and I'll use it like a cutting board. If you'd rather jump, spring off before I get there."

Jared's climb seemed deliberately slow. Hannah tried to judge the distance to the ground. It would be like jumping off of the roof of a house. She knew she'd break something, but there was a chance she'd be okay.

Jared rested on a branch. "Hannah, before you jump, I want you to promise me something. Will you?" She didn't respond, but he continued, "I want you to concentrate as hard as you can on flying when you jump. If you fly, you will land safely, or maybe even fly to a different tree. Can you do that?" Hannah still didn't answer. Jared swung the machete at her, laughing. "Will you do that, little bird?"

"Okay!" Hannah's voice was a loud shrill. She tried to make it loud in case someone would hear her.

Jared laughed, "Hannah—I told you—no one can hear you. But if my little blackbird wants to sing, I will make her sing." He resumed his climb.

Her lungs sucked in a great volume of air and she exhaled. Jared was three branches below her, so there was no climbing down to make the jump less dangerous. There was a way to make it easier, and despite being terrified, she could do it.

Hate. No one could hate Hannah more than she hated herself. A thousand mistakes brought her to that tree, and it was her fault. If she had only been smarter, prettier, or knew how to say no...she let men use her and fuck her, so it was no wonder Jared had singled her out for his plan. She now realized that everything about her was a beacon. A jump out of the tree was the least she deserved. Jared was now two branches below her and he had started swinging the machete again. Hannah loosened her grip on the tree branch and sprung off of it.

She felt the breeze catch her on the way down as her screams emptied into the night. The light passed by her so quickly—it looked like she was surrounded by stars until she landed with a loud crack on the ground, which forced all of the air out of her lungs and darkness engulfed her.

*

Small shrubs tearing at her skin woke Hannah up. *I am not dead*, was her first thought. It took her seconds to understand. Jared was dragging her body through the woods and she realized could not let him know she was conscious. In a bloody maze of disfigurement, Hannah felt that her right leg was broken below the knee and was bent in an unnatural way. Blood erupted from a cut on her head, and ran into her eyes. She was not sure if she could move even if she wanted to. She almost felt paralyzed, but as seconds passed, she realized she was feeling too much pain for that to be true.

They stopped and Hannah wondered what their destination was. As soon as Jared rolled her body into the shallow grave, she knew he would be leaving her. It was the one thought which centered her enough to keep pretending she was dead. When he lifted her legs into the grave, she nearly screamed from the pain. Tears pressed out from the slits in her eyes, but she hoped he would not notice with all of the blood.

Smelling the lavender was peculiar. The ground was damp and cold and she smelled it, too. Dirt pushed between the spaces that separated her fingers farther apart. Jared reached behind her head, pulled her hair out of the pony tail so it fell loose around her face, and spread it out to the edges of the grave. He placed the ribbon bow from her hair between her lips and began tossing the dirt over her.

As prepared as he had been, he had grossly underestimated the depth of the grave. Hannah's body took up most of the space so he only sprinkled some soil on her, and finally covered the spot with leaves and twigs from the forest floor.

"There you go—not meant for the sky, but for the dirt."

After her burial, Hannah heard him walk away. Hannah thought he cared very little for hiding her body, as though the disappointment of his effort had worn a hole in his ambition to finish the project.

Hannah remained terrified. She waited and prayed he did not come back. Even if morning came, she was not certain her body would work well enough to crawl out of the hole. The forest stirred and those sounds blended with the breeze upturning leaves. Hannah felt like Alice in Wonderland, but with a less desirable destination.

CHAPTER 43
HOBBY

Matt filled the absence of Hannah bevel up. Shooting heroin was a line he never expected to cross. But then again, he never knew he could feel such numb emptiness. The liquid plunging through his veins made him feel. In her absence, he made carpet angels and contemplated leaving messages on her answering machine.

After work on Friday night, Matt had a guy he worked with take him to Pittsburgh to re-up. He was going through the heroin even faster now that he was shooting it himself. Habits such as his became full-time jobs.

Customers were always waiting for him when he returned on re-up day. That night, Hannah number two was sitting on his porch steps when he arrived at home.

"You've had quite the crowd waiting for you tonight."

She rested her elbows on her knees and squinted at him. "I told most of them to leave until later, and some others got sick of waiting."

"Thanks," Matt murmured as he unlocked his door. Hannah followed him inside and locked the door behind her.

"I'm gonna run some of this shit up stairs. How much were you buying?"

"Just a bun."

"Okay, I'll be back." Matt had a safe bolted to the floor of his closet. Inside he put a roll of cash, his gun, and the brick of heroin he bought. Out of his right pocket, he pulled baggies of pills and weed and a few loose buns of heroin. After closing and locking the safe, he went downstairs and handed Hannah number two her bun. She gave him money and nodded.

"Do you mind if I smoke some here? I've had a shitty fucking day."

Matt had second thoughts about it, but figured his Hannah wouldn't show up this late, so he said, "Go ahead."

"Are you going to smoke with me?"Matt shot up in the car on the way back, but he answered, "Sure, light it up."

Their straws were greedy to seize the smoke before it disappeared into the air. Hannah leaned back on the couch, her skirt pulling up her thigh. Matt looked at it and she noticed. "What? You wanna fuck?"

Matt missed his Hannah, but love was new to him and he didn't know how to navigate it. Opportunity was familiar to him, so he said, "Yes."

They were quick because Matt expected customers to come soon. Like a well-worn hobby, he worked the girl until he was done with her. Afterwards, they smoked more and watched TV.

"You know, that friend of yours is creepy."

"What friend?"

"That Jared guy. He called me for a ride hours ago."

"Jared did?"

She looked at Matt and rolled her eyes. "Err...yeah, that's what I said."

"I thought he was still in jail or the hospital. Where did he want a ride to?"

"His girlfriend's house—someplace in buttfuck New Florence or something."

"Are you kidding me?"

"No—calm down. I'm not fucking kidding you."

Matt jumped up and dialed Hannah's phone number. There was no answer. He grabbed the phone book off of the top of the refrigerator and scrambled for a number. He paused to dial it, listening carefully, but there was no answer there either. "Can you take me where you took Jared today?"

"Fuck, it's late and I'm high."

Matt screamed, "You stupid fucking whore, he's going to kill her."

Hannah number two flinched. "Okay, okay, let me put my fucking shoes on."

*

The car ride fucked with Matt's hallucinations; he saw rabbits and severed fingers. To make things worse, she drove like shit—swerving and nodding off as she drove. When they arrived, Matt saw Hannah's parents' house illuminated with doors wide open. The car lights shone on the yard and Matt noticed Skye's body in the grass. He jumped out of the car and ran to the lifeless dog. Matt bolted into the house and began searching for Hannah, calling her name. He found it empty, so he returned to the car and got in.

"The phone in there is dead. We have to go to my mom's and call the police."

"Call the police? Are you kidding me? We're high as fuck."

"Walk across the street to my mom's, tell her I sent you, call the police, and leave before they get here."

Matt searched the house and the yard again before he saw Hannah number two emerging from him mother's house. "Are the police coming?" She nodded. "Then hurry up and leave." She didn't hesitate. Her eyes were saucers and she looked like she was tweaking. Matt started to run as she pulled away.

Down the road, past Olivia's house, towards the cemetery, he ran so hard it felt like sharp thorns stabbed his lungs. Like Hannah, he knew the cemetery well enough to jump over the big holes and hurry into the forest. He began calling her name, but stopped when he realized he was being too loud to hear if she responded. He looked around and screamed her name, holding his breath so he could listen for her. To his right, he heard something. He took two steps and saw the shovel leaning against a tree and then a nearby pile of soil.

Matt's stomach lurched. To him, the shovel indicated that Hannah was dead. He dropped to his knees and scrambled to rub his hands over the surface of the forest floor, searching for upturned soil.

The dry leaves made it difficult to see the grave, but Hannah's fingers sticking upwards snagged under his touch. He rushed to sweep the dirt and leaves off of her.

"Hannah. Hannah. Hannah…" Matt kept saying her name as he uncovered her.

Hannah began to cry as he brushed dirt from her face.

CHAPTER 44
FORE-RESTS

Pain sleeps. When it's too bad, it becomes a blinding white light. Shapes and sounds fragmented into trickles of things Hannah could not comprehend. Either Matt or Jared was there—she didn't know which, because they were really just different version of the same perversion, so she couldn't have told them apart even if the dirt wasn't in her eyes.

Through the breaks in the trees, he came to her on a night-colored magic carpet. He wore a turban with a syringe where the jewel and feather should have been. As though she was weightless, his carpet swooped beneath her and she rose into the sky with him. The wind on her skin chilled her enough to extinguish the pain. It blew the dirt out of the corners of her eyes and she could see stars—thousands of them waving tiny hands at her, like they were tossing light colored flowers at her feet.

Her hair trailed off of the edge of the carpet and was combed by the air. A spare twig of lavender blew loose and fluttered downward. Hannah watched it descend back to the ground, landing in the black spot in the woods where she was almost swallowed.

The smell of something musky pinched her cheeks. She wanted to say it smelled like frankincense and myrrh, but she didn't know what they smelled like.

"Is it Christmas?" she asked, but no one answered. The carpet felt like moss under her fingers and she rhythmically stroked it.

"Where are you taking me?" she whispered.

He didn't turn around. His back was towards her as he steered the carpet by holding the front upturned corners. "Heaven. You're going to Heaven so you can be a real carpet angel."

CHAPTER 45
CEMENT

"I didn't want a hole in the dirt to be the end of my story. I chose to live, even if it meant I had to break to do so." Hannah grimaced as she sat up in her hospital bed. The Assistant District Attorney came to interview her before Jared's arraignment hearing.

The woman's tears formed. "You're one of the bravest people I've ever met."

"Thank you, but not really. If I were brave, none of this would have happened. I would have been saying 'no' since the beginning." Hannah fiddled with the edging on her white hospital sheet. "I'm just glad they didn't have to pin my leg back together. A cast is bad enough, but pins are even worse."

The woman nodded her head as though she understood, but she did not. "If the psychiatrist suggests Jared go to prison instead of a mental hospital, how do you feel about that?"

"Jared in jail—a real jail, not a psychiatric hospital? I think he belongs there. He gives mentally ill people a bad name. He doesn't want to get better." The woman scribbled as Hannah looked at the cast on her arm. It had to be redone a third time because there was so much dirt between her skin and the cast.

A few of her ribs were broken, and her shoulder had been dislocated. She couldn't remember if this was from the fall, or if it was from being dragged through the forest by Jared. They shaved a small spot on her head where they needed to put in three stitches—Hannah itched her bald spot.

The Assistant District Attorney left and Hannah was alone. Her family and Donna were frequent visitors, but Hannah suggested Matt not come because he might run into her parents. Instead, he called her several times a day.

Iris worked part-time at the hospital, so she stopped in almost daily to speak with her.

"I have caverns in my mind, and I don't want to crawl into them anymore." Hannah winced as she tried to adjust her leg. "There are silent places too, but I don't mind them so much. I don't want to be quiet anymore. Maybe if I can scream in the silent place now, someone will find me. Being alone is overrated. I'm not better—

don't get me wrong—an act of violence turned me inside out, but another one didn't flip me right-side-up. I'm still broken, but the difference is, I don't take comfort in being broken anymore."

"You have hope," Iris said.

"Hope? Can I hold something like that, or do I need to put it in a glass jar so it doesn't evaporate?" Hannah laughed.

"I think it's more like a friend who wants to be with you—no need for the jar."

"That's lovely."

*

Hannah's hospital stay was longer than expected because she was administered IV antibiotics for a few days. The dirt rubbed into her compound fracture might cause an infection, so the doctors insisted on the preventative medicine.

Immediately after the accident, Hannah's parents discovered she had been spending time with Matt. They were enraged and under the guise of them thinking she needed to live in a one-story home closer to them while her leg healed. They moved her belongings into an apartment outside of town, near to where they lived.

The move upset Hannah, but she didn't say no. The hospital gown didn't hide her scars, and the revelations her parents were facing left her feeling defeated and unwilling to fight. When she was finally released, her parents took her to her new apartment and arranged things so she could manage on her own. She was fairly mobile on the crutches, but wouldn't be driving for a long time.

When they arrived at her apartment, there was something big in a wagon sitting in front of her door. It was poorly wrapped in pink wrapping paper.

"What is that?" Hannah laughed.

Hannah's mother paused and looked at her husband. "Honey, I—I don't know what it is."

"Well, can we take it inside and see?" Hannah was smiling. "If it's on my porch, it must be for me—maybe a welcoming gift."

The three of them shuffled inside and Hannah's father pulled the red wagon into the living room. Hannah had paused to look around at her new apartment, "This is nice, thank you." She leaned down and tore the paper off of the gift to reveal one of the gargoyles from the top of City Hall.

"Frank!" Hannah clapped as she tilted to the side from laughing so hard.

"What do you mean, 'Frank'?" asked her mother.

"I love it!" Hannah exclaimed. "I have stolen property in my living room, but I love it."

Hannah's father's voice was stern, "Hannah, where did

this come from?"

"From in front of my door, of course!"

"Does Matt know where you live?" asked Hannah's mother in a lowered voice.

Hannah sighed and frowned, "Mom! I can't have this crazy stuff in my life anymore if I want to get better. Matt and I both naturally live in these chaotic circles, and when they overlap, it's too volatile. Don't worry; he'll stay out of my life. I feel different now."

Her parents were quiet and exchanged glances.

Hannah exhaled. She pulled at the fraying strings at the end of her cast on her arm. "I don't want you guys to worry. I'm not going to be friends with him again—no matter what."

Hannah's mother's voice was small, "That sounds like a good start."

Hannah couldn't wait for her parents to leave. As soon as they did, she located her purse and started preparing the heroin. It was a well-practiced method for her now.

*

Hannah was folded into an envelope and sealed. She could feel the paper turn and fold, turn and fold, as she was pressed gently into the warmth of the creases. When it cracked open, she was wearing a dress covered in white origami cranes, running through wheat fields towards a swing set on a beach. It was warm, but snowing and she caught snowflakes on her tongue as she ran closer to the swing.

She sat on the seat and her dress crinkled, but she pumped her legs harder and harder until she was in the air. The high parts gave her a second of weightlessness and the backward swings blew her hair around her face. She was at the sea shore on a swing set, wearing a paper crane origami dress and she could smell the ocean salt. Her toes swung above the beach, and she knew that when she was done, the cranes would depart in a flock and she'd make angels in the sand.

"Where are you at, Angel?"

THE END

ABOUT THE AUTHOR

The most exquisite things Lucia has ever written have been on dirty napkins left in barrooms she will never return to. She spends her time:
Contemplating the difference between want and need
Staring at her palms, trying to rearrange the destiny lines with her mind
Writing about the social consequences of being poisonous

Lucia began writing as a child. Her work spans several genres, but frequently focuses on showing mental illness from the inside out. *Vein Fire* is her third novel and the first she's decided to publish. Some of her writing appears in anthologies and in literary magazines. Lucia lives in Pennsylvania, somewhere between a forest and a river, with a cute potato and her beloved chi-spaniel.

Lucia is a member of the Quark Paper Cutting Factory.

VeinFire.net

ACKNOWLEDGMENTS

I'm so *thankful* to Carolyn Violet for the use of her stunning photograph, which appears on the cover.

I am forever grateful to Paul, for without his encouragement, *Vein Fire* would have remained a short story.

A thousand thanks to my beloved beta readers for their feedback and edits, and so much more that I can't even articulate (it would be a novella): Lorri, Jane, John, and Paul.

Special thanks to my writing partner, Gerry, for taking the plunge with me; Tony, my professor, for convincing me that I'd save more lives as a writer than a doctor...*Vein Fire* started as a single thought in your class, many years ago; Sharon for always picking me up; Bill, for teaching me not to eat the free popcorn on the bar; Ross, Egads! Thenk ye fir bein' ma chum; the lovely Sarah-Jean; Susan; and for Lee, who always believes.

Sincere gratitude to Rosanna Weil for so many things.

Eternal thanks to my family for their love and support—it humbles me every day how they help me, and especially to my beautiful sister, who continually invested in my talent.